The Island Hideaway

Louise Candlish

SPHERE

First published in Great Britain as *Prickly Heat* in 2004 by Arrow Books
This paperback edition published in 2013 by Sphere

A CIP catalogue record for this book
is available from the British Library.

ISBN 978-0-7515-4124-3

Typeset in Sabon LT Std by Palimpsest Book Production Limited,
Falkirk, Stirlingshire
Printed and bound in Great Britain by Clays Ltd, St Ives plc

Papers used by Sphere are from well-managed forests
and other responsible sources.

For Nips

Acknowledgements

This book was originally published as *Prickly Heat* and has now been revised and updated as *The Island Hideaway*. In the writing and publishing of *Prickly Heat* I was championed by Claire Paterson at Janklow & Nesbit and Kirsty Fowkes and Georgina Hawtrey-Woore at Arrow, Random House. Andrew Burton, Jane Candlish and Heather McCarry were also invaluable supporters. Joanna Rahim, John Tague and Debbie Whittick kindly helped, as did David in Panarea. The press office at the London Ambulance Service supplied me with useful information. Friends Dawn Terrey, Mats 'n' Jo, Jane Sarluis, Neal Cobourne and Will Holme all contributed lines that made me laugh.

For its revised and updated incarnation as *The Island Hideaway*, the version you read here, I owe thanks to Jo Dickinson and also to Rebecca Saunders, Lucy Icke and the rest of the Little, Brown team. I'd like to thank

Hannah Wood for the new cover, which captures the spirit of the story so well, and Rachel Cross for her sharp proofread.

Particular and grateful thanks to Sheila Crowley, Rebecca Ritchie and the team at Curtis Brown.

Chapter 1

Twenty minutes late, the hydrofoil from Lipari to Panarea rose out of the water and gathered speed. Eleanor Blake, sitting in the nose of the boat, was suddenly conscious of her own breathing: for the first time since leaving London she felt the unmistakable retch of dread.

It was several seconds before she registered the sound of a man's voice above the groan of the engines: 'Excuse me! Hello! Excuse me?'

The accent was English. She panicked, instinctively guilty, but saw immediately that it wasn't what she'd feared. The man was a complete stranger; he probably just wanted the seat next to her. He was very tall and she found herself tipping her head right back as though assessing the height of a cliff. His smile was wide, patient, a little lopsided.

'Is anyone sitting here?'

When she still didn't respond, he rattled out something in fluent Italian and finally Eleanor found her voice. 'No, please, go ahead . . .' She snatched up her bag and watched as he lowered himself into the aisle seat.

'Thanks. I thought you might be English,' he said. 'Can you believe how full this thing is? I bet it's well over legal capacity.'

'Oh,' Eleanor said, alarmed.

'So much for island hideaways and best-kept secrets and all that rubbish. All paths are beaten now, aren't they, even the ones through the Tyrrhenian Sea? Are you going to Salina or Panarea?'

'Panarea. I didn't know we stopped anywhere else.'

'Only for a minute, they do a kind of bus route thing around all the islands. Salina's the next one along, between Lipari and Panarea.'

'Right.' She supposed he must be one of those know-it-alls who behaved like a tour guide. His eye contact was steady and serious.

'I'm Lewis, by the way.'

'Eleanor.' She suddenly couldn't help giggling.

He looked at her with curiosity. His eyes were an unusual golden-brown colour and strands of his longish dark hair kept falling into them. He had a distracted, crumpled look about him that was really quite attractive, Eleanor thought, surprised she'd even noticed. But it was impossible to ignore the warm, physical bulk of him – the seats were narrow and his shoulder and thigh now seemed absurdly close to hers, something that hadn't struck her about her neighbour on the window side, an elderly Italian woman with gold shells at her ears and a large cake box on her lap. Eleanor edged imperceptibly towards the cake box.

'So did you stay in Lipari long?' he asked.

'Just one night.' The Eleanor of old would certainly have enjoyed describing the hotel she'd just left, a conversation piece by anyone's standards with its 1970s cruise liner theme, the armchairs made of curled cane with orange-and-brown terry-cloth cushions, the terrace walls dotted with 'portholes', the thick twists of rope for handrails that couldn't possibly be needed on dry ground. But instead she was tongue-tied, even a little afraid.

'Don't suppose you got to the archaeological museum while you were there?' he went on, undiscouraged.

'No.' She was a bit thrown by this. *Museums?* They were the last thing on her mind.

'It's really excellent, one of the best in Sicily. I recommend it if you've got time on your way back. It's just a few minutes from the *corso*, right by the church, you can't miss it.'

Eleanor nodded, wondering what the *corso* was, but before she could ask a baleful droning noise started to seep through the cabin, making them both look up. She thought at first that it was one of the other passengers in some kind of distress; then for a split second it crossed her mind that she herself may even be the

3

drone. She'd noticed recently that she seemed to have less and less control over what came out of her mouth; like last night, in the hotel restaurant, when she'd listened to her own order with as much interest as the waiter. Then she realised that this was *music*, some sort of jingle coming through the speakers, and an ancient black-and-white TV monitor was flickering into life at the front of the boat.

She looked at her new companion, already accepting him as an authority figure, and he grinned at her alarm. 'I don't think they've kitted this thing out for about thirty years, it's completely falling apart. We'll be lucky to get there in one piece.'

'Oh.'

'So are you on holiday?'

'Yes.' Eleanor paused, before blurting, 'I'm meeting up with my fiancé on the island.'

'Ah, right.' She thought she sensed a slight retreat. 'Not travelling together?'

'No, he had more time off work than me.' This, she told herself, was probably true. 'He went a few days ahead.'

'Well, it's a small place. I'm sure we'll all bump into each other at some point.'

'Yes.' Eleanor felt another, much more painful, prickle of nerves. She really was almost there – provided the boat didn't crack in two and drown them all. What on earth was going to happen over the next few days?

She began fiddling with the ticket still clutched in her hand, tearing at its edges. Then it occurred to her that this Lewis might notice she wasn't wearing an engagement ring and she quickly tucked her fingers into the cuffs of her shirt.

'It's a volcano, you know, Panarea?' said Lewis. 'Inactive, obviously . . .'

She barely listened as he talked on about the tiny villages, the shrinking off-season population, the sense of isolation. Instead she imagined Will waiting on the jetty to wrap her in a huge welcoming hug, turning on his beauty in that way of his, like a movie star in front of the camera. For a few minutes the fantasy tricked her and she sank back into her seat, her whole body suffused with happiness.

Out of the corner of her eye, she saw that Lewis had given up on her and was reading a newspaper, pausing at intervals to unfold, flap and fold it again. She was relieved their conversation was over for now: chit-chat with a stranger required a skill she'd let lapse in recent months. She supposed she ought to try to rediscover it since the hotel she'd booked had only twelve rooms and half-board accommodation was obligatory – she probably wouldn't be able to eat alone as she had last night in Lipari. No, she'd be sharing meals with other people, holidaymakers, like the hundred or so filling this boat, most conferring excitedly about the identities of the various bumps of grey land they could make out through the window. The famous Aeolian Islands, islands that she'd never heard of until four days ago.

Glancing past the old lady to take a look too, she was shocked to see the changed colour and swell of the water. From her table on the breakfast terrace that morning the sea had looked exactly as it was supposed to look in this part of the world – flat, petrol-blue, pulling in and out in safe little breaths – but here it was ash-grey and swollen, with horrible yellow-white spittle staining the windows. This couldn't be right.

Suddenly the engines went dead and the boat lurched massively from side to side. Eleanor allowed her fingers to search for the life jacket under the seat as a murmur spread through the cabin. 'What's happening?' she said, faintly, to neither neighbour in particular, horrified that her eyes had filled with tears. The lady with the cake just looked at her and made a snickering noise through her nose, but Lewis lowered his paper, instantly solicitous.

'Nothing to worry about, the sea's a bit rough, that's all. We're just coming into Salina, see? It's only another twenty minutes to Panarea.'

His eye lingered on her. Without the noise of the engines she felt exposed, self-conscious, and wondered for the first time how she must look to this man. Her hair, she knew, might have been styled by a clown.

She'd had it cut in London yesterday in a last-minute attempt to alter her appearance and a kink had sprung up in the humid Sicilian air – not a pretty curl to brush her brow and accentuate her eyes, but big flossy curves worthy of the double-takes she'd been attracting. She hoped her face wasn't too flushed, but a few hours in the morning sun had already left her skin seared and itchy. And even her eyes – grey-green and large, undoubtedly her best feature – couldn't rescue her, for they were red from crying.

The boat docked. A small crowd shuffled off and another shuffled on: a trio of girls with backpacks and two or three couples wheeling suitcases along behind them. Expectant faces hunted for seats.

'Well, Salina looks beautiful,' Lewis said, as the boat accelerated again, and he leant over Eleanor to look out of the window. 'Incredibly green for September, isn't it? I've heard it's a lot quieter there than Panarea, not so popular with the Milan crowd.'

All at once Eleanor felt grateful for his efforts with her. He didn't *have* to be so friendly. And wasn't this the sort of distraction she should be indulging in, anyhow? The inconsequential passing of time that proved that life went on? She racked her brain for a detail from her guidebook to contribute to the conversation: 'Isn't Panarea full of celebrities or something?'

'Yeah, it's supposed to be some kind of retreat for wealthy businessmen from the north – and their model girlfriends, of course – all playing at living the simple life. You know, a bit like Marie Antoinette in her little *hameau* at Versailles.'

Eleanor nodded, pretending to know what an *hameau* was.

'It's almost all private villas, apparently. There are hardly any hotels. Actually, someone was telling me that property prices there are among the highest in Italy.'

'It sounds a bit more exclusive than I was expecting,' Eleanor admitted.

'Well, they're letting us in, aren't they, so it can't be that chi-chi.'

Eleanor, who didn't think she had ever heard anyone use the word 'chi-chi' before and certainly not a man, ignored the twinge in her stomach at the memory of the price she'd been quoted – and duly paid – for this impromptu break.

'So where are you from?' Lewis asked.

'Originally Devon. But I live in London now.'

'Whereabouts? Hey, are you all right?' He peered at her in concern. 'You've gone really pale.'

'I suddenly feel dreadful. The water seems to be getting rougher.' In the open sea once more, great smoke-coloured waves were sloshing against the boat, building up into noisy, slamming assaults. Eleanor had a horrible feeling she was going to be sick, and her eyes moved between the old lady's cake box and Lewis's thighs for a likely receptacle.

'The currents on this stretch are famously bad,' Lewis said. 'It can get quite dangerous, I heard.'

'Really?'

'Yes, a hydrofoil got dragged on to the rocks at Panarea a few years ago. No one died, though, don't worry.'

'Right.' Eleanor tried hard not to think about this latest tip as rolls of queasiness rose inside her in direct opposition to the rhythm of the water; it felt painful, like being a rider unable to get the measure of her horse's stride. Surely they were almost there by now? Breathing deeply, she tried to focus on the safety photographs on the wall by the TV monitor. A man with a moustache was neatly strapped into a life jacket, standing smiling in a three-quarters pose; the backdrop looked like a golf course.

'Here, take this . . .' Lewis passed her the white seasickness bag from the seat pocket in front of him. 'You know it's just your eyes and ears sending the brain conflicting signals? It's decided you must have been poisoned, that's why you want to—'

'Thanks, that helps.' She slapped the bag over her mouth, conscious of both Lewis's and the cake woman's eyes fixed on her as she panted in and out, causing the bag to inflate and deflate in a way that would have made her laugh had it been someone else doing it. She squeezed her eyes shut, wishing herself anywhere but here. Slowly the sickness subsided and so, miraculously, did the currents. When she next dared look up the boat was sliding serenely along a rocky coastline and before long a line of grinning faces bobbed into view.

'Panarea! Panarea!' The door was wrenched open, ropes knotted and people were standing and fussing over their luggage. Eleanor stood, too, scrabbling for her bag. Beside her, Lewis was already in the aisle.

'Where are you staying?' he asked. 'Do you need some help – you'll probably feel a bit wobbly when you get off this thing?'

'I'm fine now,' she said, half cross with relief. 'I'm sure my, er, boyfriend will be waiting for me.'

'All right, well if you're sure, I'll leave you to it. My bag's out the back.'

She watched him walk off through the cabin, newspaper tucked under his arm; he had the stoop of someone long accustomed to being the tallest person in the room. Waiting for him to disappear from sight, she fished her sunhat from her bag and shuffled down the ramp, pushing through the hugging scrums on the jetty before finding a spot to stand still and take another long, deep breath. She considered a cigarette, then decided against it: her hands were shaking too much.

In front of her was Panarea. The tiny harbour was lined with cafés, all crowded with people, some sitting right out on the rocks on a wooden deck. Red-and-blue striped fishing boats rested higgledy-piggledy on the rocks, as though arranged with elaborate artlessness by a magazine stylist. Behind, the island climbed in gentle terraces, with bright, whitewashed houses and flowers cascading over low walls. In the distance was a vast gnarl of a mountain, pocked with grey rock and glittering with silvery-purple highlights. She stared, realising that she hadn't considered for a moment how the island would actually look. Its beauty was a shock.

But right now she needed to concentrate on getting herself to the hotel as inconspicuously as possible. It was vital she look relaxed, anonymous, for it would be disastrous to be spotted now and the jetty and harbour front were teeming – clearly the whole island had piled down to inspect the new arrivals. She clamped her hat to her head, covered half of her face with oversized sunglasses and began walking down the jetty behind a family and several couples, as if attached to their party. Everyone gazed around, dazzled by their delivery into paradise, and she tried to mimic their delight as they registered that this glorious sun-drenched spot was to be their home for the period ahead.

Reaching the waterfront strip of cafés and bars, the group slowed up: a collection of three-wheelers and golf karts were knotted together in a little traffic jam.

'Rush hour in Panarea,' said a woman to Eleanor in heavily accented English, and then laughed with unexpected fierceness. She looked in her mid-forties, her forehead deeply creased, eyes vivid and intense.

German, thought Eleanor and smiled at her. German was unconnected, German was safe. And how handy it was that other Europeans knew English so well; she knew next to nothing of *their* languages. Moving on a step or two, she saw that one of the karts had the name of her hotel painted on its side in pink: 'Albergo delle Rose'. She hurried over, head down, as the driver, a tanned boy in a pale-blue T-shirt, reversed out of the tangle and indicated the passenger seat: '*Prego.*'

'Thank you.'

Safely seated, she slid another glance at the cafés, both alert for that one familiar face and entirely unprepared for seeing it so soon. She had never before witnessed such a choreography of glamour: elegant, pin-thin women with glossy brown faces were sitting watching the jetty scene, their clothes expensive wisps, gleaming black hair pinned back with flowers and silver clips. Long toned legs were crossed gracefully or stretched out in the sun, feet bare or dangling pretty sandals. Almost without exception each of these astonishing-looking creatures was paired with a heavily tanned man who had either a phone locked to his ear or a screen in his palm, his attention elsewhere.

Eleanor stared in stupefied admiration until the three-wheeler pulled away at top speed and took a right up a steep lane. Less than ten seconds later they were braking into the driveway of a hotel. The boy leapt out, pulled out her bag and set it down in an empty reception area. No sooner had she followed than he took off again in his kart without a word.

'OK.' She waited, feeling more and more ridiculous as various faces she recognised from the jetty began appearing from the lane – on foot, of course. The German woman was among them, trailing behind her a middle-aged man and teenage girl, both long haired, long limbed and, Eleanor soon noticed, long faced; they looked like a pair of sulky spaniels being taken for a walk in the rain against their will. The girl was as cool and gorgeous as any of the women at the waterfront, her blonde hair sun streaked and her skin perfectly smooth.

'You have taken the taxi?' the woman called to Eleanor. 'A nice idea, I think.' She laughed again in that oddly ferocious way. 'Holidays are for the relaxation!'

'They are.' Eleanor wasn't at all surprised to see Lewis sloping into view next, a battered brown leather bag slung over his shoulder. He was smoking, which somehow seemed to highlight his boyishness next to the German couple; he looked young enough to be their son. She avoided eye contact and the smirk she felt sure would be on his lips, but from the corner of her eye she saw him fall into easy conversation with another set of arrivals and told herself that he likely hadn't seen her climb into the buggy. He hadn't seen her climb *out*. She busied herself taking off her hat, patting down her hair and hunting for her passport.

Once a group had gathered and the desk bell been repeatedly rung, a round white-haired old woman appeared through an archway to the right and moved towards them at the pace of a sloth shrugging off deep sleep. She spoke extremely rapidly, however, and began making what Eleanor took to be some kind of welcome address in Italian. A truncated version in German followed, before she finished, briefly, in English: 'Welcome to this Albergo delle Rose. I am nime Giovanna. Give the passport. Dinner is in the owl.'

Eleanor pressed forward, suddenly feeling that she couldn't bear a moment longer in transit among all these tourists. She needed to lie down.

'Your nime?' asked the sloth. Eleanor noticed she had several teeth missing at the back on both sides.

She handed over her passport.

'Please careful yourself een sunshine,' the woman cried, loudly, leaning towards Eleanor's face. To her horror, Eleanor realised a small mole on her chin was now the object of inspection. The other guests had stopped talking and were looking over with interest as Giovanna declared, 'You's too white, *inglese*, you's will burn, get the cancer.'

'Yes, yes, I have sunscreen,' Eleanor muttered, weakly. This seemed to satisfy the old bird and she was at last despatched with her key up a nearby staircase. Behind her she thought she heard a round of titters from the waiting group.

14

The room was small and pristinely clean, with pretty pink and blue tiles and a carved dark-wood bed and desk. The only other item was a low-slung white sofa with silk cushions the colour of bougainvillea. She cleared the desk of its hotel stationery and carefully laid out her most important possessions: monocular (recommended by ornithologists and chosen over the binocular model for its lightness and discretion); digital camera and charger; torch with spare battery; notebook and pen; guidebook. Then she sat on the edge of the bed, the cover cool against her legs, and finally allowed herself to take stock of her feelings. She felt swamped with dejection. Now that she had arrived, the whole thing seemed farcical. What was it Lizzie had called it, when she'd phoned Eleanor at the departure gate in a last-ditch attempt to talk her out of it? 'Mission unhinged'. Her best friend in the world had thought she was mad, had been sick with worry for her. So why hadn't she listened?

A knock at the door made her jump and she pulled on her sunglasses before answering, faintly aware that this would seem peculiar in a shuttered room.

'Come in!'

'Hi there, I'm Sophie, another guest.' The woman was English, in her late thirties and approachably pretty, with pale, plump skin and silky blonde hair to her shoulders. 'You left your hat on the reception desk . . .'

'Thank you so much,' Eleanor said, feeling as though

she'd been caught by the teacher doodling obscenities in her maths book. She knew she needed to stop behaving so guiltily; it would only stir suspicion in regular civilians like this one. It was good to have her hat back, though. She placed it on the desk and turned back to Sophie. 'I'm Eleanor.'

Sophie looked with eager eyes over her shoulder and into the room. Eleanor supposed she was checking to see if it was larger or nicer than her own. 'Goodness, that looks very organised,' she said, indicating the desk with its neat arrangement of tools. 'We didn't think to bring a torch. D'you think we'll need one? Aren't there street lights?'

'I'm not sure. I wouldn't want to get lost at night,' replied Eleanor, lamely.

'There's no chance of that. According to my book there's only one road on the whole island.'

This was disconcerting news. Eleanor's own guide-book hadn't mentioned this, nor included a map, for that matter. She'd imagined herself prowling round a labyrinthine network of alleyways, like a medina, perhaps, with plenty of places to duck into and lie low.

'What's that telescope thingy for?' Sophie asked.

'Oh, er, that's my monocular. I got it from a shop for birders.'

'Birders?'

'You know, bird spotters. It's so I can see all the flora and fauna close up. Apparently, the island's full of it.'

16

This was pathetic, she knew, but Sophie smiled encouragingly, showing small straight teeth. 'Well, all you're missing are the infrared goggles and Swiss Army Knife,' she said, merrily. They both laughed, Eleanor a note too long.

'OK,' said Sophie. 'Well, I'm going to get a large drink after that journey from hell. We'll see you at dinner, shall we? *Otto ora, va bene?*'

'Yes. I mean *sì*.' Eleanor closed the door. Generally, she loathed Brits who insisted on showing off their language skills to their compatriots when English would have done perfectly well. But she hadn't understood much of Giovanna's trilingual address and had been wondering about dinner. Now she could look up *otto ora* in her book.

Eight o'clock. Good, that should be long enough to pull herself together.

Chapter 2

Dinner was a lot more enjoyable than Eleanor had expected. The 'owl' turned out to be a lovely vaulted hall, with low, candle-lit alcoves and tiled seats stacked with red-and-silver embroidered cushions. It was already noisy with conversation when she walked in, voices crashing off the stone walls and causing everyone to speak even more loudly. There were two long tables, one of which had been claimed by a party of Italians, the other reserved for the non-Italian arrivals. Evidently, smoking was permitted, which was very good news indeed for someone who had become somewhat reliant of late.

Sophie was already there, all showered and shiny in the kind of classic white shift dress that always looked better on the last night of a holiday than the first. She insisted Eleanor take the seat next to her.

'You've taken the shades off then? I thought you might be a pop star or someone famous.'

'I'm afraid not.' Just an idiot, Eleanor thought, cringing.

'Meet my husband Tim!'

'*Ciao*, Eleanor.' Tim was an eager-looking sort of man in his early forties, with a fleshy, still-attractive face and a jocular, well-spoken delivery that Eleanor guessed would get ten times louder after a few drinks. Dressed in well-ironed khaki, he looked as though he were ready to lead a team into paintball battle. From the pair's style and easy worldliness, she felt she could pin down their west London postcode without needing to uncover a single personal detail. She wondered if they were now assessing her with equal haste: spinster takes holiday alone to rediscover long-buried passion for ornithology? Or something more poignant, perhaps: sheltered London girl seeks solitude to recover from loss of old family pet? She wished her reason for being in Panarea were so innocent.

Next to arrive were the German woman, Katharina, and her spaniel husband, Stefan. He'd looked quite striking from a distance, with his muscular build and thick hair dusted with grey, but now Eleanor looked more closely she saw that his eyes were small and close set, screwed up as though someone had just squeezed a lemon in his face. He dressed reasonably well, though, with no evidence of the socks-and-sandals crime she might have expected. Katharina, meanwhile, with her curly dark hair down her back and fat lips coated in pearly pink, had the air of a previous, more forgiving fashion era.

'And who's this young lady?' asked Tim with barely contained lechery, holding out his hand to the Germans' daughter, who was looking disconcertingly sexy in a cropped white T-shirt with the words 'Tennis is Life' stamped across her breasts.

She regarded him with a passive, slate-eyed gaze. 'My name is Nathalie,' she said, finally, her tone conferring instant subhuman status on a surprised, but undeterred, Tim. Eleanor found her chilly self-possession distinctly unnerving.

'Just fourteen,' tinkled Katharina, as Tim took an unconvincingly long time to absorb the girl's pledge to her favourite ball sport, even cocking his head in scrutiny. Nathalie just looked bored, hooking her arms over her seat-back and looking over Tim's shoulder at the Italian table. Eleanor glanced at Katharina. Though handsome in a weather beaten sort of way, she must surely be hurt by the readiness with which this new man overlooked her to smack his lips over her nymphet daughter. Fourteen? With her glossed pout and mascara-thick eyelashes, the girl looked at least nineteen.

'Hi, all,' came a new voice. 'I think I'm with you, is there space?'

It was Lewis. He hadn't changed his clothes from the journey, Eleanor noticed, as he took the empty seat opposite her, but exuded the same freshman enthusiasm as the others. With a new round of introductions, there was palpable relief that in spite of the exotic setting they'd be sharing meals with their own kind. Eleanor was certainly pleased that she wouldn't need to struggle with her one-day-old Italian at a tableful of glamorous couples from the mainland.

Best of all, there were now no other places left at their table. It would have been appalling luck to have booked the very hotel where Will was staying. (Her strategy, given such an event, had been simple: run and hide.) She instantly felt more relaxed: no danger could possibly lurk here. Her real mission would begin tomorrow, but for now she could lower her guard and allow herself to be distracted for a few hours, make the best of meeting the other guests.

Katharina fixed her eyes on Lewis and spoke with renewed command. 'You are living in London, Lewis, so what is your job, please?'

'I'm an archaeologist,' he said, making Eleanor realise how little she'd thought to ask in their conversation on the boat. 'I teach at one of the London colleges, do research, a bit of writing. What about you, Katharina? Did I hear you're from Cologne? That's a lovely city, I was there last year.'

Eleanor opened her mouth to join in, but at the same moment Sophie pounced. 'Isn't this hotel wonderful? So spare and stylish. We tried to rent a villa, you know, but it turns out you have to organise

21

it months in advance just to get on a waiting list – that's if you're willing to stump up ten grand, or however much it was.'

'It is a lovely island,' Eleanor agreed. 'So secret and hidden away.' She brandished her cigarettes. 'Do you mind if I . . .?'

'God, no. Everyone seems to here. I don't think they bother with smoking bans in the middle of the whatever-it's-called Sicilian ocean.'

Eleanor lit her first cigarette of the evening. It tasted dry, dirty, reassuring.

'We just adore Sicily,' Sophie went on. 'You know, this is our first holiday on our own since Rory was born. We had our fifth wedding anniversary last month and we said, "Right, enough is enough, we're human beans in our own right".'

'Human beans?'

'That's what Rory calls them. God, I must get out of the habit or you'll think I'm one of *those* mums.'

Eleanor wasn't sure what *those* were, but she did know it was already too late to alter the course of this conversation. 'How old is Rory?'

'Four last month, gorgeous little teeny-weeny,' Sophie pouted. 'It feels so strange to cut the cord. I can barely remember life B.C.'

'B.C.?'

'Before Child.' Sophie adopted an excessively dramatic tone, as though performing the ogre in a children's bedtime story. 'You're still B.C. yourself, I take it?'

'I certainly am.' Smoking furiously, Eleanor braced herself for the slew of Rory-related tales to come. She was well versed in the dynamics of conversation with fond mothers: once warmed up, her friends with children would run through anecdotes like waiters listing specials. However, after a whistle-stop account of the key moments from conception to kindergarten, Sophie surprised her by switching slickly into information-gathering mode.

'So, what about you, Eleanor? What's your story? What fabulous luck to find an English girl at the same hotel. We heard Panarea was all Italian glitterati – not that Tim and I would recognise a famous Italian if he landed on us from a great height. Oh, unless it was Pavarotti, of course. Hang on, he's dead, so that seems unlikely. Who, then? Sophia Loren, is she still alive? Help me out here, Eleanor!' She was obviously the kind of person who addressed all comers with the same confidence that they would be as interested in hearing her opinions as she was in sharing them. It was not so different from Lewis's tour guiding. Eleanor found both styles comforting; they meant less effort on her part.

So why had she chosen Panarea for her holiday? Sophie now asked. Which airport had she flown into and did she have to stay overnight in Lipari en route?

Eleanor shot a look at Lewis, who thankfully was preoccupied with Stefan, and tried to keep her answers economical and bland. She knew she wasn't a good liar and even when she sounded convincing, her blushing usually gave her away. '. . . And since no one was free to go away with me, I thought I'd catch some late-summer sun on my own. Much nicer than hanging around the flat all day watching daytime TV.'

'So you're not with anyone back in London?'

Again, she checked Lewis. She should never have mentioned a boyfriend to him, a fiancé, no less. That had been silly. She prayed he wouldn't bring up the subject himself out of politeness. But surely he must be speculating already? If he'd overheard any of her check-in exchange with Giovanna, he'd know she hadn't even enquired about the arrival of another guest, had clearly not been joining anyone and was here at dinner alone. Now it was obvious the group would be sharing all hotel meals, she realised she'd have to put him right as soon as possible, which was a shame. It had given her a sweet artificial glow to present herself as someone's fiancé, one of a pair.

'It's complicated,' she said, finally, lowering her voice so Sophie had to crane forward to hear.

Her new friend nodded knowingly. 'When isn't it? Well, I think it's wonderful when girls go off on holiday solo. I did that a few times before I got married. You think it will be miserable, being away on your own, but it's total bliss, isn't it? Just non-stop reading and drinking and convincing yourself you're over whichever bastard last darkened your door.'

This was getting a little too close to the bone and Eleanor felt anxiety rise again. 'Do you work?' she asked, hurriedly changing the subject. 'I mean other than being a mum.'

'No, I used to work in the City for Tim's bank. That's how we met. He was a fund manager, head of department, actually, and I was his assistant, would you believe it?' It seemed a perfectly probable way for a husband and wife to have met, but since Sophie hooted loudly at the absurdity of it, Eleanor could think of nothing to do but giggle along.

'But since Rory, I've been at home. Picking things up off the floor, mainly. I can't imagine being released into the wild again. But maybe I'll start my own business, do a course or something. A friend of mine's just started doing mosaics, went on a fantastic course in Padua. Anyway, I'm not thinking about anything this week except being completely lazy; maybe even have a go at producing a little sister for Rory . . .'

Eleanor wondered if she had shared this scheme with Tim, and looked across the table to where he was draining the last of a jug of red wine into his own glass. His dark hair had ruffled to expose pale glimpses of scalp, but his eyebrows were strikingly plush over blue eyes. He'd slipped into the role of leader as comfortably as an old dressing gown: the atmosphere was already festive and excitable. With an easy gesture he silenced the table for a toast: 'Here's to a great gathering of Europeans and a holiday of a lifetime! To leaving our troubles behind!'

Fat chance, thought Eleanor; she for one had come to Panarea in search of her troubles and, if Lizzie was right, maybe even to make new ones. But everyone responded to Tim with happy little 'chin chins', slopping wine all over the place as they clinked tumblers around the table. Tim slapped Lewis on the back and cadged himself a cigarette before predicting that the seven of them would all be like old friends by the end of the week. Eyeing Nathalie's unimpressed face, Eleanor doubted this, too.

'She's a right little heartbreaker, isn't she?' said Sophie, following her glance. 'Just look at those pert little bosoms. Makes you wonder how all that gorgeous leanness can turn into, well, into you and me, right under our noses!' Chummily, she indicated Eleanor's stomach, a shining white portion of which had popped out above her waistband. 'No offence, Eleanor, but her trunk would fit three times over into ours!'

Eleanor felt dismayed to be categorised with Sophie in this uninvited comparison of 'trunks' (and she would have preferred a term that did not bring elephants to mind). After all, the woman had claimed only minutes ago that her body had been 'slackened' beyond salvage by the arrival of Rory ('Came into the world as though heaving himself through a manhole. Can you imagine how that feels, Eleanor?'). She had liked to believe that weight loss had been the single welcome side-effect of her own recent miseries.

'I just shudder to think of a Lolita like that getting her mitts on Rory.' Sophie gave a theatrical little quiver before straightening up to fork pasta into her mouth.

'He's only four, though, you said?' Eleanor asked.

'Yes, four and two months, but you can't help worrying about the future – they grow up faster than you think, you know. I dread the day I have to share him with another woman.'

Katharina leant across the table to join in, evidently having missed Sophie's previous comments about her daughter. 'You are getting that very right,' she said in her deep, rolling voice. 'These bambinos, they grow very quick. You pull the eyebrows only one time and now they're with the fourteenth anniversary!'

Baffled, Eleanor looked at Katharina's eyebrows: they were narrow, neatly arched, rather elegant.

'I know exactly what you mean, Katharina,' Sophie said. 'There's no time for personal grooming when there's a kiddie around. Since Rory came along, I've only had time to have my hair cut twice. In four years! It used to be so sleek and gorgeous, but now look at the state of it. It's like hay fit for a horse's nosebag. I'm totally ashamed of myself.'

Before Katharina could reply, Tim burst in from the left: 'Just look at the ladies, closing ranks as usual, and we haven't even reached the fish course!' And he exploded with laughter, causing his neighbour to wince faintly. This, and the rapid fire of Sophie's chatter, made Eleanor suspect the couple had not been out much lately.

On cue, two of Giovanna's boys appeared with a vast platter of roasted fish and dishes of sautéed potatoes and fried aubergine slices with tomatoes and capers. Everything smelled delicious. One of the boys was the teen who'd collected Eleanor from the jetty; he was very good-looking, she now saw. Predictably, he was eyeing Nathalie, who had yet to contribute to the evening's conversation.

Looking around the noisy room, Eleanor saw that all the hotel guests, with the exception of Lewis and herself, were in couples. She wondered if the Italians at the other table would assume that they were a pair. After all, they were sitting opposite each other and she had helped herself to his cigarette lighter. She watched him as he mopped up the garlicky fish juices with a piece of bread and bolted it down in a couple of bites. His hands were very pale, she thought, considering he was an archaeologist and must spend half his time scrabbling around in the dust for shards of old terracotta. Perhaps he wore special gloves.

Stefan turned to Lewis and asked loudly: 'Lewis, where is your girlfriend? Are you alone here in Panarea?'

'She's in London,' replied Lewis, colouring slightly as all faces turned his way. 'She couldn't get the time off and, anyway, I'm partly here for work myself. I'm writing a paper about the local archaeology – there's a fantastic ruined Bronze Age village on the island, and Roman traces on the islets, as well.'

'I've never heard anyone use the word "islet" before,' cried Tim, in a bid to wrest back the spotlight, and Sophie rewarded him with a whoop of laughter.

Eleanor, still panicking that it was only a matter of time before Lewis remembered to ask after her fiancé, caught his eye and gave what she hoped was a calm, sane smile. 'What does your girlfriend do, Lewis? Is she an archaeologist as well?'

'No, no, she's a teacher. She teaches pre-school kids.'

'How lovely,' Sophie said. 'Those girls are angels from heaven, if you ask me. Well, except for the ones you read about who leave the kids to play with loaded guns while they text their boyfriends.'

'There are no guns in Chiswick, darling,' Tim said, and began to explain to the table the extraordinary talents of little Rory's nursery teacher, how she'd trans-formed singlehanded the boy's Terrible Twos into the delightful brand of infant maturity they were confident would lead to Oxbridge and the Cabinet. 'No more tantrums from the little bugger, thank Christ, it's all proper sentences now. Quite the young philosopher, isn't he, Sophe?'

As Sophie picked up the tale, Lewis looked as relieved as Eleanor felt at the change of subject. She decided he was probably the sort of man who felt uncomfortable talking about himself, but could drone at length on subjects like sport, tax returns and, of course, museums.

'So is that what you studied at university, archaeology?' she asked him.

'Yes, and ancient history, at Bristol. That's where I met . . .' He paused to take a final mouthful of bread and she waited patiently while he swallowed. '. . . Where I met Rebecca, my girlfriend.'

'Right.'

'And what do you do, Eleanor?'

'I'm a designer for an advertising agency – we do a lot of Internet stuff.'

'Where are you based?'

'Hammersmith. I haven't been with the company long. Actually, I'm not sure it's for me – or that I'm for them.'

'Why's that?'

Because I'm completely obsessed with something else and have no energy or imagination left for work . . . Her spirits dipped at the thought. It was true that during the last few months she'd barely noticed her work life and had as much presence round the office as a zombie: slow, dead-eyed, tripping people up as they tried to pass. She was lucky she hadn't been formally warned or even encouraged to leave: there'd been a lot of late mornings and she'd been less than sparkling in creative meetings.

'Oh, no reason,' she told Lewis. 'I'm just not sure I'm cut out for that kind of thing. I get frustrated dealing with clients. There are too many compromises in the work.'

That sounded reasonable enough and she hoped Lewis would view her as a purist, committed to her true artistic values in a cynical commercial world, but he just smirked and said, 'What did you expect, going into advertising?'

'I know, you're right,' agreed the purist. As she tried to come up with something more intelligent, Stefan cut in and she watched gratefully as Lewis asked him about his job (which, from what she could gather, amounted to the occasional gig as a jazz guitarist). While part of her was enjoying the old tingle of first conversations with new people, another was already exhausted by it, craving instead the usual occupant of her waking mind. How strange it was to find herself on the subject of work, to be asked to think about her career, when she'd spent the last few months talking about one subject and one subject only: Will. When he wasn't being discussed with her friends, she was replaying conversations with him in her head or scripting new ones, constantly refilling herself with his presence.

At last, dinner was finished, including a whole flask of lemon liqueur Giovanna had brought out with the pudding and coffee. Even Nathalie had been allowed to dip into that, not that it had sweetened her demeanour in the slightest. Eleanor tried not to meet the youngster's unpleasant gaze.

'*Andiamo*, let's get this holiday off with a night to remember!' declared Tim, getting clumsily to his feet. 'Drinks down at the harbour, no excuses!'

Stefan relayed the call to arms to the Italian table and one or two stood gamely. They lacked the urgent alcoholic flush of the Brits and Germans, Eleanor saw, that sense of an emergency mission. She knew it was impossible for her to go too.

'I won't join you, Tim, I think I'll get an early night. I still feel a bit queasy after the journey.' This was desperate, particularly given the appetite she'd displayed for the huge meal and bottomless jugs of wine, but Tim let her off with a bit of slurred teasing and Sophie even gave her a kiss goodnight before she was able to escape up the stairs. She wondered if it was too late to call Lizzie in London. But there was nothing to report yet and, in any case, Lizzie was not a great fan of her plan. She was on her own here.

Lingering on the open walkway outside her door, she listened to the voices of her fellow guests, loud and bright with wine, and to their fading laughter as the group made its way down the lane. She felt a twist of envy for the holidays they would all have here, long, fun-filled days on a beautiful sunny island.

The normal holidays of normal people.

Chapter 3

Three days earlier, London had already had the air of a new season about it, worn out, palely lit, not quite ready to welcome life back indoors. It didn't suit the hot bubbling Eleanor felt in her blood as she watched Lizzie come into the bar and settle into her seat. She had to scrape her chair forward and lean right into the table to allow a group of men to squeeze by – City types whose faces looked preposterously young for their expensive suits, like sixth formers dressed up for a family wedding.

'I've got some news,' she burst out, as soon as Lizzie had ordered. 'A plan!'

'What plan? Sounds excellent,' Lizzie said, hopefully. 'Are you going on holiday, like I suggested?'

'Actually, yes,' said Eleanor, 'though it's not *exactly* as you suggested. I'm going to Italy. Miranda told me Will and the new girl have just left for some secret island hideaway in Sicily. I thought I might like to hide away, too.' She tried to stop her lips from widening idiotically. Will! She would be seeing him again within a matter of days.

'Oh, Eleanor!' Lizzie's pretty, open face always expressed precisely what she was feeling. Now, with her pale eyebrows raised high and the dark eyes wide as circles, Eleanor could see in her friend's face a mixture of pity, affection and plain alarm. 'You can't be serious? Confronting them when they're on holiday – it's crazy, you'll be humiliated!'

'Who said anything about confronting them?' Eleanor was impatient to get the objections over with. 'I just want to see them.'

'How do you mean, see them?'

'I mean go there, hang out, keep a low profile, you know . . .'

'A low profile? What, in disguise? Please tell me you're not intending to *stalk* them?'

'That's not what I mean,' Eleanor said, testily. Lizzie was disappointingly difficult to convince when it came to Will.

'OK, so what? You're going to bump into him accidentally on purpose and say, "Hey, long time no see! Since we're both here, in the middle of nowhere, let's rake over what happened between us yet again – I'm sure your new girlfriend won't mind if I join you for dinner"?'

'Oh no, nothing like that,' Eleanor said, nervously. She

started playing with her drink, using the plastic stick to stab at the lemon slice until there was just the rind left.

'What then? What's the point in going all the way to Italy if you're not even going to talk to him?'

'I may not get the opportunity,' Eleanor said. 'I have to prepare myself for lots of different scenarios.'

'So it's not a plan at all.'

'It's a *loose* plan.'

'It's a *mental* plan.' Lizzie switched to her patient, rational work voice. 'OK, best-case scenario: you go and have a lovely holiday, you find Will and at the sight of you he changes his mind, dumps the new girl, and you get back together. Agreed?'

Eleanor didn't answer but the thumping in her ribcage was so loud she felt sure Lizzie could hear it.

'Look,' she said. 'I just know this is the right thing to do. Things will be different out of context. You could be a bit more excited for me.'

'But it's so extreme, so risky! I'm just worried there won't be the happy ending you're looking for.'

'I'm not looking for a happy ending, just an ending.' That sounded good, Eleanor thought. She hoped it were true. 'I just think that going there and seeing them together, seeing Will with her, might really help me move on.'

Move on. There they were, out there between them after just five minutes, the most frequently uttered words of the last few months. No quick drink after work had been complete without them, no phone conversation satisfactorily concluded.

'Bloody Miranda!' Lizzie exclaimed. 'I can't believe she told you where Will is. How does she even know? How come they're suddenly so close?'

'I guess she must still be in touch with him. They did get on really well when we all lived together.'

'Well I think that's totally disloyal. She just wants to stir trouble.'

Eleanor sighed. They'd had the Miranda debate before. Lizzie had never really warmed to Eleanor's younger office friend, had made up her mind after the first meeting that Miranda was a little lightweight, a little junior for their intensely analytical round-table sessions. But Eleanor knew that Miranda's fatal mistake had been to tire too early of the subject of Simon, Lizzie's new boyfriend. They were cut from the same cloth, all of them, and the cloth had men's names embroidered into it.

'But she has passed on the information to me, so she's not exactly being loyal to him, either, is she? Anyway, Miranda is a friend. I live with her and work with her and I can do without a big falling-out.'

'Oh, Eleanor,' said Lizzie again. 'Why don't you just wait for Will to come back to London and then go and have a look at the girl? You know where he works, even if you're not sure where he's living now.'

This was a huge concession and they both knew it.

Until now Lizzie had sternly discouraged Eleanor from making any contact with Will at all.

'You might not even run into them on this island, what's it called?'

'Panarea. I looked it up. It's tiny – it'll be easy to track them down. And if I don't, well, I'll just enjoy a bit of sun.'

'You've already booked the whole thing, haven't you?' asked Lizzie. 'God knows what you're really planning. And what about work?'

'Oh, they were fine,' Eleanor said. 'I haven't taken any holiday since March, not since New York.'

It was not quite true that the office had supported her request for time off. Her account director Rufus had been livid, though he'd hidden it well enough. There was a lot of new business at the moment, he'd said, baring his teeth in a little clenched grin, and he needed to throw a lot of people at it, including Eleanor, especially Eleanor, who had once had a dream in which her boss had entered a dwarf-tossing competition and she had been his dwarf. But he'd agreed in the end. No doubt Miranda had told him about the sleeping pills incident; he was far too delicate with her for it to be put down to luck.

Eleanor said: 'I'm off on Friday. I've booked a hotel for ten days, but I can always change it if—'

'If what? If Will calls the police and gets you thrown off the island?' Lizzie was laughing now, at least.

'Sicilian jails aren't very comfortable, you know. They're filled with Mafia.'

'Neither the police not the Mafia will have the slightest interest in me,' Eleanor said, whose great fear was that the same might be said of Will.

'Bloody hell, Eleanor. Well, what can I say? Good luck, I suppose.'

Even through her head rush, Eleanor felt a bit sorry for her friend. For almost twelve years, since they'd first met at college, Eleanor had followed Lizzie's lead. But recently the dynamic of their friendship had shifted: Lizzie, the single-minded one, the one who ran a team of thirty people, had been defeated by the sheer force of Eleanor's gloom. 'Another thing I got out of Miranda,' she said. 'This new girlfriend of his, she's an actress.'

'An actress, really?'

This was surprising, Eleanor agreed. They'd assumed the new interest was someone from Will's office.

'Well, that can mean one of two things,' said Lizzie, finally sounding more excited. 'Either she's a leading-lady type, so good-looking and thin, like Angelina Jolie, or she's a character-actress type, like . . .' She cast around for an example, '. . . Maggie Smith!'

'Maggie Smith?' Eleanor was starting to feel faintly hysterical. 'Well, I hope it's her rather than Angelina!'

'Me too,' said Lizzie.

But they both doubted it.

*   *   *

The next morning Eleanor avoided breakfast and, from what she could hear through her open windows, so did most of last night's other revellers: just the occasional ring of cutlery on china over the low chunter of italian television.

She showered, dressed and looked at the equipment laid out on the desk. Her private-eye starter kit. How very organised she'd been. But now the time had come she was at a loss as to how to begin her search for Will. She supposed she could sit in one of the waterfront cafés full of beautiful Italians; that was obviously Panarea's parading ground and he'd be sure to appear sooner or later. But she'd been right to avoid going down there with the others last night: it meant only that he would be able to spot her as easily as she could him.

She looked at herself in the mirror, unsure of what she might find. Her light brown hair, newly chopped to chin length, still looked unfamiliar, but at least it was less comically bushy than yesterday. She wasn't at all sure it suited her. Her pale skin, with high colour in the cheeks, was familiar enough – no seductive Mediterranean shimmer quite yet. She smiled at her reflection, trying to imagine herself animated and friendly, as she had been last night. That looked better, if a bit maniacal.

She'd packed painstakingly, but now her clothes seemed a disaster: the grey T-shirt and white linen shorts she'd just put on looked as though they'd been screwed into a ball and squeezed in someone's damp fist before being released for wear. No, while she looked like this the idea was definitely not that Will should stumble across her on the first morning and take the offensive in a public spectacle watched by half of Milan's modelling community. She would head in the opposite direction to the harbour, inland.

Outside the day was already hot, startlingly so. The sun bounced off the walls as though someone were redirecting the rays into her face with a magnifying glass, and Eleanor felt herself respond in optimistic little stabs to the beauty of the place. The alley was lined with simple sugar-cube houses with blue shutters and pretty wrought-iron balconies and gates. Flowers spilled from every garden and terrace: lilies, bougainvillea, hibiscus, all painted exotic hues by the sun. And in the distance stood that great knuckle of a hill; that was Punta del Corvo, according to her guidebook, the highest point on Panarea. About halfway up, neatly splitting its pelt of gorse, stood a line of slim, elegant trees, cypresses, perhaps. Even the trees were tall and graceful in Panarea, Eleanor thought. This reminded her that she would need to get up to speed on her flora and fauna: Sophie would be sure to tell the others about her special interest and it would be just her luck that there was a botanist – or zoologist – in the group. Lewis struck her as the kind of person who might even know all the Latin names; she'd be outwitted in a flash.

The painted tiles that passed for Panarea's street signs

told her that Sophie was right: the island did have just one main road, and it wasn't even a road, just a swept lane, wide enough for the three-wheelers but nothing bigger. The signs gave the distances in times: if she turned left out of San Pietro she'd reach the beach – *spiaggia* – in thirty minutes and the *Villaggio Preistorico* in forty; that must be Lewis's Bronze Age village. If she turned right she'd get to Iditella and Calcara, whatever they were. It was bad news, this one-road arrangement. Unless Will and his actress were getting around by boat, they'd surely be using this road too. And she knew from her own holidays with Will that he prided himself on adopting local transport methods, in this case a scooter ridden barefoot as though fleeing Pompeii from the wrath of Vesuvius. Already she'd had to spring out of the way several times as scooters zoomed by.

She decided to start with the beach, striding up the lane as it curled and climbed, picturing herself as a celebrated sleuth, a hunter. A sense of purpose had taken hold of her, an exhilaration she hadn't felt for months. Would it feel so very different, she wondered, if Will were actually expecting her, if she really were here for a lovers' reunion? She'd be skipping along the path just the same, aching for that first glimpse just as she ached for it now. But when it happened, if it happened, she had to be ready to hide, possibly even make a run for it. A fiancée wouldn't need to do that.

She picked up her pace, already sweating in the heat, and listened for voices on the path ahead. If Italian she would continue with confidence, but if English she would lower her head and pretend to study her guidebook, so anyone passing would see only the white disc of her hat. Where possible, she even slipped into the nearest doorway out of sight, but this grew more difficult as the shops and restaurants petered out, replaced by smart private villas, each one securely walled and gated.

She caught the chatter of Italian coming towards her and glanced up as another group wandered by, everyone murmuring '*Buon giorno*' to her. One rake-thin woman was wearing nothing but a vivid red swimsuit and turban, apparently made from one seamless flow of fabric. It was what Eleanor's mother would call a 'get-up'. It looked extremely elegant.

It was soon clear that the times on the signs were for people walking at Giovanna's snail pace, for the beach came into view after only fifteen minutes. There was a café to the near side, half full already, the warm smell of bread in the air. She used her spyglass to scan the outside tables for Will – no sign – before padding down to the sand. It was soft and squishy, the colour of ground pepper.

The beach wasn't crowded, just a few groups of Italians grilling themselves, not a tube of sun lotion in sight. At the back, in the beach's single scrap of shade, there had gathered a clutch of creatures with pallid bodies and red faces. The English, though no one from her hotel was among them, as far as she could see.

Spotting some steep steps on the far side of the beach she decided to take them. This brought fresh anxiety, for they were narrow, barely wide enough for two people to pass one another; if Will happened to be coming down the other way he would see her at once. But pulling her hat down over her ears would affect her balance – she was nervous about heights. She decided to risk it. Thankfully, only one family passed her on the way, with much shouting of their dog's name, Uno, a snappy little thing that hurtled past her legs and flung itself into the water. She watched it splash around a group of women, all standing thigh-deep in the water smoking cigarettes.

She pushed herself on and up, stopping only when she'd reached the top. It was dizzyingly high, the sea a distant floor of twinkling cobbles. Ahead a promontory jutted out into the ocean like a hammerhead – that was the Punta Milazzese headland, her book informed her – and beyond it lay a dark-grey heap, Salina or Lipari, presumably. On the top of the hammerhead people were picking their way through tracks of stones, some with heads bent over guidebooks – this must be the prehistoric village, Eleanor thought. She scanned the faces systematically: Lewis obviously hadn't made it here yet and nor, more to the point, had Will. Perhaps

Lizzie would turn out to be right, she might not see him at all the whole time she was here, her trip no more than a costly near-miss. Then it occurred to her that Will and the girl may in fact just be holed up in their hotel room, in bed. It was a new romance, after all. She remembered it herself, those first few months with Will . . . But she wouldn't think about that now. Remembering his face, his voice, caused excitement; remembering his touch caused pain.

She was just about to turn back when she noticed a couple disappearing down some steps to the right, so she followed and peeked over the edge. Below was a small stony cove crowded with bodies, the sunbathers splayed out on the rocks like sacrifices. The smooth grey stones made Eleanor think of the pebble sweets she used to be given by her parents as a treat at English seaside towns – she remembered selecting each one carefully from the tube and sucking it right down to a tasteless little kernel. Another train of thought to avoid: her mother and father, proud of her, confident of her path through life; what they might think to see her now, to know what she was doing here.

Again, no Will. The water looked wonderful, aquamarine and limpid, and snorkellers were slicing off at angles from its edge. Her eye was caught by the movements of a beautiful black-haired girl at the back of the cove, who stood up, pulled a snorkelling mask out of her bag and started making her way towards the water. The stones must be tricky to walk on, Eleanor thought, but the girl danced from one to the next with ease, making it look as simple as a game of hopscotch. She snapped the goggles over her eyes, dropped into the water and pushed off, snorkel bobbing. Several faces had turned to watch her. Who *were* all these women? thought Eleanor. Was it some kind of genetically engineered secret race? Did they come here specifically to mix with their own kind?

'Eleanor! Eleanor! What are you looking at? Feasting on the local talent?'

She straightened to find Sophie, fresh and smiling in a blue sundress, her straw-coloured hair scraped back by a wide band decorated with blue flowers. Tim trailed behind carrying a bag of groceries and calling out, 'Hello, hello. *Come stai?*'

'Hi.' Eleanor concentrated hard on looking natural. 'I thought I saw a, um, parrot,' she told them, waving her monocular about in no particular direction. A parrot? How ludicrous, they'd think she was deluded. She was seized by a sudden impulse to rush to the cliff edge and leap off. But Tim and Sophie both cackled appreciatively.

'Oh yes,' said Tim, 'I've heard about the attractive birdlife in Panarea myself and I have to say that early sightings are proving *very* gratifying . . .'

'Shut up, you twit,' Sophie said. 'This must be Cala Junca. The snorkelling's supposed to be the best on the island. Just look at the water! Are you coming down, Eleanor? We've got *panini* and *formaggi* from the *supermercato* – you're more than welcome to join us for a picnic? Then we can all splash around with the fish. What's the word for fish again, Tim, is it *piscine*? No, *pesce*?'

'Thank you, no,' said Eleanor, suppressing her irritation at Sophie's insistence on Italian terms. 'I forgot to put my bikini on, so I think I'll just carry on wandering.' Before they could think to notice the straps of her swimsuit showing at the neck of her T-shirt, she added, 'You look lovely, Sophie, that colour really suits you.'

'Thank you,' beamed Sophie. 'That's sweet of you. One has to make an effort in the company of all these Latin goddesses.'

'I know,' agreed Eleanor, regretful once more of her own choice of clothing. Judging by the way the other two were looking curiously at her oversized hat, she decided that the best she could expect was to be filed under 'eccentric'. She added: 'The women here make Nathalie look like a gawky teenager, after all.'

'God, yeah, we saw the brat earlier,' said Sophie. 'She was arguing with Katharina, not wanting to go on some boat trip. Said she just wanted to sunbathe on the roof terrace. We think she's got the hots for one of the waiters, Carlo, and you know he and Rico are both Giovanna's grandsons? Or even Lewis, maybe? She's a man-eater. I wouldn't have a clue how to deal with a child like that. I feel so sorry for Katharina.' Hands on hips, she looked set for an hour-long gossip, but Tim was already making impatient noises. 'Sophe, I need to lie down before I collapse and die. Sorry, Eleanor, not feeling too bright-eyed today, bit too much of the old sauce last night.' He pulled off his sunglasses and Eleanor saw how bleary and bloodshot his eyes were.

'Oh, how was the harbour last night?' she asked, suddenly unwilling to let them go. While Sophie chattered on, it occurred to her for the first time that Miranda might have deliberately misled her about Will's holiday plans. What if he'd never been in Panarea in the first place, was somewhere completely different? How long had she known Miranda, anyway? Less than a year and she hadn't had much time for her lately. Perhaps her flatmate's loyalties had switched to Will since he'd moved out. Most friends felt they had to take sides in these situations, but Miranda gave the impression of being comfortable in both camps.

Realising she was frowning, she forced herself to tune back into the conversation.

'. . . So it was all very civilised,' Sophie was saying, 'with the notable exception of my own husband. But that's the Italians for you, they just don't seem to get as rowdy as us. They've got so much more style, haven't they?'

'Any other Brits about?' Eleanor asked, casually. She longed to cut to the chase and describe Will in detail;

ask if they'd run into a software consultant from south London, amazing light-grey eyes, thick blond hair, irresistible charm. Perhaps with a theatrical-looking girl declaiming loudly and throwing her hands about.

'A few couples, maybe,' Sophie said, 'but we were wrapped up with the hotel crowd. It was great fun; you must come out with us tonight.'

They issued happy little *ciao*s, Sophie snapping her fingers and thumb together like a hungry beak, and trotted off down the steps. Eleanor watched foolishly, cheeks burning again as she remembered her parrot remark. Why had she said something so far-fetched? There couldn't possibly be parrots in Panarea. She sat down heavily on the top step and drank from her water bottle. She had no idea what to do next. The path clearly ended with Cala Junca; wherever Will and his actress were they weren't on this side of the island. And she could hardly continue sitting at the top of the steps in the roasting heat like Little Orphan Annie.

She decided to have a look at the Bronze Age ruins; at least she'd then have something to talk to Lewis about. But after ten minutes of listless picking about she still found it impossible to visualise the piles of rubble as an actual village, so wandered dispiritedly back to the beach. It was busier now, with little circles of sunbathers tearing at packages of bread and ham and passing bottles of wine amongst themselves. Other camps had been deserted for lunch at the beach café.

Several small yachts were gathered near the shore, barely stirring the still water. At least she could swim freely, as there'd be no chance of bumping into Will underwater. She was drenched in sweat. Her sunglasses slid greasily down her nose and when she took her hat off her hair was pasted flat to her head. She flung down her bag and clothes at the water's edge and eased backwards into the coolness as though lowering herself, weightless, on to a mattress. The water was quite clear and when she looked down her legs were bright white, the disembodied limbs of a floating corpse. Alarmed by this, she kicked them energetically; now it looked like someone was batting the fish away with the legs of a statue.

She swam out slowly, watching the deck of one of the boats, where a gleaming, olive-skinned woman was rocking in a hammock, magazine in hand. A man appeared and handed her some wine – the glass blinked in the sunlight – and then lit her a cigarette, placing it between her lips, stroking her face. How adored the women were here, how adoring the men. To Eleanor, it was the picture of bliss, off shore, out of reach.

On the sands, a gaggle of teenagers began screeching and making sinister little miaowing noises to each other, an unexpectedly hostile chorus that broke her reverie. She suddenly felt absolutely alone. Tears began pumping and she plunged her head underwater, thinking, 'What am I doing here?'

Chapter 4

Back at the hotel Eleanor found Lewis chatting with Giovanna, heads bent over the reception desk studying a large map of the Aeolian Islands. Eleanor took off her hat and sunglasses to have a look. How tiny Panarea was, she thought, just like a little round jewel.

'Everything OK?' asked Lewis, looking closely at her face. 'Have you been crying?'

'No, of course not,' Eleanor said, defensively. 'I've been swimming and the salt got in my eyes. I've got very sensitive eyes, you know.'

'They do look very red,' Lewis agreed. 'And my skin will be that colour tomorrow, I guarantee you. The perils of being an English rose, eh?' Eleanor noticed he was wearing full-length trousers and long-sleeved white shirt, presumably in the interests of skin protection. It gave him a dapper 1940s sort of look and it struck her that he was far more stylish than she'd noticed yesterday.

'Met up with your boyfriend yet?' he asked, inevitably.

'No, I'm not sure he's arrived yet and I can't get a signal on my phone,' Eleanor said, as casually as she could manage. She dared not catch Giovanna's eye in case she began quizzing her about the possibility of a new guest.

'You're welcome to try my phone,' Lewis offered. 'I haven't had a problem getting a signal.'

'Oh, don't worry, we'll find each other sooner or later.' Now avoiding his eye too, she hovered closer to the map and her hair began dripping all over it. Clearly she was still going to have to find the right moment to explain to Lewis that she'd lied on the boat. But how? There was always the truth: that she'd been indulging in a moment of delusional fantasy – just as she spent most of her time these days – having never expected to lay eyes on him again. No, far too humiliating. What then? That a fictitious fiancé was her way of putting off unwelcome advances from other men? No, frankly implausible in this colony of beautiful people, where she just looked like an English girl with a flapper hairdo who'd caught the wrong flight. Perhaps some kind of adjustment to the original lie would work? That her fiancé wasn't joining her after all because of a work emergency – had she mentioned that he was a leading cardiac surgeon? No, too melodramatic; no need to get into occupations. How about they'd argued on the phone and he'd flounced off to another island, they'd agreed to have some time apart? After all, she'd told Sophie that her situation was complicated. But she wasn't sure she could keep even that up for a week or more, especially with Sophie's nose for detail.

She decided not to attempt anything at all in front of Giovanna and opted for a safe change of subject. 'Now where are we exactly, is that us there?'

'San Pietro,' said Giovanna, slowly, as though enunciating the words to an infant with learning difficulties. ''Ees main village in Panarea.'

'And there's Stromboli,' said Lewis, pointing to another rugged shape. 'Where the active volcano is.'

'Active?' Eleanor said in alarm. 'Is that safe?'

Giovanna laughed, an odd breathy, cheeping noise.

'As safe as active volcanoes can be, I suppose,' said Lewis, cool and amused. 'You can climb right up to the top and see the lava spurting out. It's supposed to be an amazing experience. I might do it while I'm here.'

'You see thees fire in Panarea,' said Giovanna, adding something to Lewis in Italian.

'She says that if you look over at Stromboli after dark you might see a little flash of red lava in the sky,' he explained. 'Like a firework. But some people go months without seeing it, so it's probably not worth us investing the time staring into the dark.' He listened as Giovanna twittered on. 'And if you don't fancy the climb, you can take a boat trip at night and watch the lava falling into the water.'

He really does see me as a simple tourist, after all, just like everyone else, thought Eleanor, heartened. For a moment she allowed herself to share in the pleasure of a holiday just beginning, the happy scheduling of sights and excursions for the days ahead.

'Anyway, I was just going to have a proper look around Panarea,' Lewis said, cheerfully. 'Fancy a walk, Eleanor? We could get some lunch, maybe down at the waterfront?'

'Oh, no thank you, I feel exhausted already.' She wasn't about to explain that she couldn't risk being seen in the public hub of the island at an exposed terrace table. And Lewis, with his unfailing courtesy – not to mention his own pale complexion – would be sure to choose somewhere in the shade, so she'd look silly if she didn't take her hat off. It was beginning to strike her that the hat and the haircut might not provide sufficient disguise for her purposes. Weren't people instantly recognisable by their gait, their mannerisms, their voice? This situation would work a lot better if *she* were the actress. 'I just want to get a bit of sun up on the terrace, maybe a snooze. Sorry.'

'No need to apologise,' Lewis said, shrugging. 'Well, mind the sun – your nose looks a bit burnt.'

And he turned back to Giovanna and the map, not the slightest bit disappointed.

The roof terrace was a happy discovery, and luckily the sourpuss Nathalie had been and gone. Used by the bar in high season and evidently abandoned now, it had a perfect view of the harbour cafés and the jetty. Eleanor sat on a blue-tiled seat, took out her monocular and began watching. She could see almost every table in the café strip, even the watches and chains sparkling at the customers' wrists. It was early afternoon and as busy as the previous day, with crowds of tourists negotiating with the fishermen for boat trips. She knew from last night's dinner conversation that boats went out daily to various spots around the island, including Panarea's archipelago of rocks, and that snorkelling and diving trips were considered excellent here.

On the jetty people were standing around with luggage waiting for the hydrofoil from Lipari, which skied smoothly into view after just a few minutes. A new crowd of delighted faces streamed out, one group laden down with suit bags, hatboxes and large packages. Eleanor watched them idly as the boat moved off again. A succession of three-wheelers departed San Pietro, the crowds thinned.

The pace of life was so relaxed here, so easy, its rhythm set by the sea, really very soporific—

Wait! Suddenly, her body was rocked with a jolt of adrenalin, and there was a moment of painful suspension before she realised what was happening.

It was Will.

He was standing with four or five other men on the jetty, watching as an older bare-chested man, probably an islander, loaded equipment of some sort into a nearby boat. She had to swallow hard to stop herself from shouting out his name. Her hands were trembling so badly it was several seconds before his face appeared in the viewfinder again. He kept jumping around, chatting all the time, eager and high-spirited. His blond hair was longer than she'd ever seen it, curling around his neck, smoothed back from his brow, and his face was darkly tanned: he must have been in the sun for at least a week. Greedy for every detail, she traced his eyebrows, cheekbones, jawline, lips – she'd forgotten how his mouth turned upwards at the corners, giving his face an expression of permanent amusement. He was wearing only a pair of knee-length denim shorts and his chest – in concession to his Britishness – was much paler than his face. She couldn't believe he was so close; just to see him again felt like all that she wanted from the world.

Adjusting the eyeglass, she watched as he now poked around in his pockets and pulled out his phone. Who was he talking to? Maybe the new girl, as there seemed no sign of anyone likely on the jetty. She must be somewhere else, Eleanor thought, perhaps in their hotel taking a siesta, the heat too exotic for her English blood. After a short conversation, he slipped the phone back into his pocket and leant down to speak to the man in the boat. How gorgeous Will looked, she thought happily, hugging her waist with her free hand. And what incredible luck, seeing him so soon; this was the perfect stakeout.

But her euphoria didn't last long, for moments later Will and others were jumping down into the boat, the older man helping them aboard in turn. Everyone was laughing as the small vessel wobbled about with the weight of each new body, then the engine was fired up and they were chugging away, waving to people in the cafés. Before long, she couldn't distinguish his figure from the others', and the boat was just a tiny dancing shape on the ribbons of blue.

It had happened far too quickly. She sat down heavily, breathless, cheated, close to tears. She felt punch after punch of yearning, blows that seemed never to lessen and only to grow more forceful. Had she really travelled all this way, risking her life on that ancient hydrofoil, not to mention the taxis driven by madmen, for this measly crumb? For another departure, an agonising replay of the man she loved heading away from her, just as he had on the worst day she could remember.

She tried to steady her breathing, reassuring herself that Will's was obviously just a short trip; there'd been no luggage, nothing to suggest he was leaving Panarea. She looked again, hoping the boat would be bobbing back into view, and for the first time noticed to the north a pale cone rising out of the sea, gently chuffing smoke into the sky: Stromboli.

She longed to have him back in sight, but the boat was long gone.

'So tell me all about your complicated love life, Eleanor?' Sophie said that evening. She tilted forward, avid for scandal, her lips shiny with oil from the olives they were wolfing.

Lewis wasn't at dinner, to Eleanor's intense relief, but she still couldn't face dishing Will up as entertainment.

'Oh, it's a long story,' she said, trying not to sound too dismissive. It was impossible not to warm to Sophie's friendliness. 'I think I'll save it for another night.'

'Make sure you do,' Sophie said. 'Tim and I are *very* intrigued. That's the problem with happy marriages – the gossip's so mundane. I mean, what's the best I can come up with? I loathe the way he gnaws an apple, like a rodent? Or he annoys me when he leaves a glass of water by the bed to stagnate? We depend on people like you, Eleanor, you're still living, having new experiences!'

There was little chance of Tim's wine stagnating as he presided once more like a suburban Sinatra over his rat pack, most of whom had come to dinner looking as though they'd been in an explosion. Eleanor, thanks to the hat, seemed to be alone in having escaped first-day beach sunburn. Even Nathalie had a hot face.

'Anyone get over to Lewis's islets today?' Tim asked the table in general. 'I heard there's nude bathing there, which makes the idea of getting in a boat again vaguely more appealing.' Eleanor thought she saw his glance linger on Nathalie at this.

'You grisly old lech,' Sophie said. 'Who wants to see your middle-age spread? Or my rear end, for that matter. But what the hell, who cares when the food's this good?'

Everyone agreed greedily. Eleanor was happy to note that her appetite hadn't deserted her, even if her will to live seemed to have come and gone a dozen times in the last twenty-four hours. In the haze of the day's events she'd forgotten to eat, and Giovanna's first course now sat steaming irresistibly in front of them: a huge dish of porcini risotto, with fresh herbs, parmesan and cracked pepper heaped on top. She wondered if she was the only one pleased that they'd be able to share Lewis's portion, too.

She found it impossible to concentrate on the dinner conversation. Luckily, with Tim, Sophie and Katharina eager for centre stage, it was easy just to drop out and listen. But she was careful to look as though she were following the chatter, laughing, groaning and gasping along with the others, adding particular feeling when Tim brought the house down with his description of Sophie's nether regions bobbing into the path of a passing kayak as she snorkelled at Cala Junca.

But all the time she was privately chewing over the same questions. Will had been on his own – surely an excellent sign? Could that mean he was already so tired of the new girlfriend that he was desperate for time to himself? Maybe they'd argued, split up, even? A thespian was sure to have a tempestuous approach to relationships. She imagined him checking out of his hotel and finding a single room somewhere else, flummoxed by the early failure of his new relationship, the one that had 'felt so right' (these had been his exact words to her, as though indescribable forces had left him no opportunity for personal choice). But that would be too easy; it also didn't fit with how he looked, as radiant and relaxed as she'd ever seen him.

'Coming for drinks tonight, Eleanor?' Sophie asked later, pulling out her lipstick and setting about some deft retouching, while Nathalie looked on with contempt. 'It's still gorgeously warm out there.'

But all Eleanor wanted was to lie on her bed, cool and still under the fan, forget about Panarea and relive for the thousandth time that soaring optimism of a perfect evening in New York.

'There's something else I need to do,' she said.

Chapter 5

'Eleanor, Eleanor! Stop fiddling with that camera, I want to ask you something.'

'I'm just taking a couple of pics and then let's get out of here. You know how scared of heights I am.' Her palms were actually damp with anxiety. This was far worse than the morning's horror, the Guggenheim Museum, with its apparently innocent spiral and the sniggers of the other tourists as she stood limp-kneed against the wall.

'You romantic soul,' laughed Will. 'Come and stand with me, it's less scary here.'

'In a second.' She gazed across to the tip of the Chrysler Building, with its gleaming scales; it looked like a giant pendant hanging against the evening sky. Funny how it felt perfectly safe to look across at other tall buildings, while the smallest glance at the crawling dots below made her want to weep.

'So, what is it?' She went to join him, clicking her

camera in his face. He looked curiously unnerved for someone who loved high places. Then she watched with terrified delight as he dipped down on to one knee.

'Eleanor, will you marry me?'

Her eyes, ears and brain tangled for a second or two. She'd dreamt of the moment for nearly three years, yet now it was here it didn't seem any more real than a voice in her head. How devastating it would be if it was just another of Will's hilarious pranks. If she said 'yes' then he'd dine out on the anecdote for years and she'd be fondly pitied by all who heard it. But how could she say 'no' when there was a chance he was serious? Weren't those grey eyes really staring up at her, their usual self-assurance splashed with something she'd never seen before: self-doubt?

'Yes.' She closed her eyes and held her breath.

'Thank God for that, I'm getting cramp down here.' He pulled himself up and took her face in his hands to kiss her. Blood racing, Eleanor heard clapping from some onlookers, and grinned at them over Will's shoulder. One woman, a middle-aged American with spun-cotton hair and very white tennis shoes, was even nudging away a tear.

'Well, here we are. Engaged. At the top of the Empire State Building. I suspect I'm not the first to think of this spot,' Will said, shifting his feet around like an actor with chronic first-night nerves.

'I can't believe it,' she whispered, finding his hand

with hers. 'I had no idea. Did you plan to do this all along?'

''Course I did. You didn't think this weekend was just for your birthday, did you?'

She pressed her head into his neck, fuzzy with euphoria. It felt as though she'd just done a flawless dismount off the beam and won Olympic gold.

'Shall I take your picture together?' It was the cotton-head lady. Eleanor handed over her camera and clung to Will's body with the trust of a newborn being lifted to safety.

'There you go, good luck, you guys. You must be on a real high!'

'I think we all are,' Will joked, gesturing to the new groups emerging on to the observation deck.

'Thank you,' Eleanor called after the woman, not wanting the scene to end. But Will was already striding towards the exit.

Later, in the big bathtub at the hotel, she wondered if she'd ever be so happy again. It was all the sweeter for being so unexpected. On the few occasions they'd talked about marriage, or when Will had been teased on the subject by his more settled friends, he'd shrugged off the idea, not ruling it out exactly, but taking the 'all the time in the world' position, as Eleanor and Lizzie called it. Women, of course, knew differently about time and its perils.

He now appeared in the bathroom with two huge

tumblers. 'Fuck the champagne, we need hard liquor to digest something of this magnitude.'

She took an icy gulp of vodka. 'So why did you decide to do it?' she asked.

'Oh, you know, it just felt right, what with you knocking on the door of thirty.'

'Well I'm glad I got your sympathy vote! Will there be any pension benefits in it?' She flicked bath foam at his face and watched a blob of it roll into his glass.

'This will have to be the toast at the wedding,' he laughed. 'Vodka, tonic, and a drizzle of some kind of overpriced bath stuff.'

'Lavender and ginger, actually.'

'Lavender and ginger it is.'

'Are you coming in?' she asked, longing to cocoon their bodies together under the water.

'No, and I hate to do this to you, but we're due downtown in under an hour.'

'Oh, are we still meeting your friends?' She didn't think she'd be able to spare any attention for anyone else.

'Of course, I want to show them my beautiful bride-to-be.' He was kidding again, pantomiming his American TV ad voiceover voice. But the words still sounded wonderful.

Eleanor sat up with a loud whoosh of warm water and handed him her glass. 'I should ring my mum. Tell her our news. Now that will make it seem real.' She pictured her parents speculating about grandchildren with the woman in the village shop, snaps of local kiddies on the corkboard behind the counter. Her mother usually saved a comment for Eleanor about each new arrival ('The Gilberts' daughter called her baby Mercedes, can you believe it? Mercedes! In Devon?').

'Oh, let's not bother with all that till we get home,' Will said.

'OK. So when d'you think we should do it?' she asked. 'Late summer, if we hurry?' She imagined Lizzie and Miranda flanking her in some dazzling Renaissance colour, scarlet maybe, or a deep ochre. 'Or what about a winter bash?' Now her mind clattered through rails of cashmere wraps and jackets with fur cuffs.

'Yeah, winter, maybe,' said Will, draining her drink for her. 'There's no hurry, is there? Haven't even sorted out a ring yet.'

She'd wondered about that.

'Don't worry,' Will said. 'It will happen.'

'What do you do today, Eleanor?' Katharina asked through a mouthful of bread and ham. 'Going to the rocks?'

Opposite Eleanor, Stefan brooded privately; he had yet to speak. It was just the three of them at breakfast today – three, that was, not counting the faces on Katharina's leopard-print top. Eleanor hadn't noticed them at first, but moments ago the German woman had turned to get the waiter's attention and she'd been startled to make out two pairs of leopard's eyes peering back at her from their snug lycra forest. She felt sure she saw the waiter's lips twitch when he came to refill their coffee cups. It was Carlo's brother, Rico, on duty this morning.

'Well, I may go swimming later,' she said, at last. 'But this morning I just want to work on my tan.' She didn't add that she intended sprinting straight up to the roof terrace as soon as she could reasonably get away from them. The last thing she needed was Katharina offering to join her, then chattering in her ear all day and distracting her from the job in hand. 'Where's Nathalie this morning?' she asked, changing the subject.

'She is with this Carlo boy. He is taking her on the tennis court,' Katharina said.

'Is he, indeed?'

'She is at championship in Köln for two weeks' time.'

Eleanor imagined the chilly teen pelting tennis balls at Carlo's body like a marksman at the firing range. 'Does she play competitively then, in Germany?' she asked.

'No, no, for the fun.'

Eleanor had trouble believing Nathalie knew the meaning of the word fun. *Spass*, that was it, she remembered it from beginners' German lessons at school, before the teacher had suggested she might like to drop it in favour of something that came more naturally to her. No, Nathalie and *Spass* didn't mix.

'So, have you seen Sophie and Tim today?' she asked.

In response to this, the left side of Katharina's face began convulsing strangely and it was a second or two before Eleanor realised she was winking. 'They are having, I think you know, another honeymoon?'

'You mean, second honeymoon?'

'We are being in the room next door.'

Eleanor giggled. 'I see.'

Stefan gave a snort of contempt at this, his first effort to communicate since grunting hello. Katharina merely rolled her eyes skywards and muttered something at him in German. He muttered something back and then it was Katharina's turn to snort. Eleanor tried to stop giggling but found she could not.

She could barely get through this meal, so anxious was she to resume her vigil. Having now convinced herself that Will must have been doing some sort of snorkelling trip the previous day, she felt certain it must be part of a two-day, or even week-long, course. Panarea specialised in this kind of thing, after all. He could be climbing back into the boat at that very moment for the morning session. She checked her watch – it was already ten o'clock – and quickly swallowed the rest of her coffee.

'I think I'll make a move,' she said, standing. 'I can't wait to get into the sun. Have a great day, you two.'

She grabbed an extra pastry for later and, leaving Katharina and Stefan sitting side by side in silence, sneaked up the spiral steps to the roof, where she settled in the spot with the clearest view. It was another shimmering day and she surrendered happily to the first hit of sun on her face and neck. The sea was noisier and more spirited today, slapping against the rocks and throwing up thick white foam at the feet of the throngs of people already in the harbour. It was only her second morning in Panarea but already she recognised several local figures: the dark-skinned islanders offering boat trips to the tourists; the waitresses expertly picking their way round the tables, delivering cups of espresso, *cornetti* and, despite the hour, shots of grappa. Her eye soon fell on Nathalie and Carlo, waiting on the jetty with tennis rackets and sports bags, Nathalie looking altogether more coquettish than usual as she twirled her racket like a baton. She was in supreme shape, thought Eleanor, her limbs so long and lean, skin young and clear; how could she be so physically unblemished with all those adolescent hormones washing through her body? And Carlo was a beauty, too, with his soft floppy black hair and strong nose and jaw. The blue of his Albergo delle Rose work shirt suited him. Was he not on duty today? He and Rico seemed to run the bar and restaurant between them, Giovanna generally nesting behind her desk or out of sight.

There were footsteps on the tiled steps and two of the hotel's Italian guests, another young couple, appeared. They greeted Eleanor with matching friendly smiles. '*Parla italiano?*' asked the man, whose closely cropped hair accentuated his rather square head.

'No, no, *inglese.*'

'You like Panarea?'

'Yes, very much.' She was like a simpleton, unable to ask a question of her own.

'You watch for the birds?' He'd noticed her eyeglass, and Eleanor smiled confidently; after the parrot gaffe with Tim and Sophie, she was prepared for this.

'Butterflies,' she said. 'It's my hobby. There are so many of them here.' She turned away, dashed the monocular to her eye and began jerking her head about as though following the swirling flight of a butterfly. She felt mean and guilty as she sensed the couple tiptoeing tactfully out of her way, but was not willing to get involved in any more holiday chit-chat. She had business to attend to. After a safe pause, she glanced in their direction; they had settled hip to hip on sun-loungers, the girl reading a novel with a picture of a couple nuzzling noses on the cover. Eleanor sighed and refocused on the waterfront.

Hour after hour oozed by, the air getting steadily warmer and silkier. For those on the beach and in the cafés it must be bliss, she thought, just the slow, lazy unfolding of holiday nothingness. But for her, squirming constantly from sunlight to shade and never letting her eye leave the waterfront below, the nothingness was agonising.

The last of the morning boats had left, writhing off one after another over the water – so much for her idea about Will's morning session – and it was now later in the day than it had been yesterday when he'd set off. Could it be she'd somehow missed him, or was yesterday just a one-off expedition, the only time he intended leaving his hotel and the new girl?

Tim and Sophie now wandered into view, approaching one of the waitresses and pointing up to the terraces above. They must be asking about a good place for lunch, thought Eleanor. Sophie was buzzing with energy, her hair yellow and electrified in the sun. She pinched Tim's cheek and kissed his nose as though petting a toddler and their yells of laughter turned even the more idle heads in the cafés. There'd been less talk of little Rory the previous evening, Eleanor thought.

Still she sat fixed to the spot. She felt like a pregnant woman waiting for the next contraction. Her arms ached; she needed to go to the loo; she wanted to sprint down to the shore and plunge fully clothed into cold water; or just make it to her room to change her top, which had now glued itself to her back. She was hungry, had eaten the pastry ages ago, but most of all she longed for a cold beer. Could she risk a foray down-stairs, she wondered, perhaps combining a quick trip to the bathroom with an order at the bar? She could collect her drink on the way back or ask Rico to bring it up to the terrace. But what if she bumped into Lewis? He always seemed to be popping in and out. Or Katharina? She couldn't risk getting stuck with her.

At last the Italian couple left. Probably going off to feed each other courgette flowers on some gorgeous whitewashed terrace, thought Eleanor, surrounded by oleander trees and butterflies. She had to concede that Panarea was an incredibly romantic place, all heart-warming colour and sparkling light. She must surely be the only person on the island that day – with the likely exception of Stefan – who wasn't rolling on her back and purring with satisfaction.

Suddenly she recognised the abrupt kick of adrenalin and knew Will was in view. This time he was getting out of a boat, the same boat as yesterday, with the same group of people, their dripping dark heads like a row of otters. She could make out masks and diving equipment and then the marine blue logo on the boat, the same as the sign in the diving shop by the jetty. So he was taking a course, after all, a diving course. But why? Will had never shown the slightest athletic bent beyond hiking an extra hundred metres up the hill to a pub he favoured over the one at the end of their street (the 'climb' raised the heart rate, he always said).

As she watched him help the others on to the jetty,

she wondered what else he might have reinvented about himself. His job, perhaps. How would it sound to an actress, someone working in the world of theatre and TV – showbiz – that he worked for a bland mid-sized software company that no one had ever heard of and was basically a salesman with a smart job title? It wasn't going to be his career for long, he'd always insisted; what he really planned to do was write and direct plays, but he never seemed to get any further than deciding on the barest of plot-lines and a selection of well-known actors he might consider casting as his leads. As she watched him unzip a daypack and pull out a crumpled green towel, she found herself playing back a conversation they'd had in New York the day after he'd proposed, about how he thought it would make a great opening scene for a play.

'Just think of the set with that skyline – it'd be spectacular!'

'So what would happen,' she'd asked, 'after the man proposes, I mean?'

'Well, obviously the course of true love wouldn't run smooth at all,' Will said, using his hands in that 'creative' way he always did when in ideas mode. 'Maybe an old lover could appear on the observation deck. No, no, that's been done before. What about the mysterious intervention of a stranger, who will tear the lovers apart forever, though they don't realise at the time? A man – no, a woman would be better! A woman with a disturbing agenda of her own.'

Now his words seemed tragically prophetic: just a couple of months later and it had all been over, thanks to a woman who had an agenda of her own all right. It was as if Will had longed for this drama all along, cast himself as the object of a tug of love. Well, here Eleanor was with him back in her sights, not at all certain that he had plotted *that*. Her head crackled with curiosity and fear as she watched him drag a V-neck shirt down over his damp torso. The triangle of skin at the open neck looked sunburnt and she felt a lurch of tenderness towards him. But then she saw that he was holding out his right hand, beckoning to someone, and a tanned, dark-haired woman was skipping up the jetty to join him, gripping the hand and pushing her whole body right up against his. She was wearing just a pale blue bikini and, tied across her narrow abdomen, a wispy sarong no larger than a scarf. A silver-and-green bag twinkled at her hip. Now Will squeezed his body closer to hers and nibbled her shoulders. Then she kissed his neck. They looked like honeymooners, and not fond, comfortable 'second' ones like Tim and Sophie, but ardent, besotted, red-blooded ones, ones who couldn't stop touching each other, even in public. Something leaden started to replace the adrenalin in Eleanor's system and she felt a painful twist in her intestines. She thought she might gag.

With a flash of glossy black hair, the girl at last pulled away and began walking towards the nearby café terrace. Her figure was flawless, Eleanor saw, slim and graceful, with a waist so tiny it lent her breasts and hips a striking curvaceousness. Then, as she moved, she pulled her hair back into a knot at the back of her head and Eleanor saw her face for the first time. There were no two ways about it: she was truly beautiful, cheekbones and high-bridged nose finely drawn, neck and shoulders smooth and delicate. It was a moment or two before Eleanor recognised her: she was the girl from Cala Junca, the one everyone had been watching, the one so stunning she was a standout even here.

This was a disaster.

She turned to study Will again. Like several others on the jetty, he was watching the girl twist between the tables and greet a male customer sitting alone with a beer. 'Can't take his eyes off her,' thought Eleanor, miserably. A minute later the girl was up again, kissing the man's cheeks, Will was joining her and they were walking away hand-in-hand, heading towards the San Pietro lane – they'd be passing the Albergo delle Rose in less than a minute.

Eleanor snatched up her things and rushed down to the hotel entrance in ten seconds flat, heart thudding hideously. Sure enough, the couple sauntered by, just a few metres from where she hid to the side of the gate. There was just time to fully take in their faces:

his handsome, alight, turned eagerly towards the girl; hers glimmering and youthful, dominated by huge dark eyes. Alone now – or thinking they were – they each wore the expression Eleanor had come to recognise in new couples, that intimate, unveiled one reserved purely for one another and replaced in an instant by something quite different as soon as any third party clattered in and broke the spell. Even so, she felt her own moment of pure delight at being so close to Will again, imagined she could catch the scent of his hair and skin in the air.

She forced herself to count slowly to ten, by which time a noisy family had also passed by, and then set off behind them at a safe distance, her hat pulled low over her ears and eyebrows. Two small children were pushing and yelling at each other and their mother struggled to prise them apart, but Eleanor was more concerned with her own breathing – it sounded far too loud, amplified, like the panting of a big dog after a bolt through the park. She had never before felt so much adrenalin attacking her body.

Now the family veered off to the left and once more she had an unbroken view of Will and the girl. Even from a distance she could see how easily their bodies worked together, arms curled lazily around each other's waists, never allowing themselves to lose contact for a second. She strained in vain to hear their voices. Turning out of the top of the lane, she was just in time to see them stooping over crates of fruit and vegetables outside the *alimentari*. She stopped dead, leant against the wall and hid her nose in the pages of her guide-book. Peeking over the top of her sunglasses, she saw that they were choosing tomatoes and aubergines, squeezing, smelling and comparing. This caused fresh pangs. For all his laziness, Will had loved shopping and cooking, and her favourite evenings had been when they'd cooked together, whiling away the evening drinking wine until it ran out and then whatever brandy or unidentifiable Christmas liqueur they could unearth.

Now the two of them had paid, had their shopping in brown paper bags, and were heading up the lane to the right, the one signposted to Iditella. A part of Eleanor's brain knew that this was the moment to retreat, to return to the hotel and do something normal, like order a late lunch or ask Giovanna about day trips. In all her imaginings, she'd never expected to tail Will any distance, only to watch him from somewhere safe, perhaps passing him at a crowded corner, catching her breath as he walked on. He would never notice her because he would never expect her to be there. But now the dilemma presented itself she was hypnotised, unstoppable.

The lane wound up the hill, steeply in places; it was even narrower than the path she'd taken to the beach, and extremely quiet: they passed just one person in five minutes. She prayed for noisy scooters, feeling sure

Will would hear her footsteps and swing suspiciously around. But he didn't, just wandered on, his body locked so closely to the girl's they were limping along together like kids in a three-legged race.

Slowly, she was catching up, was soon close enough to hear them talking. The girl had a low, rolling laugh and, despite her Italian colouring, a deep, well-modulated English accent. For some reason the voice was a shock. It occurred to Eleanor that she had equipped her rival with a squeaky helium-voice, something girlish that might quickly grate.

'All right, little mister Wilful, have it your way,' the voice said, playful and sultry, followed by laughter from Will and a sudden shuffling halt. Eleanor stopped short, too, out of sight, just a corner away from them. She supposed they must be kissing again. It was unbearable to picture it, even more unbearable not to be able to see it.

Finally, they were on the move again, but within seconds the trail went dead once more at the sound of a vehicle braking and an exchange of voices in Italian. Now she could make out new male voices, speaking in Italian with the girl. She listened, barely drawing breath: was it her imagination or did the exchange sound serious, even angry? A blue kart rolled into view containing two uniformed officers: the island *carabinieri* – police. She felt them eyeing her up and down and could do nothing but stand there, stricken and guilty. It was all clear to her now: the game was up. Will and the girl had seen her, after all, and had pointed her out to these officers. She closed her eyes, imagining herself being escorted to the jetty as Tim and Sophie and the nice Italian couple watched in disbelief from a restaurant terrace. But when she looked up again the kart was accelerating past her, the two officers nodding a little lecherously in her direction before continuing their own banter.

Eleanor relaxed in ridiculous relief. What on earth had she been thinking? This was Panarea, not a Nazi occupation. Turning the corner, she realised that in her panic she'd lost all sight and sound of Will. Then, out of the corner of her eye, she caught a shiny sliver of green and silver disappearing down a side lane and into a blue door. She edged forward and saw the house properly: it was a traditional cube-shaped villa with a large terrace, the low terrace walls framing the most perfect view of Stromboli in the distance. Eleanor remembered Giovanna's promises of spurts of red lava and gazed transfixed for a moment, before slowly tiptoeing down the side lane. She was close enough to read the nameplate on the wall, a square tile painted with an island scene and the words 'Casa Salina' in clumsy calligraphy.

Suddenly, a creaking above her head made her start. The shutters were being eased open and she could hear the girl's voice again, calling from somewhere in the distance: 'Darling, can you grab the wine?' She must be out on the terrace, Eleanor thought, holding herself in a tight squeeze. Insanely, she was reminded of a game of musical statues, one in particular, at a school friend's house in the next village. The hosting parent had tried to trick the girls by calling 'Come for ice cream, everyone!' just as the music stopped. Eleanor alone had dashed to the kitchen.

Then she heard Will's voice, much closer, quite clear – 'What happened to that cheese with the peppercorns? I think we must have left it in the shop . . .' – and the sound of it so engulfed her with yearning that she thought her ribcage would combust. The last time she'd heard that voice was four weeks ago, on the phone and hardly in the easiest of circumstances, thanks to Miranda and her ridiculous 999 call, but here it was again, as familiar to her as her own.

'No, I've got all the cheese out here.' It was the girl again. 'We just need the vino and glasses – you might have to rinse a couple out.' This was followed by the tip-tapping of heel on tile, then the girl's voice, closer than before, fading to a groan: 'Mmm, that feels really amazing . . .' More groans and murmurs, then Will: '*You* feel amazing.'

Oh God, thought Eleanor, they had to be standing in the window right above her head. They were obviously kissing again. She thought she could even hear them breathing, but quickly realised it was her own, still coming in painful pants. She started edging uphill in retreat, inch by inch, willing herself to resist the impulse to whimper.

Just as she reached the lane leading back to San Pietro, her body clenched again at the sound of a man's voice. Instinctively, she darted into the nearest gateway and crouched down, pushing her head between her knees. The spot was barely hidden, raised just a step or two from the lane, and she caught the sweet, optimistic smell of fresh laundry flapping on the washing line a few feet away. Pulling her hat right down over her ears and squeezing her eyes shut, all she could hear was the choking sound of hot, muffled air. It had to have been Will's voice. He had finally spotted her.

She counted torturously to thirty before opening her eyes, prepared, once and for all, for capitulation. But the lane was completely deserted, not a footfall to be heard. The next thing she made out was a clattering noise, getting louder and louder and filling her whole head with its din. Then she realised it was the sound of her own shoes on the flagstones: she was running. She ran all the way back to San Pietro, downhill and off-balance, dodging the scooters, vaguely registering the *carabinieri* kart parked outside the tobacconist, desperate to put other bodies and vehicles between herself and Will, between herself and Will's girl.

She didn't think she'd ever felt so out of control. She'd petrified herself.

Chapter 6

In her room Eleanor closed the shutters, turned on the fan and lay on her bed in the dark. In an effort to cool down, she flung out her legs and arms to make a star shape, remaining in this position for almost two hours. She didn't sob or groan or even sigh, but tried to close her mind completely. Eventually, almost at the point of sleep, she forced herself to get up. She needed a shower and a drink.

The hotel bar was quiet. Rico was pouring a beer for Stefan, who sat alone at the bar, hot faced and flat haired, still in his beach clothes. Eleanor slumped into the first chair she came to and pretended not to see him. She felt listless and itchy at the same time and was developing a headache from blacking out the image of Will and his new girlfriend: the kissing, the horrible voices of mutual rapture.

Rico approached. '*Prego?*'

'Um, *vino tinto, grande, por favor.*'

As he nodded, there was a cheerful 'Evening, guys', and Lewis appeared in the bar, lugging over his shoulder a heavy-looking backpack. Stuffed with bits of smelly old stone, Eleanor supposed. He had the same second-day flush as everyone else, but looked enviably relaxed, as though Panarea were delivering precisely the experience he'd anticipated. She longed for the same contentment.

She said hello and watched as he ordered himself a beer and, uninvited, took a seat at her table.

'Was that Spanish I heard you speaking to Rico?' he asked her, mock-admonishing. 'You are aware that Sicily is part of Italy?'

'Oh, sure,' said Eleanor, feeling her cheeks go red. 'I just get Spanish and Italian mixed up sometimes. It's no big deal, I wouldn't care if someone ordered a drink from me in . . . in Welsh or whatever . . .'

'No, but would you understand them?' He chortled, his face creased with amusement.

Eleanor was not in the mood for teasing, however playful. With some effort, she kept her tone polite: 'How was your day? What have you been up to?'

'Very good, yes, thank you. Bit knackered – I walked as far as you can go in both directions. The views are out of this world. This island just gets more and more beautiful.' All of a sudden his expression became dramatically more intense. 'Look, Eleanor, I know it's got nothing to do with me, but I saw you in Iditella earlier. You looked like you were *hiding* from someone. Is everything OK?'

Eleanor blushed even more deeply. 'Have you been following me?' she cried. 'You certainly seem to be popping up everywhere I happen to be! On the boat, here, Iditella!' At this point Rico reappeared with their drinks and stood uncertainly, startled by her raised voice. She grabbed the wine from his hand and took a huge slug.

Lewis dug out some euros and thanked Rico for the drinks. 'Of course I'm not following you,' he said, turning calmly back to her. 'What on earth do you mean? I saw you when I was walking back from Calcara – you know, beyond Iditella where you can see the volcanic emissions?'

'I'm not interested in emissions,' Eleanor said, childishly.

He sighed. 'Anyway, you were squatting in a doorway down the hill, at least I assume it was you, I couldn't see your face, just your hat. I called your name but by the time I reached you you'd gone . . .'

Eleanor continued to avoid the gaze that she knew was searching her face for clues to her peculiar behaviour.

'And I can hardly be blamed for being on the boat, or here, can I? The boat is how you get here and a hotel is where you stay. I'm on holiday, too, you know.'

'I know, I know, I'm sorry.' Eleanor gulped more wine; she'd almost finished the glass already.

'So why were you hiding?'

'I wasn't hiding. I was resting. It was a coincidence that the police happened to pass by.'

'I see,' said Lewis, who had not mentioned the police. He was drinking as quickly as she was. 'Well, you're obviously upset about something. Is it your fiancé? Have you still not been able to get hold of him? I can help you ask at the other hotels if you're worried about speaking Italian.'

His concern brought on a surge of raw longing for a friend, for Lizzie, Miranda, anyone she could pour it all out to. 'Look, Lewis,' she said. 'Look, I'll come clean with you.' Her tone had tripped from pathetic to pompous and his eyes widened in surprise. 'I'm not in Panarea to join my fiancé. Actually, he has no idea I'm even here. He's not my fiancé any more, anyway, or even my boyfriend, because we've split up. And now I seem to be stalking him. *That's* what you saw me doing earlier: stalking a human male.'

Lewis looked astonished. There was a pause as he appeared to grapple for an appropriate response. 'You can't be serious?' he said. The very words Lizzie had used.

The wine suddenly rushed to her head. 'Of course I'm bloody serious. Would I be in such a state, confessing to a stranger, a . . . random archaeologist, if I thought this was some kind of . . .' She struggled to develop this, '. . . some kind of a comedy?'

Lewis looked puzzled and a little hurt. She regretted calling him a random archaeologist. There was no doubt he must think she was unhinged – and she was beginning to agree.

'That's why you were in Iditella? You saw him there?'

'I followed him from the port,' Eleanor said, limply. 'I was watching from the roof terrace and I saw him down at the jetty.'

'Did he see you?'

'No, he was all wrapped up with, with someone else – his new girlfriend, I think.'

There was a short silence while Lewis patted his pockets for his cigarettes. 'I take it you weren't the one to initiate this split?' He lit himself a cigarette and then offered the pack to her. There was something about the gentleness of his questioning that made her hopes leap; could it be that she'd found an ally, someone to root for her in all of this?

'Thanks. No, he left me. For her,' said Eleanor. Her hand was shaking so much Lewis had to steady it with his own to light her cigarette. Fighting the impulse to bury her head into the nook of his arm and weep, she added, 'To make matters worse, she's an actress.'

'Well, in that case there's no hope for you.' He was smiling, no doubt hoping to ease the atmosphere, which had become highly charged very quickly.

'Well, thanks for your sympathy.' She drew her face away from him as self-pity coursed through her veins. Unfortunately, this meant she was facing Stefan, who was looking over with interest while feeding himself peanuts from the palm of his hand.

Lewis smoked, silent until she turned back. 'I'm sorry, I didn't mean it like that. It's just that this all sounds so mad. What do you want to achieve? Won't seeing these people just make you upset?'

'Of course, that's why I *am* upset! I'd been hoping she might be more of an ugly sister type . . .' She instantly wished she hadn't admitted this as she saw the twitch of distaste on his face, and found herself rushing on: 'I mean, she's so amazingly gorgeous, way out of my league, I've got no chance of getting him back. *I'm* the ugly sister. Though I'm not an actress, of course, but if I was then I'd be the ugly sister. She's the star.'

There was another, longer, silence. Her words echoed horribly in her head: *no chance of getting him back*. It was the first time she'd actually voiced this thought.

'Is that your plan?' asked Lewis, carefully. 'To get back together?'

'I don't know, I just don't know. I suppose I thought that once I'd seen them in the flesh this whole thing might solve itself, in my head, you know? Help me move on.'

The phrase did not appear to possess the same

magical cachet for Lewis as it did for her girlfriends, for he just snorted incredulously. 'Move on? This is about as far away from moving on as I can think of. Sinking into quicksand, more like, and dragging other people down with you. They're here on *holiday*, Eleanor. Everyone is.'

'Except me.' Typically, tears were now spilling on to her burnt face, hot and stinging, making the end of her cigarette damp. She stubbed it out and Lewis automatically passed her a fresh one. She longed for the sympathy she'd sensed a minute ago; sharing this humiliating tale with him was no good if it just notched up another person determined to bundle her on to the next flight home.

'So what did you do when you saw them?' he asked. 'Did you speak to him? What's his name, anyway?'

'Will. Will Miles. No, I didn't, I just listened and looked at him through my bird-spotter thing. And then I thought they'd heard me so I hid. That must have been when you saw me.'

'Well, I don't know what to say,' said Lewis. In Eleanor's experience, this declaration was generally followed by quite a lot to say, more than she cared to hear. 'Break-ups are awful for everyone,' he ventured. 'He probably feels terrible about the whole thing as well. It just takes a bit of time, a few distractions.'

'Yeah, I suppose,' said Eleanor, sniffing. She'd heard every conceivable variation on this theme over the last few months. Seeing some of the other guests now coming into the bar and exchanging greetings with Rico and Stefan, she made a huge effort to stop snivelling and grabbed a paper napkin from the dispenser. She emptied her nose with a wet snuffle, mumbling, 'Didn't take *him* long to find a new distraction, did it?'

'When did you split up?' Lewis glanced at his phone, checking the time, perhaps. Eleanor could tell he would have preferred not to have been cast as a Relate counsellor in this little melodrama.

'June the 16th. Just under three months ago.' She didn't quote the days and hours as she might have done with Lizzie; Lewis would be sure to mistake such preciseness for obsession.

'Still quite new, then. I'm sorry, I really am. You're having a tough time.' He crushed out his cigarette and got to his feet. 'Look, let's talk more at dinner. I have to go, I'm late meeting someone.'

The custodian of the Bronze Age village or some other dullard, Eleanor thought, sulkily. But she felt grateful for his interest; approving or not, he was getting to be the nearest thing she had to a friend on this island.

'Thanks, but I don't think so,' she said. 'I can't face talking about it in front of everyone else.' She imagined them all chipping in with advice, Sophie and Tim storyboarding potential follow-up scenes, Nathalie sneering from the sidelines. 'Actually, I think I'll give dinner a miss tonight,' she added, also standing. 'I'll get some food in my room. But thanks for trying to help. It's not the cheeriest situation, I know. I wouldn't like to think I was dragging you into the quicksand with me.' She hoped there was none on the island: it had been a very specific analogy.

'Don't be silly,' Lewis said. 'That's not what I meant. Look, we won't talk about it if that's what you want, but you should come to dinner. It'll take your mind off things for a few hours.'

'No, I'm shattered, really, I just want to sleep.'

'OK.' He hovered awkwardly for a moment, fiddling with the straps on his bag. 'What are you doing tomorrow? More stalking in that ridiculous hat? Which by the way is only going to draw more attention to you, not less.'

She forced a smile.

'I've got an idea,' he said. 'Meet me in the morning at ten o'clock on the jetty. Will you do that?'

'Why?'

'Just meet me. I promise you'll have a good day.'

'I can't go down there,' Eleanor said. 'I might bump into Will.'

'No you won't – there'll be a boat coming in, so just go straight to the end of the jetty and keep your head down. Blend in with the crowd. I'll find you.'

'All right.' She was too exhausted to argue; her mind craved the oblivion of sleep.

'Excellent – oh, and bring your swimming stuff, you'll need it.'

And off he loped, leaving Eleanor to blot her tears with the sodden napkin and stare blearily after him.

Chapter 7

Eleanor loved to think about her first date with Will. It was her favourite morning fantasy, before she'd even lifted her head from the pillow and allowed the reality of her new life without him to properly take grip. She was surprised by how frequently her mind took delivery of a new detail. Sometimes she carried the reverie with her into the shower or on to the tube to work. By the time she reached her desk, however, too much of the present had usually started to interfere.

They'd met, but not really spoken, at a birthday party at her old boss's house. She'd been amazed by Will's call a couple of days later, remembered him as the very sexy sleepy-looking blond one on the sofa, the one groaning with laughter all night with his own little crowd. There'd even been a girl in tow, too, attached to his thigh like a limpet.

But when she turned up for their date, forty minutes late after a coronary-inducing succession of transport mishaps, she found him sitting at the bar with a jug of margarita – and another girl. Whipped up by her row with the bus driver, she picked up his glass and threw the drink in his face. She could still see the frosting of salt on his nose.

'Don't go mental again,' he said to her, fifteen minutes later, when the eyewash had been applied by alarmed bar staff and they were both settled with fresh drinks. (The other girl had by now retreated to a table as far away from them as possible.) 'But seriously, I thought she was you.'

'What?' Eleanor looked guiltily at his sore red eyes.

'I was so out of it that night at Ian's, I couldn't remember what you looked like, not exactly. She came up and said "I'm Ella, remember me?" I thought that must be short for Eleanor. It started to dawn on me after a bit, but it seemed rude to just walk off. Especially as we'd ordered a jug. Plus there was no sign of the real you.'

'That's very hard to believe,' Eleanor said, 'though I'll give you points for artistic merit.'

'So did you remember *me* exactly, then?'

Eleanor had to admit she'd pictured him as a little taller and a little blonder.

'Well, if I said that to you,' Will laughed, 'I really would deserve a slap.'

'Shall we just start again?' he asked a bit later. They were too late for the table he'd booked at the restaurant by the river, so they went instead to a Japanese noodle place in Battersea. The bar seating arrangement meant they were side by side, so close that if they turned towards each other at the same time their noses bumped together. A man eating alone occupied the corner spot by Eleanor's other elbow, making obscene slurping and smacking noises throughout the meal. Will whispered to her that from where he sat the guy looked exactly like a ventriloquist's dummy perched on Eleanor's shoulder, and kept asking her what her little friend was called. Eleanor felt bad laughing so openly at a stranger.

It was not an elegant occasion. She dribbled miso soup down her new top, he knocked the sake over and soaked their legs, only to discover when the bill came that the bottle they'd spilled cost £85. Will suggested doing a runner at this point, but they paid up after persuading the waiter to sell them a bottle of plum wine, which came wrapped in brown paper like something from Prohibition. And then they went back to her place.

It had only been a few months since she'd split up with Alex but she was confident she was ready for someone new. Alex. Laugh-out-loud funny Alex, cry-out-loud frustrating Alex. He'd driven Eleanor to distraction with his mixed signals, tempests of hot and cold that continued long after it had been established that they were going out and not merely having sex. He was the sort of man who referred to his girlfriend as 'current', as though it were only a matter of time before she'd be succeeded by the next. Once, when they were rushing to get ready for work, she'd smudged make-up on his work shirt and he'd sighed, 'Not to worry, El, you're not the first and I daresay you won't be the last.' She'd been distressed by this but felt helpless to retaliate, a dynamic that continued as long as their relationship. What made it doubly disheartening was that if she'd made a similar remark to him he would *daresay* have taken it with great cheer: he enjoyed being kept on his toes, it helped him hotfoot it round every pub in south London with his all-male posse of mates.

Yes, thank God for Will, Will and his straightforward ways, his relatively straightforward ways. He'd never shown much of an interest in playing games; he was committed right from the start. He believed in seeing someone as little or as often as 'felt right' and had no interest in any other dating principles. Everyone agreed he was a much better bet than Alex: his laid-back good nature calmed her more anxious one – he enjoyed teasing her for her habit of viewing a blocked sink or missing shoe as a global crisis. And he thought the larger issues, like her loathing of her job designing greetings cards for Ian's company, should be dealt with straight away – in this case, with her resignation. It seemed far too churlish to point out that his own work frustrations and writing ambitions seemed destined to stay on the back burner, especially when it was he who'd heard about the job in Rufus's team, got her all excited about it. A friend of a friend had just left the agency, what was the harm in Eleanor giving the account director a call?

After a year together he moved into the flat and life felt idyllic. They would lie like a pair of spoons on the sofa, draining bottles of wine and eating a hodgepodge of treats, wrestling each other for the remote control. She'd recognised early on that he was the man she wanted to marry, but knew better than to voice the thought: even the most emancipated males needed to believe that sort of leap was their own idea – all women knew that. Instead, she saved the subject for long debates with Lizzie and later Miranda, until, finally, there was New York. The trip had been planned with Miranda's help as a surprise for Eleanor's thirtieth birthday, and she'd managed to miss all the hints (Miranda was not a talented keeper of confidences, as Eleanor came to learn).

But all along, even when she despaired that they'd still be lying on the same sofa with the same easy arrangement between them until they were collecting their pensions, it was never disputed that they came as a package: Will and Eleanor, Eleanor and Will, depending on which side the speaker came from. Right from that first night, in fact. That was another thing she was convinced about – she'd never have such a fun first date again.

When they pulled into the harbour at Vulcano, it seemed to Eleanor that they were docking in hell.

Everything looked scorched and hostile: jagged black rocks stained with yellow – surely human skin would sizzle at the barest contact with it? And the smell: it was as though they'd been spooned into a burning vat of rancid eggs.

Lewis laughed when he saw her face. 'Grim, isn't it? Don't worry, you won't notice after a while.' He began marching off towards a cliff of brittle ochre stone, and she saw that most of the other passengers from the hydrofoil were also heading in that direction. She trotted to catch up with him, holding her nose; if anything, they were ploughing deeper into the sulphurous stink.

'Wait till you see our first activity for the day,' he said.

He'd been very secretive about the trip so far. When they'd met at the jetty in Panarea, he'd already bought the hydrofoil tickets and would say only that they were going to Vulcano, the Aeolian island closest to the mainland. 'You can climb right up to the lip of the crater and see the sulphur vapours,' he'd said, adding that they probably wouldn't have time for this.

Eleanor was pleased to hear it. There were far too many smouldering volcanoes in this part of the world for her liking. She felt unexpectedly nervous, and not because of the crossing: the sea was as smooth as a bowl of cream today.

A moment later they arrived at a large pool of

yellow-grey gloop, which was filled with dozens of apparently naked tourists. Some were smearing the stuff on their arms and faces and all over each other; others just squatted there, still as ducks. The yellow made them look quite frightening, like overfed savages, Eleanor thought, and how could they bear the heat? It was midday, the sun was ferocious, and there was no shade anywhere. She couldn't believe this was the same climate as Panarea, with its cascades of late flowers, sprinklers feeding water to every last petal.

'What on earth?' she asked, looking at Lewis. She had a horrible feeling he was going to make her get into that stinking emulsion. Taking a closer look, she saw the surface of the pool was pocked with bubbles. It made her think of teenage acne.

He was laughing at her face. 'You look totally appalled! Come on, it's the famous *fanghi* mud pool, it's supposed to be good for you. We're going in, no arguments!' He was so high-spirited it was impossible to resist, and they started pulling off their clothes and shoes. Eleanor noticed he had surprisingly thick, muscular legs; she'd imagined them to be meatless. He was very pale, though, and only his face and forearms had any colour. She tried not to linger too long on the sight of her own body: although less wobbly of late, thanks to her summer season of misery, the parts of her that weren't flushed from her roof terrace sessions were now bleached an unflattering pearly white in the sunlight.

Underfoot, the mud was baked hard and furnace-hot in the sun, so they had to dash the few steps to the pool. 'This is sulphurous mud,' Lewis explained, dipping his toes in the squelching liquid. 'It's not that hot, come and try. It's supposed to heal arthritis and a whole load of aches and pains. Maybe it will fix your heartache?'

Eleanor doubted that, but followed obediently. Sitting in the mud pool felt like being plopped in a giant rain puddle, unless you were unlucky enough to scald your buttocks on one of the bubbles, like Lewis, who shot up shouting, 'Fuck, I've burned my arse!'

Eleanor laughed out loud. She couldn't think of anything more absurd than sitting with a man she barely knew in a huge yellow puddle. 'I feel like we're on the moon or something,' she said, looking round. 'This is so weird.'

'Don't knock it, you girls would pay through the nose for a treatment like this in London,' he said, rubbing some of the gunk into his elbows, then flicking a globule at her midriff.

'I think we're all paying through the nose here,' she replied. 'The pong is gruesome.'

He grinned. 'I hope that's not a designer bikini, the white's turning a charming yellow colour . . .' She found the idea of Lewis looking at her breasts slightly unnerving – they were barely covered with the little triangles of fabric – but he was right, the white edging on her bikini top was already stained and grubby-looking. She imagined the elegant turban-headed woman in Panarea sitting in the mud; not even she could make this look glamorous.

'Have you noticed how all the women in Panarea are incredibly beautiful?' she said.

'It had crossed my mind once or twice. It's a bit of a celebrity haunt, isn't it? And the rich blokes from the mainland obviously like their trophy girlfriends the same as the rest of the world.'

'Yes, I suppose.' Eleanor paused, images of Will's gorgeous new attachment invading her head. She tried to spear them away and pay Lewis the attention he deserved. 'So tell me about your girlfriend, Lewis, is *she* attractive?'

Lewis looked as though he'd never been asked to consider this before. 'Well, yes, obviously *I* think she's attractive.'

That made it sound as if he doubted anyone would share his view. 'What's her name again?'

'Er, Rebecca.'

'I thought you'd forgotten for a minute,' Eleanor laughed. 'You must be spending too much time with your stones.'

'No doubt she'd agree with that.' He didn't follow up with any details of Rebecca's appearance, but this didn't surprise Eleanor. What was the percentage of men who didn't even know their girlfriend's eye colour? She wondered if Will could remember hers.

'What did you say she does?'

'She's a teacher. Infants.'

Now she had her picture of Rebecca: a wholesome girl with hazel eyes, a wide smile, ponytail swinging behind her head as she scurried around after her little charges. Lewis would meet her from school at the end of the day, help her extract the last child from the sandpit or goldfish tank, or wherever it was they played these days. Maybe she wasn't beautiful like Will's new girlfriend, but *he* thought she was and that was all that counted.

They caked the gritty clay on their arms, legs and faces, then hopped across the hot rocks to the beach, where everyone was washing off the mud in the sea. The water was warm and bubbly with thermal currents; it felt much more soothing than the mud, and Eleanor leant back in the shallows on her elbows, looking out to sea.

'You've still got a big blob on your cheek,' Lewis pointed out, and before she could sit upright he was leaning across and gently rinsing the mud off with his hand, his face intent, like a parent. His body was so close to hers they could have been in a bathtub together.

'Thank you.' She looked back into his face, at the jut of the nose and jaw. His eyes were squinting in the sun and she noticed how long the lashes were, rather like Will's, unusually long and curled for a man. Miranda had made her laugh when she used to liken

Will to a camel – both for the lashes and his capacity for storing endless pints of liquid without needing to relieve himself.

She sighed to herself. Would she never be rid of these details? How simple life would be if Will were no longer of any significance; had never existed. For a wild moment she imagined returning to Panarea to discover the news that a couple from London had tragically died that day, been swept off a cliff when their stroll took them off the beaten track, or trapped under the boat in a freak diving accident. Or maybe someone had let poisonous reptiles loose in Casa Salina . . . it would be easy to do if the shutters were open.

'What are you thinking about?' Lewis asked her. 'You look very serious – not plotting something, I hope?'

'No, no, I was just wondering if there were any poisonous creatures on these islands. You know, snakes and stuff?'

'Another one of your phobias?' he smiled. 'I think there might be a kind of spotted grass snake or something, probably some lizards. I don't know about venomous, though. But don't worry, I'm sure you're quite safe.'

'Oh good,' Eleanor said, feeling guilty.

'Come on,' he said. 'Let's go and crash out on the beach. I need to put some sun stuff on.' It was impossible to stand and balance on the rocks with the water pulling and pounding at their legs, so they had to slither backwards on their bottoms, which made Eleanor terrified her bikini would be dragged off by the current. Lewis got up first, took her arm to pull her up and steadied her as she stumbled on to dry beach.

They collected their clothes and flopped down on the dark sand. The beach was more crowded than in Panarea, with a greater variety of shapes and sizes. It didn't feel like such an insult to neighbouring eyes to stretch out, stained bikini, white skin and all.

'When in Vulcano . . .' Lewis insisted, when she suggested shade. She noticed he used a thick sun lotion like lard, which took several minutes to rub in and made him even whiter.

'You look embalmed,' she said, giggling.

'You're too kind,' Lewis said. 'I prefer to think of myself as pale and interesting.'

She thought how much she liked it that they'd settled into this cheerful banter. It struck her that this was the first time she'd really relaxed in months.

'Look at that guy,' said Lewis, pointing to a very dark, long-haired man who was clambering to the top of a high spiky rock. He stretched up like a gymnast and dived gracefully into the water. A couple of girls clapped as he surfaced. 'Twat,' Will would have said, a little too loudly, and they'd have had fun fabricating some absurd gigolo lifestyle for him. But Lewis just said, 'He looks genuinely Sicilian, don't you think?

A local, not one of the Milanese pack – he doesn't look groomed enough.'

'No, he's not wearing Prada swimming shorts, with a BlackBerry surgically attached to the palm of his hand.'

'Not shorts,' Lewis said, 'briefs.'

Eleanor giggled. 'Not briefs, micro briefs.'

'All the better to be seen preening in.' He flopped down on to his elbows. 'It's good to escape from Panarea for a day, isn't it? Not that I don't like it there, but it's almost too perfect – like some theme park, Glamourworld or something.'

'I know what you mean. It *is* nice to escape; keeps me out of trouble.'

'Well, I can't guarantee that,' said Lewis. 'But at least you've got a day off from your big hat.'

'Ironically, now is when I need it, my face feels burnt already.' Her legs and midriff were already alarmingly pink and her whole body felt stripped and itchy. She fished an ancient sarong from her bag and wrapped it around her shoulders like a cape, trying not to make comparisons with the elegantly knotted garment Will's actress had modelled.

Suddenly everyone was scrambling to their feet and gazing up at the sky to watch a chunky yellow plane that had buzzed into view and was swooping steeply down towards the sea. Eleanor stepped back, thinking for a moment it was in trouble, but to her surprise it soon climbed sharply back up into the sky. There were shrieks and excited chatter all round; some people were even pulling out cameras. Lewis shouted an enquiry to a nearby Italian couple.

'What's going on?' Eleanor cried.

'That, my dear, is your local fire engine,' he said. 'Look at the body of the plane, it's shaped more like a boat. It collects water from the sea and then drops it on to the fire. It'll be back in a bit for more. This is so cool, I've never seen one before.'

The plane seemed to be climbing towards the volcano crater. 'What, are they trying to put the volcano out?' Eleanor shouted in fear. Lewis roared at this, as did several Italians within earshot, all of whom could obviously understand English. She flushed with humiliation and cried, 'What? What is it?'

'Apart from the fact that the volcano hasn't seen any action for over a century,' said Lewis, 'if there was an eruption I think we'd all be making a run for it, don't you? A few gallons of water won't save us!'

'Oh, yes, of course.' She wished her blushing would calm down. She saw him glance at her, then quickly away, probably to spare her embarrassment. He was sweet. She thought about telling him that her lack of geographical knowledge, not to mention common sense, was fairly well known in her circle. Once, swimming in the sea, she'd remarked to Will that the horizon wasn't quite straight. 'That'll be the curvature of the earth, then,' he'd replied. He'd had to go back to the shore he was snorting so much water through his nose. She decided against sharing this with Lewis. It would be better to dig out some anecdotes that showed her in a more intelligent light.

'My guess is there's a forest fire,' he was saying, still transfixed by the action. 'But I can't see the flames, can you? Only smoke, up there by those villas.' She followed his gaze as the excitement continued, with a helicopter now appearing from the direction of the Sicilian mainland. It was dangling a large bucket.

'What a simple idea,' she said, 'just scooping up the water from the sea.'

'Bloody expensive, though,' he replied. 'That helicopter must have come all the way from Messina.'

'It feels like a local festival or something!' It was true, everyone had crowded on to the roads and beach, exclaiming and cheering, with children carried aloft on fathers' shoulders and people aiming cameras at the aircraft. Then, after several more minutes of diving to the sea and roaring up to the fire, both plane and helicopter climbed higher into the sky and headed off to the mainland. It all seemed fantastically exhilarating and heroic.

Gradually, everyone settled back down to their baking, but Lewis remained standing. 'I reckon we deserve a drink after all that high drama,' he said. 'What d'you think?'

'Yes please,' said Eleanor. 'Anything but eggnog.'

Chapter 8

They found a bar just off the beach for *panini* and cold drinks, managing to grab the last table from under the noses of a couple lingering at the roadside over their scooters. It was all getting so familiar now: the tanned bare legs, the mouths never quiet of conversation, the flicking of cigarettes, the smell of warm bread and bubbling cheese.

Lewis ordered a beer, she falteringly requested Limoncello, the sweet, icy after-dinner favourite at the hotel.

'You know, I wouldn't worry about the language thing,' said Lewis in the casual tone Eleanor had come to recognise as having been chosen to make her feel less self-conscious. 'Italians never expect the English to know a word. And Sicilian is practically another language anyway. Sounds like Italian spoken by Sean Connery, if you ask me.'

They laughed. 'I'm just not used to being so out of

control,' said Eleanor. 'Coming here, not knowing where it was I was heading, I'd never heard of the Aeolians before last week, let alone knew how to pronounce them. This whole situation is insane. And I can't even make myself understood in a bar. I feel like some kind of village idiot.'

Lewis grinned. 'You could always try your Spanish strategy, you seemed pretty fluent in that.'

'You're not going to let me forget that, are you?'

They lit cigarettes and watched the rest of the sunbathers gradually retreat to the roadside cafés to be fed and shaded. Eleanor was only vaguely concerned about this new compulsion to chain-smoke; she supposed she must subconsciously be aping the locals. They smoked everywhere: riding along on their scooters, sitting in the back of the little three-wheelers, on the beach, talking on mobile phones while water slopped around their thighs.

'You know the first time I came to Italy I was in this small town, didn't know the language at all,' said Lewis. 'I was having a look round and kept seeing these big signs saying "*senso unico*" I thought it must mean "unique place", so maybe the cathedral, since that would be the most important building in the town. I followed those signs for ages, round and round like a mug. Then I gave up and looked in my guidebook. Turned out *senso unico* just means "one way street".'

Eleanor laughed. 'How come you know so much

about these islands? Have you been out here before?'

'No, but I've studied them, done a lot of reading. There's so much stuff here. You know, they've been inhabited for 3,000 years, but have only really opened up since the hydrofoil service began. The stories are incredible – volcano eruptions, prisoner-of-war camps, shipwrecks. They found a shipwreck off Panarea a few years ago, with hundreds of beautiful terracotta vases still perfectly intact. Who knows where they were being taken or who they were meant for.'

'How romantic. Just so long as our hydrofoil back doesn't meet the same fate.'

'You really are a nervous sailor, aren't you?' he smiled.

'I know, I'm fine about flying, but boats always give me palpitations . . . even a rowing boat in the Serpentine. It used to drive Will crazy.'

She realised this was the first time she'd said his name aloud that day, though it had been on her lips a hundred times. She marvelled at the pleasure it gave her to speak that simple syllable.

'How long were you with him?' Lewis asked.

'Almost three years. We got engaged in March, but that didn't last long. By April he'd met the actress.'

'I'm not sure her profession is of any great signifi-cance,' said Lewis, eyebrows raised. 'Not unless she's researching a part about stealing other people's blokes and intends handing them back over when she's finished. She's probably out of work, anyway, they mostly are.'

'It just sounds so glamorous,' said Eleanor. 'And now I've seen how amazing she looks, it's obvious that she *is* glamorous. She's just so . . . Panarea. Her life must be a thousand times more exciting than mine.'

'Oh, come on, what you do must be pretty interesting, too? Most people would say that being a designer sounds quite cool.'

'I suppose. Everyone at work takes themselves so seriously, though. But it's just ads and websites, it's not like we're producing the Lindisfarne Gospels . . .' She slid a glance at his face, hoping he would be impressed with the reference; she was still feeling stupid after the volcano blunder.

'Oh, people take themselves seriously in every industry,' he replied, evidently not tempted to discuss illuminated manuscripts with her. 'That's why we need holidays. Another Limoncello?'

'Ooh, yes, a large one, please.'

As he waved his arm to get the waiter's attention she thought how much she liked talking to him. He was so clever and funny – Rebecca was very lucky to have such a mild-mannered, thoughtful boyfriend. There was no way he would be off at the first sniff of an actress's greasepaint. But he didn't say much about himself, she noticed, beyond a few details about the archaeology department at college and a flat in Maida Vale, where, from what she could gather, he lived alone. And he clearly wasn't going to respond to probing about Rebecca. Eleanor decided he was being tactful, not wanting to flaunt his happy pairing with the ponytailed Miss Perfect in the face of her own romantic slump.

'How long have you been with Rebecca?' she asked, trying again.

'Oh, a couple of years.'

'I thought you said you met at university?' she said, shocked. Surely Lewis couldn't still be in his early twenties? He was ten times more worldly-wise than she was.

'That's right, but we were friends for years before we got together. We're both twenty-eight now.'

Younger than she was, then. She'd liked Will being a few years older, it made her feel more protected somehow, as though he was always there to try everything first. It crossed her mind that it was getting to be about the time she'd seen Will yesterday. She remembered the desire in his voice as he spoke to the black-haired girl, the sound of them kissing and murmuring to each other, and felt the familiar contraction of distress in her stomach. It was no good. How would he ever be of no significance to her?

'You know, you shouldn't define everyone by their partner, or whether they've even got one,' Lewis was now saying, in best counsellor's style. 'It's just one part of someone's life, not everything.'

'I know,' she said, a little prickly. How humiliating to require a feminist pep talk from a man, a man she barely knew. 'But the reason I'm here in the first place is because I want to see my ex-boyfriend with his new girlfriend, crazy as it may be. As it obviously is. So couples are on my mind. I can't help it. Besides, look at Panarea – just about everyone's in a couple, it's a honeymoon spot, a place for lovers. You're quite unusual going on holiday on your own – unless you're following someone too?'

'Damn, you've caught me out,' Lewis said, deadpan. 'Actually, I've admired Katharina from afar for years. I could barely control myself yesterday when I saw her in her leopard-skin.'

Eleanor giggled at the thought. Clearly she wasn't going to get any more information from Lewis than he was prepared to give. Perhaps she'd made herself far too vulnerable by pouring out her own story so readily. She cast around for a change of subject. 'So did you say you're from Durham originally?'

'Yes, I couldn't wait to escape, to be honest. My sister's still up there, though. She's a painter, claims to be inspired by the bleak and blustery northeast.'

'How wonderful. I'd love to be a real artist. Is she with someone?'

Lewis pulled a face of mock despair. 'She is not, so there you go, a single female role model for you. Would you like her number?'

She sighed. 'Sure. I need all the tips I can get.'

'Where did you grow up? Did I hear you tell Sophie you're from Dorset?' he asked.

'Devon. A little village near Exeter, you won't know it. Just me and my parents.'

'You must all be close then, being an only child?'

'Yes, we are, though I have to admit I haven't seen so much of them in the last year or so.'

'Why not?'

'I don't know – I suppose I got the feeling Will wasn't that excited by them, so I stopped going down so often, except on my own.'

'That's a shame,' said Lewis. 'Doesn't sound like this Will character made much of an effort?'

'Oh, it wasn't like that.' Eleanor couldn't stop herself rushing to defend Will. 'He's just the sort of person who gets bored if he's not entertained, and he just found them a bit unentertaining. You know what parents are like, with their routines and domestic stuff?'

'I do indeed, though my parents recently split up, so I'm still getting used to the new routine there.'

'Really? Were you surprised?'

'Not really, they always seemed to despise each other. There's an element of Stefan and Katharina that reminds me of them, actually. Silently warring. Takes you a while to work out that they never actually speak to each other. But with Mum and Dad, I suppose once my sister and I were grown up they felt free to finally get rid of each other.'

'Funny to think of people staying together for decades, just because they have children,' said Eleanor.

'I know. Our generation wouldn't dream of doing that.'

'Or feel the need to have kids at all.'

'Oh, I don't know about that,' Lewis said.

Again, inevitably, Will was on her mind. There'd been a conversation about children a month or so after they'd got engaged, which of course turned out to be a month or so before they split up. She'd ventured a time-frame, nothing too threatening, but his response had been disappointingly opaque.

'Will wasn't keen to start a family,' she said. 'He never actually said it explicitly, but you know when you just know? But I suppose most men are quite reluctant, aren't they?'

'I don't think that's true,' Lewis frowned. 'If I think about all the blokes I know, I'd say only one is dead set against having kids at some point. Your Will might be the exception rather than the rule.'

Eleanor didn't like this interpretation at all, though she enjoyed the phrase 'your Will'. 'Sorry I keep going on about him,' she said. 'You must think I'm completely obsessed.'

It had not been a question, but she could see Lewis was considering his answer. His verdict. 'I think you still seem to believe your relationship can be resurrected, even though you've seen him with someone else.' She felt his stillness as he watched for her reaction.

'It's not that I *believe* it,' she said. 'It's just that I *want* it. I can't imagine going back to London and being on my own again.' She met his eye and saw the pity there.

'You'll be fine,' he said, seriously. 'People always are. You just need to get into the habit of thinking about other things.' With this, he jumped up. 'Hang on here a minute, I have an idea.'

Eleanor watched him talk for a few minutes to the barman and then return, grinning widely and twirling a set of keys. 'Your next entertainment, signora . . .' He pulled her out of the bar by her arm and she found she liked it – it felt like being steered by a friendly bear. Now he was climbing on to a cream-coloured Vespa parked at the kerb, one of the smart ones with brown leather seats Eleanor had seen around Panarea, and started up the engine. 'Hop on, we're going for a little ride.'

'But there's not room,' she protested.

''Course there is, come here.' He pulled her into position behind him. It felt snug and intimate. She hadn't been pressed this close to any man since Will. She was glad she'd pulled a long T-shirt over her bikini.

'Whose is this thing?' she asked.

'The guy behind the bar lent it to me for an hour for a few euros.'

'Won't he worry you'll steal it?'

'Oh, Eleanor, not everyone expects high drama and betrayal all the time.'

They zoomed away from the harbour, past the mud pool, where people were still squatting in little clusters, and up a long, gentle slope. 'This is Vulcanello,' Lewis shouted back to her. 'It was created by an eruption from the main crater, so they called it "Little Vulcano".'

They were winding up the hill, passing villas with vast fenced grounds. It was dusty, parched, much drier than Panarea, and with a more forlorn atmosphere. Some of the walls were topped with ceramic pots with faces, and at the edge of the gardens Indian figs stood like prisoners, forcing their spiked little ears through the holes in the fencing. Sad that their bid for freedom only locked them more firmly in place, thought Eleanor. There was no one else around and that made her enjoy the human contact all the more. Hugging Lewis felt safe and cosy, and the breeze on her stinging skin was delicious.

Finally the road petered out and they were by the sea again. Lewis pulled up and stepped off the scooter.

'This will take your mind off things,' he said. 'It's the *Valle dei Mostri* – Valley of Monsters.'

Eleanor looked around. The 'monsters' were scorched gnarls of black lava, and there were countless numbers of them as far as the eye could see in an unsettling clifftop assembly. The sun was lower now and they looked sinister, as though harbouring something evil.

'Isn't this incredible?' called Lewis, leaping down and exploring happily. 'You can see why they named them monsters, they are quite spooky, don't you think?'

Eleanor saw that there were flies and bugs everywhere, living on the monsters. It felt unearthly, as though they'd landed on the wrong planet. She didn't join Lewis as he jumped between the rocks, examining crevices and spikes and picking up bits of loose matter here and there. Feeling as though the warmth of the bar and the sun had never existed, she lit herself a cigarette and shivered.

On the hydrofoil trip back to Panarea, she noticed her silver charm bracelet had turned dull and discoloured since the morning. The little charms were badly tarnished.

'Look what's happened to my bracelet!' She showed Lewis, suddenly feeling far more distressed than she knew was appropriate.

'It must have been damaged by the sulphur in the mud and maybe even the sea, too,' he said. 'I meant to warn you to take off any jewellery. Should be all right, though, if you soak it in some lemon juice.'

'Hmm.' She still felt dejected. His Boy Scout practicality annoyed her all of a sudden.

'Did Will give it to you?' he asked.

'No, but I bought it to match a necklace he gave me. I've become very attached to it.' Her tone was so girlish and pathetic it offended even her own ear.

'Well at least you're not wearing the necklace today,'

said Lewis, sitting back and glancing out of the window at the darkening sky.

'No, I haven't worn that since the day we split up,' she said, morosely.

'Right.'

He was tired of the subject of Will, as anyone would be once they'd heard the story and offered an opinion on it. The interesting bit was her having followed him here; his rejection of her was in itself nothing special. It happened all the time, it happened to everyone.

They lapsed into silence, not speaking again until the boat delivered them to the dock in Panarea.

Sophie was to be put off no longer. As soon as they walked into the dining hall, Tim cornered Lewis and Sophie pounced on Eleanor as though they'd planned the ambush in advance and deemed anything less than a full confession unacceptable.

'What was today all about?' she asked Eleanor in a lowered voice. 'You know we were up for going with you guys to Vulcano? We thought it would be fun, all four of us, but Lewis made it quite clear it was just you two. Was it some kind of date?'

'Of course not,' Eleanor said, taking a deep breath. 'Lewis has a girlfriend in London. He was just being a good citizen, cheering up a potential suicide.'

Sophie gasped and gripped Eleanor's forearm. 'But, Eleanor, you're not suicidal, are you?'

'No, but I needed cheering up, I'm a bit down about something.'

'Oh?' Sophie's mouth and eyes were three huge circles on her face.

'Yes, I split up with my boyfriend recently and, I don't know, this place is just a bit coupley, I suppose.'

She had decided the story of the break-up would be quite enough for the others; there was no need to let them know about Will being here in Panarea. Lewis was to be trusted, she was certain – she didn't think she'd met anyone so upstanding, so sure of his values. As she talked, describing to Sophie the romance of Will's marriage proposal, followed by that final conversation in the flat that had left her feeling so terminated, she felt strangely detached from the action, like a storyteller trotting out a well-worn tale. Maybe the heat was making her too tired to care.

Sophie, however, became more and more invigorated with each new nugget of information. 'And you'd been together three years? What a complete *bastardo*! Have you met the new woman?'

'No, but I saw her once. She's spectacularly gorgeous.'

'Typical,' Sophie growled. 'Younger and thinner than us, I suppose?'

'I think so.' Eleanor felt a twinge of protest at the implication that she shaped up to the opposition alongside Sophie as little more than a pair of swollen has-beens. She let it go.

'Well, it won't last,' Sophie said. 'I bet they work together, do they?'

'No, she's an actress, I think.'

'What's her name?' Sophie asked, briskly. 'We'll look her up online and get some gossip. Shall I go and get Tim's laptop from upstairs?'

'No, I don't actually know her name,' Eleanor admitted. Her investigations had been rather poor so far, she realised, considering it was now Tuesday evening and she'd been in Panarea since Saturday.

'Well, who cares anyway?' Sophie said, sloshing more wine into their glasses. 'She's obviously not successful or you'd know about it. She'll just be some ditsy tart not quite tall enough for modelling and too stupid for a real job.'

Sophie's unconditional support, not to mention the vindictive tone, was refreshing after Lizzie's well-intentioned pessimism and Lewis's platitudes ('You'll be fine; people always are'. Well, she was not 'people'). Perhaps Sophie was exactly the ally she needed.

'Don't worry,' Sophie said on cue. 'You'll get your revenge. She'll ditch him, I should imagine. I'm a great believer in karma.'

Eleanor saw that Stefan had fallen silent after a conversation with Nathalie and was now listening to theirs, following their exchange with his eyes like a game of ping-pong.

'What's your manly hunch on all of this?' Sophie

asked him. He looked at her, bewildered. 'Come on, what do you think Eleanor should do to get over this ex-boyfriend?'

He shrugged. 'There are two sides to every cake.'

Eleanor pressed her lips together and tried not to look at Sophie.

'You are lucky, I think,' Stefan added, 'if it is possible to run here, away from him.'

'My thoughts exactly,' Sophie cried. 'You've done the right thing, leaving the country and going on holiday. This way, you can't be tempted to go begging for him to take you back. That's just what I told Rory when that dreadful brat Hugo from the nursery wouldn't let him sit next to him for golden time.'

'What time is golden?' Stefan asked, lost, but Sophie had finished consulting him.

'Now don't you worry, Eleanor, we'll keep your mind off things. Do you fancy the beach tomorrow? Tim and I are planning a lazy day with a strict no-activities rule, maybe lunch at that beach restaurant? Apparently they do the best *pasta con le sarde* in the Aeolians.'

'Maybe,' Eleanor said. 'It's so nice of you to include me, thank you. I do have a few things I need to do in the morning . . .'

Will, her spyglass, the roof terrace: she knew she'd be back there. She wouldn't follow him again, she promised herself, but she still needed her fix. There

120

was also the small matter of three messages she'd received on her mobile from work, all from Rufus and the last sounding quite unfriendly.

'But I'll try to come,' she promised.

'That's what I like to hear. We'll sort out a plan at breakfast,' Sophie said. 'Now where's our fish? Has anyone else noticed how they always seem to serve the Italian table first?'

Chapter 9

Rufus loomed at the head of the long, pale-wood conference table, shifting his weight from foot to foot, arms motioning in big shrugs from the shoulder, as though warming up ringside for a big fight. He looked crazed.

'We need to get leaner, meaner, sharper, greedier!' he yelled. Then he slowly, dramatically, spelled out a word – 'B-U-S-N-E-S-S'. He must mean 'business', Eleanor thought, not anything to do with London Transport, but he'd missed out the 'I'. 'Business, new business, we need more of it, we can't get enough of it. It's time to get our fucking act together, guys, it's time to be hunters, predators!' His face had turned the colour of a tomato about to split.

Eleanor wanted to giggle, but looking round the table at the rest of the team she realised this outburst was being received in all seriousness. A line of account handlers sat along one side of the table, each with phone, tablet, laptop (in some cases, all three) laid out neatly in front of them. When one of their gadgets gave a bleat or pulse, they would deaden it instantly, fingers deft in deference to Rufus's address. She tried to catch Miranda's eye, but she too was watching their account director with rapt face. Perhaps such fits were a regular feature of these weekly status sessions. This was Eleanor's first.

'Otherwise,' Rufus was now saying, 'you know what the bonus ball will say . . .' Eleanor had no idea what the bonus ball would say and hoped he wouldn't ask for suggestions from the floor. She decided that if challenged she would just say 'Seven', everyone's lucky number. She sensed a general stiffening of backs as Rufus groaned a game show sound effect for the wrong answer and held up his right hand, index finger and thumb coiled together in an 'O' shape. He was breathing very heavily.

He'd just got back from a business trip to Singapore and this was the first time she'd seen him since her interview three weeks ago. She remembered it well. What was it the agency did, exactly, she'd asked, sitting in her neat little skirt and jacket, smiling interestedly.

'Whatever the fuck our clients want us to do,' he'd snarled, like something out of a *Wall Street* spoof. 'We're whatever they want us to be. While they pay, we kiss butt. We're whores. Does that answer your question?'

'Right, yes, of course,' Eleanor said, face solemn as he continued, seamlessly mixing cliché with technical jargon too new for her to decipher. Only when he'd finished laughing at her ignorance of engagement platforms did he add that as a studio designer she might be creating websites, brochures, press and outdoor ads: above-the-line, below-the-line, through-the-line.

As it turned out, lines were important in the company. There was no traditional hierarchy, merely lines that shouldn't be crossed, and if you needed to ask whether you could cross a particular line, then you could rest assured you weren't entitled to cross it. It was like a sophisticated home security system with infra-red rays criss-crossed all over the place: you only knew you'd walked into one when you heard the sirens screaming.

A girl needed a friend to navigate a place like this. Miranda was the only other woman in the design studio and she made no bones about enjoying her captive little court of male admirers. Not that many of the men bothered lowering their headphones for long enough to have a conversation with her (they were mostly DJs, really, just marking time), but their glances were admiring and there was undeniably a steady stream of them heading up to the bar with her after work. Eleanor was no threat, it seemed, especially once she was safely engaged to Will.

Miranda was in her mid-twenties and obsessed with her looks, which were petite and vulpine. Everyone said she could have been a model if it weren't for her height, five foot two. Sometimes she got very bitter about the lack of commercial demand for mini-models. But shallow as Miranda could certainly be, Eleanor liked her very much. For one thing, she enjoyed going out for a glass of wine at lunchtime every day, in itself exceptional behaviour at the agency, which had turned out to take a rather puritanical line on such things. They'd laugh and gossip, dissect Miranda's latest love interest, tell each other they needed to stick together in the passive-aggressive male environment. When Miranda was looking for a new place to live it was only natural that Eleanor should offer her her own spare room. Gradually, as Eleanor grew disenchanted with the company and convinced she'd made another wrong career move, Miranda helped make office life bearable.

She was a good friend, Miranda. She'd told Eleanor about Panarea, hadn't she?

On Wednesday morning, Eleanor made an early start on the roof terrace, determined to be there before Will turned up at the waterfront. It was sheer masochism, she tried to tell herself sternly, like a child pressing her own loose tooth deep into the inflamed gum and then weeping at the pain. But she knew she wouldn't rest until she'd seen him again.

As she waited she rang the office on her mobile; to her dismay, Rufus's came straight on the line.

'Eleanor, where the fuck have you been? I've been trying to get hold of you all week?' She imagined him taking the call standing, like a trader surveying the skyline as he sealed his latest deal. Perhaps he would even punch the air.

'I've had trouble getting a signal. I've just managed to pick up your messages now.' She crouched down to minimise background noise – a hydrofoil was approaching the jetty – but the line was helpfully faint.

'Can you come in later today? We're really up against it. We've got three new pitches out of the blue and I'm talking to everyone in the boardroom at two o'clock.'

'But I've booked this whole week off, and part of next,' Eleanor protested. 'You signed my form.'

'I'll give you a couple of extra days next month to make up for it, when we're a bit quieter.' This was serious, Rufus was stingy about days off; he really must need her.

'Sorry, but I can't. My dad's not well, he's lost his voice and is in agony. And my mum's out of town.' She'd rehearsed this; it sounded exactly right. And her father *had* once lost his voice, so she would be able to bring authentic detail to the tale when she eventually did return.

'What can *you* do about a sore throat?' Rufus demanded, rudely. 'Anyway, didn't that happen before? He survived all right, then, didn't he?'

Damn, she'd forgotten she'd told them all the story of Will meeting her parents, that peculiar weekend when her father couldn't speak and her mother couldn't

126

stop – it had seemed so comical in retrospect. It was the night the whole team went out for drinks to celebrate her engagement, she remembered; she'd already squandered every last authentic detail.

'Yeah, it's an ongoing thing. Someone has to be here in case he needs to make contact with the outside world.'

'That's what email's for, for Christ's sake! I know they're in the back of beyond, but they're connected, right?'

'A lot of older people are uncomfortable with technology,' Eleanor said, playing for time. The boat she'd seen Will in before was being loaded at the jetty and a waiting group approached to board, too much of a huddle for her to make out individual faces.

'I haven't got time for this,' Rufus said. 'Just buy your dad a litre of Benylin and get yourself on the next train back.'

But she'd stopped listening. Will was there, climbing on to the boat. She used her free hand to adjust the monocular and feed on his face: he looked tired today, hungover, more like the Will she knew and loved, but his body was still brimming with that new, unfamiliar energy.

'I'll see what I can do, but don't count on me,' she said into the phone and hung up. Rufus's dilemma was instantly forgotten.

But her exhilaration at the sight of Will seemed

fainter than on previous days, and as she saw him bob off into the distance she suddenly felt overwhelmed with dissatisfaction. This wasn't enough, this glimpse, especially after a whole day of no glimpses at all.

She picked up her bag and hat and wandered through the hotel bar, which was empty except for Nathalie and Carlo, limbs woven together as they whispered at the foot of the stairs, the German girl wearing only slinky white hotpants and a tiny bikini top. Eleanor knew that Stefan and Katharina had already set off with Lewis for the Bronze Age site – they'd been discussing it at breakfast. She had to admit she'd felt slightly disappointed when they'd made their plans without inviting her to join the little excursion. Could it be, she now wondered, that she felt a little proprietorial about Lewis after their day alone together? Or perhaps he was simply being sensitive to Sophie's new claim on her, the waif of the group with no special mate. No doubt he thought it best that another woman should take over the job of distracting her from her dangerous obsession.

'Come and join us at any time,' Sophie had said to Eleanor the previous night. 'You really shouldn't be alone too much – you'll only brood. And there are some quite tasty specimens to be seen at the beach, I can tell you. Anyway, we're there all day – we'll be the fat white ones not beating off the paparazzi!'

Eleanor waved hello to the teenagers, who cast unimpressed glances in her direction. At least Carlo followed his up with a polite nod: she was a guest, after all. They looked like beautiful adolescent panthers eager for some adult savagery, thought Eleanor. She felt plain and weary in their presence; the flesh on her arms and legs seemed to judder where theirs rippled. Suddenly she couldn't wait to be out of their sight.

She found herself strolling down to the waterfront. She hadn't set foot there since arriving on Saturday, had viewed it as strictly out of bounds. But now she felt confident she had the measure of Will's day, and if there was one benefit of him disappearing out to sea for a few hours each day it was that she could at least move about the island freely, rather than skulking and sneaking about: in a few short days, she'd started to feel more fugitive than hunter. And with Will out of range she could even take off the hat, she hated the way it flattened her hair and made her neck tickle with sweat.

She sat down in one of the cafés, choosing a corner table in the one closest to her getaway lane, and ordered a large cappuccino and pastry. The blue of the water and painted stripes of the fishing boats seemed more dazzling at ground level; the heat more oppressive. She felt sweat run over the bumps of her spine and put her head in her hands, massaging her eyes and temples with her fingers. Near her feet, beyond the edge of the wooden deck, she could see tiny geckoes threading their way across the rocks. She let out a little whimper of frustration.

'Are you OK? You're English, aren't you?'

Eleanor recognised the voice before seeing the face, the words smooth with sympathy, as though rolled gently towards her. Feeling her heart pound and blood hiss, she forced a smile. 'Yes, how can you tell?' A foolish question: her hot skin and heavy cotton clothes would be enough to mark her out, even if her English-language guidebook weren't laid out on the table.

The girl had appeared at the next table, smiling and blinking in the direct sunlight. She looked cool and freshly showered, her skin a radiant golden colour next to the white of her sundress, which appeared to be made of a fabric no denser than tissue paper. She had no guidebook, lotion or silly hat; just her twinkling sequinned bag. She was thoroughly poised, looked as though she'd never been more at ease in her life than exactly as she was here and now.

'I'm Frannie,' she said, beaming. 'A fellow Brit abroad. How long are you in Panarea for?'

Startled by such beauty at close range, Eleanor felt herself flush. Above the perfect wide smile, the girl's eyes gazed like headlamps, huge, dark and intense. 'Ten days. How about you?' Eleanor's mind raced. She couldn't give this girl her real name; she'd be sure to report to Will that she'd come across an English woman called Eleanor. 'Nice, but a bit strange,' she imagined her telling him. 'Had her head in her hands.'

'Three weeks,' Frannie was now saying. 'But we're

already into the second week. It's going sooo quickly. The less we do the faster the days whizz by – doesn't make sense.' Eleanor noted the 'we'. It made her feel sick.

'Lucky you.' Three weeks with my boyfriend, she thought. 'I'm Jane,' she added. This was true: Jane was her middle name.

Frannie nodded, then turned to the approaching waitress. '*Ciao*, Anna,' she smiled, and began chattering in fast fluent Italian. Eleanor hoped she wasn't staring. The heavy hammering in her ribcage had subsided, but she knew she was still flushing. She'd never seen anyone so extraordinary-looking before, it was disarming, those huge intensely brown irises, fine cheekbones and perfect high-bridged nose. Her hair was a dark highly polished drape, so effortlessly natural it had to have been expensively cut.

'Oh, I love long holidays,' Frannie said, turning back to Eleanor with a kittenish little sigh. 'You can totally forget about the real world, can't you? I always feel I should take them when I can. My work means that I have to do really long stretches without a break. It just kills you.' She paused and leant forward on to her elbows, elegant fingers tucked under her chin. 'I'm an actress,' she explained. 'I've done a lot of theatre this year, so this is my first real time off.'

'That sounds fun. Are you based in London?' Eleanor was pleased that some kind of autopilot had kicked in to make her voice sound both natural and friendly.

131

'Yes, not much choice, really. But I'm from London, anyway. That made it easier when I started out, because I could just live at home.'

Her drinks arrived: espresso and mineral water. Even this seemed more stylish than Eleanor's choice. She noticed that flakes of her pastry had been lifted by the breeze and scattered on to her chest and lap; she brushed them off.

'How about you, what d'you do?' asked Frannie.

'I'm a designer for an ad agency. At least I was. When I get back I'm going to leave my job.' Eleanor was astonished to hear herself say this out loud, although she knew the idea had been germinating for a while. She'd only had the job ten months, always told Will and Miranda she'd give it at least a year.

'That's so exciting!' exclaimed Frannie. 'Changing jobs is like, I don't know . . . like shedding a layer of skin. You'll be all new underneath. It's very healthy. What will you do next?'

'I'm not sure yet, just something more fun, I suppose, or something totally different. I don't really do any real designing anyway. People always think designers spend their day with some big marker pen and flip chart, you know, having ideas, visualising. It's not like that at all. I spend most of my time answering emails about meetings.'

'I know exactly what you mean,' said Frannie, repositioning her chair closer to Eleanor's so her face was in the shade. 'Whenever I say I'm an actress, the first thing people ask is "Is it hard to learn your lines?" But that's such a tiny part of it, like me asking you how you turn your computer on.'

Eleanor didn't want to ask Frannie about learning her lines. She wanted to ask her about Will, how she thought it might feel to be cast aside for someone new, shed like a layer of skin, you could say. Instead, she sat grinning admiringly at her rival like the president of her fan club. 'What's your next project?' she asked.

'I start filming a TV thing in Spain next month for the BBC. I play a Latin temptress type. That's partly why I'm here – I've been told to tan.' Frannie gave a deep, flirtatious laugh. 'So if I end up like a wizened old walnut, it'll probably be my first and last TV appearance.'

She was utterly charming, thought Eleanor, instinctively liking her. There was nothing self-conscious about her beauty; she didn't hold herself like a sculpture to be admired, the way some of the women did around Panarea. Her manner was sincere, her eyes and smile genuinely engaged. It was so unfair, beautiful people had such a head start – literally – you just couldn't help feeling well disposed to them because they were so lovely to look at. Eleanor felt flushed and graceless compared to this poised creature. She couldn't believe this meeting was even taking place, that she was taking part in it. It had never occurred to her that she might find herself in conversation with the girl. She needed to remind herself that Frannie was the enemy, the she-devil who'd swooped down from nowhere and made off with Eleanor's most treasured possession. She willed herself to stop gawping and start using this opportunity to dig for information.

'So are you in Panarea with friends?' she asked, lightly.

'With my boyfriend,' said Frannie, sipping her water. 'And a couple of other friends have been popping in and out, which is good, because he's off on a diving course all this week.' She looked out to sea as though searching for Will's boat, just as Eleanor had done twenty minutes earlier. So it was confirmed: Will was busy recasting himself as an action hero. It made sense that a woman like this would require more from her man than the occasional offer to slouch to the corner shop for cigarettes.

'Is he really into it?' she heard herself ask. 'The diving, I mean.'

Frannie smiled indulgently. 'He loves it, a typical new convert. He's never done anything like it before but it turns out he's pretty good and now he can't stop going on about it. He's one of those naturally fearless types. Just goes for it.'

Will, naturally fearless? Eleanor supposed she could sort of see it. He'd never been a scaredy cat, certainly, even if he had preferred to curl up on the furniture in his spare time rather than take up anything too taxing. Another thought now clamoured: was it possible that she had held Will back somehow, that she was the reason he'd become so complacent and neglected his writing? Maybe she'd stifled his creativity, his spontaneity? In their three years together the surprise New York trip was the only unpredictable thing he had done, yet here he was in Panarea, out in the middle of an ocean famous for its vicious currents, 'just going for it' in a pair of flippers. Who exactly was this new muse?

'Didn't you want to go too?' she asked Frannie, spooning the foam from her cappuccino into her mouth and licking off the chocolate. It struck her that this might look English and provincial to Frannie's eye and put the spoon down again.

Frannie shuddered. 'God, no, I'm scared of deep water, I'd be frightened the sun would go in and I wouldn't be able to see the surface and work out which way was up. I went canoeing in St Barts last year and practically had a panic attack.' She laughed. 'It's crazy, I know. Apparently there are no childhood traumas to account for it; didn't have my head pushed into the paddling pool by the nursery bully, or anything like that!'

Eleanor laughed, too. She was already struggling with the idea that this delightful creature was her nemesis.

'And you, are you here with a boyfriend?' Frannie asked.

'No, on my own, but I've met some nice people at my hotel, some English and German couples.'

'Where are you staying?'

'The Albergo delle Rose, just up the road.'

'Ah, Giovanna's place. She's a funny old bird, isn't she? There were rumours about her husband when he was alive. This is Sicily after all.'

'Do you know Panarea really well then?' Eleanor asked, curiously.

'I've been here quite a few times, but I know Salina a lot better. That's the next island along, where my grandmother was from.'

Eleanor remembered the name of Frannie's villa, Casa Salina. Her family must own it then, she thought. No budget hotel accommodation for Will.

'Really, have you . . .?' Eleanor began, but at that moment a man and woman appeared from inside the café and waylaid Frannie with a flurry of kisses and exclamations. Eleanor recognised the woman: she'd been sitting in the same café on previous mornings, talking into her phone, looking sullen and bored. She now seemed far more pleasant, and, as Eleanor inspected her oversized smile and low pink gums, rather less intimidatingly perfect.

'Jane,' said Frannie, and they all turned to look at her. Eleanor realised her mouth was still open and closed it quickly with a little snap. 'This is Emilio and Rita. They're here from Naples. They've got a house near us in Iditella.'

136

They shook hands politely. Emilio, immaculate in dove-grey linen and waving Fendi sunglasses as he spoke, said: 'You are *inglese*? A pleasure to meet you.' He seemed to mean it, too, offered her a cigarette, and, for the first time, Eleanor felt her status soar above that of an undertanned, overcharged tourist. It was a good feeling.

'Oh, are you off?' asked Frannie, as Eleanor took the opportunity to hand some euros to the waitress, anxious to conceal her poor Italian in front of this sophisticated trio. 'Why don't you stay and join us for lunch?'

'Oh no, thank you, I'm meeting some people at the beach. It's getting so hot.' It was enough, she decided, this brief contact. She didn't trust herself to stay for more, felt certain she'd give herself away if they got back on the subject of Will. The deception of Rufus was one thing, but this was face to face, it was barefaced. She felt unprepared.

'It's been great meeting you,' said Frannie, warmly, as Emilio and Rita looked on approvingly. 'Perhaps another day? I'm supposed to be going to Stromboli tomorrow, but maybe we could get together on Friday? It makes a nice change to chat to another London girl.'

'I'd love to,' said Eleanor. As Frannie talked on, suggesting times and restaurants, it occurred to her that she hadn't mentioned she was from London. She supposed as much could be assumed, since London was where most of the advertising agencies were based. She felt quite flattered that Frannie had just taken it for granted that they had a city in common.

And a boyfriend, she reminded herself.

Chapter 10

Unexpectedly energised by this encounter, Eleanor walked back up the lane to the hotel and, without thinking, made for the roof terrace. She hadn't really intended going to the beach, where Tim and Sophie would certainly be cooling their bodies in the water by now, but the sun was high and she longed for the relief of the sea.

Training her eyeglass on the café, she saw Frannie still standing with Emilio and Rita, all talking at once, heads tipped back with laughter. The waitress, Anna, reappeared and set down three shot glasses on the table, before removing Eleanor's cappuccino cup. Even when she took the monocular away, Frannie's face still filled her mind. She couldn't quite take stock. The horror of realising her successor was not only beautiful but charismatic and kind, too, mingled bewilderingly with her instinctive liking for her. How could it be that in a matter of minutes she was already admiring the same charms that had so recently devastated her life?

Now she'd tasted freedom from her perch, she wanted more. With Will out for the day, why shouldn't she go to the beach for some holiday fun like everyone else? It was no different from spending the day in Vulcano, and she could still be back in time for his return, maybe get a couple of photos this time. The only problem was her bikini, grubby and smelly from yesterday's mud bath; she'd been too tired to rinse it out last night. She needed a new one, she decided, something more glamorous.

Humming with a strange new voltage, she skipped down the steps, made straight for the nearest boutique and began rattling through the racks of swimwear like a demented filing clerk. Which one would Frannie choose? There it was, dark red, sexy, plenty of plunge for showing off her cleavage, and tiny low-cut bottoms – a bit too tiny, perhaps, she'd have to remember not to frighten anyone with a sudden roll on to her stomach. Changing in her room a few minutes later, she was elated with the effect, and left for the beach before she could change her mind, still buttoning up a long white shirt as she waved to Giovanna at reception.

As she hurried along the coastal path she replayed her conversation with Frannie in her head, savouring the phrases, hunting between the lines for anything that might throw new light on the situation. But somehow it came back to the feeling that she was cheered by Frannie, almost inspired. Hadn't Frannie totally approved the idea of her leaving her job? Someone like Frannie wouldn't put up with Rufus's bullying, that was for sure. Screw Rufus, she decided, maybe she should simply never go back to the office again; it wasn't important to her, not like this.

Arriving pink and puffing at the packed sands, Eleanor was surprised to find not only Tim and Sophie but the entire dinner contingent camped at the water's edge on a patchwork of towels – including Lewis, who was sitting slightly apart on a large patterned sheet. Stefan and Katharina were lying together in the middle, heads propped up on their elbows but faces turned in opposite directions, like a particularly sweaty Janus. The Bronze Age expedition was obviously over, thought Eleanor. She couldn't understand how it could take anyone more than five minutes, anyway.

She tried to catch Lewis's eye, bursting to share the news of her Frannie encounter, pleased that there was now someone who understood her plight. But as she approached she saw Nathalie stretching towards his legs, kicking her heels up and down in the lapping water. Her feet wore socks of wet ashen sand, but the rest of her was the colour of liquid caramel, stunningly set off by those tiny white shorts and bikini top. She was very close to Lewis's body, practically wriggling between his legs; why not go all the way and dribble an ice lolly on to his thighs, Eleanor thought, instantly irritated with the ubiquitous Lolita. Now was obviously not going to be the best time for a debrief with Lewis; he didn't even look up at her arrival. She bit down on her lip with impatience and settled herself between Sophie and Stefan.

'I'm so glad you came!' Sophie exclaimed. 'We couldn't find any shade, but the bar's nice and cool if the sun gets too much. How are you?' she added, meaningfully.

'Good, fine, feeling much better today,' Eleanor said. 'How about you? Any news from home, from Rory?'

'We phoned after breakfast, but he was out at the park with his grandpa. I feel guilty just lying here doing nothing . . .'

'Oh, the little bugger won't be giving us a second thought, I promise you,' Tim interrupted. 'What do you think of my round towel, Eleanor?' He stood up to show her the soggy yellow circle he'd been slumped across. 'Our friend markets them in the States. "Suntowels", they're called – the idea is that you never have to move the towel, just edge yourself around as the sun moves.' Judging by the reddening strip down one side of his body, he'd clearly not followed this methodology himself.

'Cool,' Eleanor said. 'It would be handy for lining a coracle, if you needed to, you know, escape from a desert island or a shipwreck.' She looked to Lewis again, but still no reaction.

'Yes,' Tim said, doubtfully, and sat back down again.

'You must be roasting in that big shirt,' Sophie said, linking her fingers above her head in a long stretch. Her reassuringly solid proportions were bikinied in standard British black. 'Aren't you going to take it off?'

Lewis chose that moment to look over and raise a hand at Eleanor, squinting into the sun and grinning. She was suddenly less confident about the new bikini; the strap visible at her collar looked too vivid, like a grisly dribble of blood. She decided to keep the shirt on for a while.

'We've been hearing more about your trip to Vulcano,' Sophie said. 'I love the idea of the pongy mud pool. Is it worth us going there, too, d'you think?'

'Yes, it was great fun, totally different from here,' Eleanor said, searching eagerly for Lewis's agreement.

He turned to Sophie. 'Actually, you might be better going to Salina or Stromboli if you're just doing one day trip while you're here. There's a bit more to do there and Vulcano's a bit of a trek, to be honest.'

Eleanor drooped a little at this dismissal of their day together, and hardly listened as Katharina began singing Lewis's praises about that morning's tour of the archaeological site.

'He is bringing history alive,' she cried. 'He is our *Lehrer*, our professor!'

Lewis at least had the good grace to look embarrassed by this.

Eleanor's euphoria was slipping away with each new rivulet of warm sweat; she couldn't keep her clothes on for much longer under this laser sun. But at least she'd lotioned up at the hotel and wouldn't have to perform an all-over body massage in front of everyone. Slipping her arms out of the shirt, she almost recoiled at the sight of her own skin; what had looked creamy and even in the half-light of her room now resembled a striped collage of sore pink and newborn white. She felt as though she'd just unveiled a giant neon stick of rock in a Blackpool shop window.

'Great bikini,' Sophie exclaimed, loud enough, as Eleanor had feared, to turn everyone's heads, including a few from neighbouring groups. Clearly Sophie had no intention of neglecting her new commitment to boosting Eleanor's self-esteem. 'Don't you think, boys? Check it out. Very sexy and Italian. Did you buy it in Panarea, Eleanor?'

'Yes, from the shop by the hotel.' Her head felt like a giant red-hot dome.

'They're so much braver about colours here, aren't they?' Sophie said. 'None of this black and grey business. We're such slaves to understatement in Britain.'

Katharina, who was wearing a floral patterned one-piece that suited her surprisingly well, laughed at this.

'It is funny in London, everyone looks as if they are entering a funeral.'

'It's not just the clothes, believe me,' Tim snorted. Eleanor noticed that the book in his hand, *More Total Detox*, had a cigarette burn through the cover.

'This crimson is a remarkable colour,' Stefan said to Eleanor. She noticed him properly for the first time, a soggy-lipped puppy about a foot from her newly scaffolded cleavage.

'Thank you.' It occurred to her that she hadn't made much of an effort with him last night at dinner, had possibly bored him for longer than necessary with the whole Will dilemma. She decided to attempt a charm offensive that might also serve to get the collective gaze off her red breast. 'Your German is so good, Stefan! I mean English, your English is so good.'

The others hooted at this, of course; was there no end to her humiliation? She feared she might be becoming a running gag to them – wasn't there always one on holidays where people were thrown together like this? The one who provided the pratfalls? Thank God Will couldn't see her at this moment, making gaffes everywhere she turned, constantly revealing too much of everything, the object only of laughter and pity. She was the diametric opposite of Frannie in every possible way.

'Oh, most English people know a little German, too,' Stefan said, generously. 'Lewis is very good, I am discovering.'

Lewis would be, Eleanor thought.

'Well, we're not all complete Philistines,' Sophie said, adding in her gruff ogre voice, '*Sprechen Sie Deutsch? Ja, natürlich.*'

'*Jawohl, zwei Biere,*' Tim chipped in. '*Sehr grosse, bitte.*'

Even Nathalie was giggling now. Everyone looked at Eleanor again. She racked her memory for similar phrases but could think only of a scrap or two of German from *The Great Escape*. '*Ihren Passe bitte,*' wasn't that what the SS officer said to Dickie Attenborough at the bus stop before tricking him into giving himself up? No, perhaps not the best contribution.

'Er, *Neun-und-neunzig Luftballons?*' she offered to fresh hilarity that took a good minute to die down. Only Lewis and Nathalie did not roar.

'Oh dear!' cried Sophie, finally recovering with a theatrical wipe of her eyes. 'The singer with the hairy armpits, what was she called, Tim?'

'Nena,' Tim supplied. 'I would have thought you'd be too young to remember that song, Eleanor.'

'My mum had the single. She loved it.' Eleanor saw Lewis wink at Nathalie, whose pout twitched reluctantly into a secret little smile. It was all getting a touch too smouldering for her liking.

'You have no languages in your job, Eleanor?' Stefan asked, with another hungry look that made her feel like a lap dancer.

She tried to explain that the only language of any use in her workplace was mumbo-jumbo, but Stefan struggled with the sarcasm and she had to field several more questions about office life before she could eavesdrop properly on Lewis and Nathalie. They seemed to be engaged in a playful quarrel about who could swim the furthest and whether the rocks would make a race to Cala Junca too treacherous. A minute later they'd jumped to their feet and announced a plan to swim to the cove and decide the matter.

She watched them splash into the water with growing regret. Her lovely Lewis of yesterday had found himself a new playmate, one half her age and with twice her energy. Meanwhile, the hairy, salivating creature at her side wasn't going anywhere. Stefan didn't seem the slightest bit concerned that his wife was positioned just a couple of feet away from where he ogled Eleanor and had now turned towards them to join the conversation.

A little comfort, at least, was to be had from Sophie's critical gaze. 'She's very sporty, Nathalie, isn't she?' she asked Katharina, nodding out to sea as the swimmers veered smoothly around an outcrop of rocks. 'Did you say she plays tennis on the junior tour?'

'Only a little, but she is improving if she pulls her socks together.'

'I'd like to be around to see that,' Tim said. He sighed deeply and threw down his book. 'I don't know what it is about this detox thing, Sophe, but it really makes me want a beer. I'm going to the bar. I shall make my order in German.'

'Ooh, can I have a *gelato*, as well?' Sophie called after him. '*Nocciolo*, if they've got it.'

'I wonder if there's anyone famous on the beach,' Eleanor said, rolling closer to Sophie in an effort to cut off Stefan's full-frontal view.

'I think they must be on the yachts,' Sophie said, scanning the horizon with authority. 'That's where the paparazzi always seem to shoot supermodels, isn't it? I bet Kate Moss has been here. It's so frustrating not being able to recognise Euro celebrities, don't you think?'

At least Frannie wasn't famous, Eleanor thought, as Sophie had pointed out so witheringly the previous night. How appalling that would be, seeing her and Will nuzzling each other in magazine features about stars and their favourite romantic hideaways, reading quotes about how they'd never experienced real love before.

Tim padded back with Sophie's ice cream and an armful of dripping beers. 'Got to be careful we don't dehydrate,' he said, handing them around. Eleanor noticed he reserved two for himself.

Everyone gulped greedily and settled back to sun or read, or, in the case of the two men, peek over their sunglasses at nearby breasts. Eleanor stretched out on her back, partially covering her body with her shirt, and shaded her eyes with her hand. Instantly she slipped into a torment of images: Frannie, swishing her dark hair and widening those seductive eyes; Nathalie, curling her perfect plump lips and kicking her cute little feet; and herself, a heifer in a wide-brimmed hat. She wasn't sure how much time passed before the montage was interrupted by Lewis and Nathalie's return, but looked up just in time to see Nathalie emerge from the water like a Miss Teen Bond Girl, skin shimmering with water and hair weighed down to her waist. Lewis helped her as she stumbled, and Eleanor half expected the girl to pull a hunting knife from her shorts and hold it to his throat as she grappled with his crotch. How could Katharina allow such a wanton display?

Eleanor sat up, remembering to smile hello with the others, and waited for the dizziness in her head to settle. Now she saw that Nathalie was snuggled up against her mother, gasping out a torrent of excited German and English about the swim and squealing as Lewis prodded her with his foot. Katharina began towelling her daughter's hair, while Lewis crashed out flat on his back, recovering his breath loudly and brushing off some teasing remark from Tim about being an old man and a loser. It seemed he'd been beaten in the race to Cala Junca.

'Perhaps you should think twice before taking on a teenager again,' Sophie giggled, with just the blend of amusement and disapproval Eleanor had come to admire. She longed for such tone control.

Lewis just laughed, flicking black sand at Sophie's

stomach. In retaliation, she packed a tight fistful and aimed at his leg. Soon, inevitably, the others were joining in.

All but Eleanor. Before she could fight it, she felt a hot veil of despond wrap tightly around her head. Her own traumas were meaningless to these people. To Sophie she was just entertainment, a project to occupy her maternal urges in the absence of Rory; and as for Lewis, Panarea's resident All Round Mr Nice Guy, she was – what? – probably just an unwelcome reminder of the neurotic London scene he'd been trying to escape. She'd been silly to think she could be one of the holiday gang.

A quick check of her watch reminded her that Will would be back within an hour: she needed to reprioritise.

'Well, I'm heading off,' she said, pulling her shirt back over her sweating skin. 'I think I might be burning. Cheers for the beer, Tim.'

'Oh, you just got here!' Sophie said. 'Don't you want to swim?'

'Hang on a minute and I'll walk back with you,' Lewis said, sitting up, still breathing heavily, 'before I get roped into any more athletic duels I can't handle.' He exchanged grins with Nathalie, who was now wrapped in a huge green towel, cheeks pink and glowing. She looked as innocent and fragile as a woodland creature peeking out from the safety of a tree, sitting patiently while Katharina proudly patted and smoothed her hair.

'No, don't bother,' Eleanor said, then realised she'd been much sharper than she'd intended as Tim and Sophie looked up with enquiring frowns. 'I mean, I need to make a few phone calls on the way,' she added, more pleasantly.

'Sure,' Lewis said, slumping back on to his elbows. 'See you later, then.'

'See you at dinner,' Stefan added.

'Just knock on our door if you fancy a tipple before dinner,' Sophie said.

Even Nathalie offered her a little wave goodbye, and as she flounced up the hill Eleanor wondered how it was that she was suddenly the one behaving like a fourteen-year-old.

Later, after dinner – another boozy occasion when even the staff had betrayed their surprise at the amount of wine consumed at the table – a sleepless Eleanor padded back down to the bar. It was empty but for Carlo wiping down tables and collecting up the last glasses and ashtrays.

'Good to see you hard at work for once,' she said, aiming for a warm, teasing tone but producing something closer to that of an inebriated butler who'd found his footman with the key to the drinks cabinet. 'A gigantic Limoncello, please.'

'Of course.' Carlo uncorked a new bottle and started pouring her a shot glass.

Eleanor snorted impatiently. 'That's far too small. Oh, just give me the bottle.'

'The bottle?' He looked at it in confusion, and she knocked back the shot glass before he could whip it away.

'Yes, charge it to my room.'

He stood aside as she skipped past to the spiral stairs. She saw that she'd forgotten to put on any shoes. After the whipped chill of her room, the air felt sultry, salty, and she imagined she could taste the spray from the sea. In fact, it was clear enough to see a generous smattering of stars above. Music carried across from a terrace bar at the waterfront: some club anthem she recognised and a chorus of voices shouting the lyrics, a second or two out of time. This was much nicer than the horror of closing her eyes; each time she'd tried the room had swirled with a kind of sorority of Frannies, taunting her from every corner with that perfect, gleaming allure.

The despondency that had descended on her at the beach had not lifted. The Frannie incident, so adrenalising at first, had left her feeling overwhelmed. It hadn't helped that she'd tried to call Lizzie twice to discuss it but got her voicemail both times. Worst of all, she was starting to suspect that bringing her traumas out into the open with the others had just served to make the wound all the more livid. It was three months since she'd split up with Will, yet now it felt like it had happened three days ago.

She'd lost him, any halfwit could see that. It was

what Lewis had been trying to make her see yesterday in Vulcano. Even he didn't want to be her friend any more; he'd made his preferences quite clear at the beach, and hadn't even turned up for dinner. She was well and truly on her own.

She settled back in contented self-pity and drank the Limoncello in big mouthfuls from the bottle, needing it like lemonade after a thirsty game of hide and seek. Another song began, who was it again? she wondered. That singer with the big hair from the Eighties, a leonine mane, wasn't that how they always described it? She laughed out loud, then found herself intoning the lyrics in her head: it was all to do with turning around with bride eyes and keeping the heart totally equipped.

Exactly right, she thought, emphatically, as she listened. Just who was this talented lyricist who'd predicted her plight with such aching precision? She glugged back more yellow goo and closed her eyes. Instantly, the terrace whirled sickeningly around in her head, so she opened them wide again.

As the song was finishing, she thought she heard a voice say, 'Hey, bravo!'

'What?' Eleanor said, crossly. 'Who is it?'

'Me.'

'I have no idea who "me" is,' she called out, rudely. Now she made out Lewis's outline; he was sitting on the low wall at the top of the steps. 'What are you doing here?'

'I was attracted by your sweet song,' he replied.

'What? I wasn't singing!'

'Er, yes you were. And with some feeling.'

She didn't care for his jaunty tone. 'Liar,' she muttered and licked the neck of the bottle. She noticed the stickiness on her fingers and began lapping at them, too, gripping the bottle between her thighs.

'Why would I make it up?' Lewis laughed, by her side all of a sudden. 'You do a fine Bonnie Tyler.'

'*That's* who it is!' She smiled delightedly, then slumped back against the wall, sulking: no one would compare Frannie to Bonnie Tyler; oh no – she'd get some siren with proper sex appeal, like Marilyn Monroe or Jane Birkin or . . . Her thought trailed out of reach, and she realised Lewis was still perched on the wall next to her. 'Want a bit?'

He took the bottle. 'Ah, more Limoncello, lovers' ruin.'

'How d'you mean?' Eleanor asked, puzzled.

'What are you doing up here on your own, anyway? I didn't even know we had a roof terrace.'

'What do you care?'

'Where are the others?'

'How would I know?'

'Is this entire conversation going to consist of questions?' Lewis grinned.

Eleanor tried and failed to think of a query to trump this. 'Well, if you must know,' she declared, 'everyone's probably still at the bar down the hill, at the Whatsit Bianca hotel, they went there after dinner. And I'm up here pondering the total something or other of my heart, y'know, like Bonnie.' It occurred to her that she might be slurring slightly.

'I think "eclipse" might be the word you're looking for.'

'Yeah, whatever.' She frowned up at him. 'Oh, and I met Frannie. Not that you're interested.'

'Frannie?'

'Will's new woman, you know, the gorgeous goddess one I told you about. Not much chance of eclipsing her.'

'How did you meet her?' he asked, and even in her drunkenness she could hear the carefulness in his tone.

'Bumped into her in a café down there. Anyway, I don't want to talk about it with you.' She threw back her head, ignoring the uncomfortable pull in her neck, and looked up at the stars, now a vast buzzing circuit board too lively for her eyes to follow. Then, after much fumbling, she located her eyeglass and tried to focus on one particularly bright twinkle.

'You may need something more powerful than that,' Lewis said. 'A telescope or something. Then you'd be able to see the—'

'Oh, hush,' she cried, turning with what she imagined to be a seductive Scarlett O'Hara flounce – but she was still holding the eyeglass and his nose and chin loomed massively into view. 'I just want to soak up the, y'know, magnitude of it all.' She dropped the eyeglass to her lap and rolled her eyes for emphasis.

'I see.'

'It's crucial to remember the bigger picture when the chips are down,' she said, wisely. 'I mean, what would you do . . . what would you do, Lewis, if a giant tidal wave, a tsunami, swept over the island without any warning at all?' She made huge swooping movements with her arms.

'That's a tricky one,' Lewis said. 'I suppose I'd head for the highest point on the island, Punta del Corvo, up there, and sit it out till the tides settled.'

'There wouldn't be time,' Eleanor said, dismissively. 'It would be here in seconds, with a big roar!'

'OK, then I'd grab one of those plastic sunloungers and hope to surf to safety.'

Eleanor pondered this and could think of no objection.

'What would you do?' he asked.

'Drown, I suppose,' she said. 'Can I have the Limoncello?'

'You've already got it, on your lap.'

She took another huge swig and passed it to him. 'OK. Well, what would you do if Stromboli erupted and hot deadly lava was pouring in our direction?'

'You're very fond of these disaster scenarios, aren't you?' Lewis said.

'I'm serious,' Eleanor slurred. 'Go on, what would you do?'

He sighed. 'Well, I guess escape would be out of the question so I'd just have to hope my ashen remains might tell future generations about the nature of holidaymaking at the beginning of the twenty-first century. What we ate for dinner, perhaps.'

'You weren't at dinner,' Eleanor said in triumphant accusation. She'd known she was annoyed with him about something.

He ignored this. 'What would *you* do?'

'I'd throw myself off this roof to my death before the deadly lava reached me, so as not to feel my own flesh boil.'

'Cunning,' Lewis said. He opened a new pack of cigarettes and she watched him light up. He didn't offer her one.

'Of course.' She was struck with sudden inspiration. 'I'd pen a love note to Will first! Wouldn't you pen one to Rebecca? Just a little chit! We could put them in this Limoncello bottle and hope it floated to the mainland.'

'I thought you said there wouldn't be time.'

'No, that was the tidal wave, ridiculous stupid person.'

'I see, I'm getting confused.' He was struggling not to laugh.

'Or maybe your note would be to Nathalie?'

That put a stop to the smirk on his sly-fox face, she was satisfied to see. 'Um, I don't think so,' he said. 'Look, Eleanor, I wonder if you've got the wrong end of the stick.'

'What about?'

He shrugged. 'Nathalie, Rebecca, everything, really.'

'No, I've got the right end of the stick, thank you very much. Are you saying I don't know which end of the stick is which when it's poking me in the eye?'

'OK, OK,' he was guffawing openly now, which incensed her more.

'I'm going to bed!' She stood up, chin lolling against her collarbone.

'Very good idea, you've had a lot of sun today.' He sprang up, 'Mind the steps, they're steep. Let me help.'

'You go first,' she said, wriggling aside and bumping her hip hard against the railing. There was no pain. 'I don't want you looking up my skirt.'

'That only works when you're going *up* stairs,' Lewis said. 'But don't worry, you can look down my neck if you like.'

'I wouldn't dream of it,' she said, primly.

She watched him disappear downwards and took a couple of steps to follow. 'Lewis, wait! The steps have gone! Right in front of my eyes!'

'They're spiral,' he called up. 'You have to turn as you step.'

She heard his feet on the iron frame and he emerged below her. 'Come here, take my hand.' Once the steps were negotiated, he helped her along the corridor to her room. 'Where's your key?'

'Here!' She pressed it so forcefully into his hand that he took a step back. She rocked forward towards him. 'Would you like to come into my, y'know . . .?'

'Your what?'

'I'm very, what's the word? Nice. I'm very nice.'

'I'm sure you are,' Lewis said, laughing very loudly now. 'But I think you need to sleep.'

'No!'

'In you go.' He turned the key and tried to nudge her through the doorway. Eleanor slouched heavily against the door frame for at least thirty seconds, becoming distracted as she tried to hunt out bits of dried Limoncello from the corner of her mouth with her tongue.

'Oh, how embarrassing,' she said, finally noticing Lewis still standing there, and she slammed the door shut between them.

She could hear him laughing softly as he walked down the corridor.

Chapter 11

'Hop in,' Eleanor's mother cried through the teeming rain of Exeter station car park, 'before I cause a pile-up. Hello, Will, we did meet once before, at Eleanor's flat, but you were on your way out. I'm Carol.'

'Hi, Mum, you look well, new hair?' Her mother had a sleek new blond and silver bob she hadn't seen before.

'Oh, it's been like this for ages. Now who's going in the back? Seems like forever since you've been down, darling, when was it, Easter?'

'Didn't I come in the summer?' Eleanor frowned, starting to clamber into the Polo her mother had driven since she was still at college.

'Can I go in the front, El?' Will asked. 'I get motion sickness in the back.'

'Of course.' She dragged their bags into the back with her, drawing her legs up to her chin and sliding out a road atlas from under her bottom. As her mother pulled off, she chattered out her news, excited and nervous – it had taken much persuasion to get Will down here, but she knew it was all going to be a huge success.

'Does she ever let you get a word in edgeways?' Carol asked him. He was slumped against the window with his eyes closed and didn't respond.

'Oh, he had a heavy night,' Eleanor laughed. 'He'll come alive later.'

'Talking of which,' said her mum, 'Dad's got a terrible throat infection and can barely croak out a command for a cup of tea. Try not to laugh, will you?'

'Has he seen the doctor?'

'Twice, but you know what they're like, just dash off a prescription, don't even look up at you. Now, what I thought we'd do is pop into the market at Bideford on the way – I need to pick up some cheese and pickles and things. Your granny's coming over for supper and I've invited her neighbour as well. Honestly, Chris is an absolute angel, always round there, even weeds her garden, and does it all out of the goodness of her heart.'

'Maybe she's after the family inheritance,' Will piped up.

Carol laughed gamely. 'Oh, Granny Blake's got nothing to leave, unless you're interested in a cabinet full of china robins.'

'No thanks. Shoot me, Eleanor, won't you, when I start buying those things.'

Eleanor tried anxiously to remember whether her

parents had any porcelain creatures of their own. There was definitely some sort of Labrador thing on the mantelpiece. Certainly not the beautiful collection of antique tiles and seascapes she'd seen at Will's parents' place last month when they'd gone down for Sunday lunch.

'Where do your parents live, Will?' Carol asked.

'Guildford,' Will said.

'You'll find us hopelessly provincial then,' she said.

Eleanor wished Will would get on with denying this, but he didn't seem to have heard. His cheekbone was grinding against the steamed-up window.

'Are you OK?' she whispered as they entered the icy cold open market, where pensioners wittered over 75p lavender soap. A sign offered two for £1.40. 'You seem a bit dazed?'

'No, I'm fine. All this travelling . . .'

'Ellie,' her mother called from the cheese stall, 'come and have a look at this truckle. Too much for tonight but I could get it in for Christmas.'

Eleanor dragged Will over. 'Christmas isn't for six weeks,' she pointed out.

'Oh, you don't think it will have heaved before then?'

Will was looking dangerously like heaving himself – all over the organic cheese display. 'Is there somewhere to sit down?' he groaned.

'Why don't you wait in that little café and we'll collect you on the way out,' Carol said, gently pushing at his shoulder as she might a donkey bothering her for treats. 'Has he been drinking?' she asked Eleanor, when he was out of range. 'I don't remember him being so odd last time.'

'He's just a bit hungover,' Eleanor said.

'Well, if he has got a drink problem you do know there's nothing you can do to change him, don't you?'

'That's quite right,' the cheese woman put in. 'You can't change a drinker, no matter how hard you try.'

'Just look at George Best,' Carol said.

'He's dead,' Eleanor said.

'Precisely.'

'Will doesn't need changing,' she said, firmly. 'He's fine as he is. I just know you're going to get on brilliantly this weekend.'

'Well, it looks like we've got our work cut out,' her mother said. 'Dad's been a right pain in the proverbial. I'm sure his throat is better but he just enjoys the attention. You know, a couple of days ago if he wanted my attention, guess what he would do? Go on, guess?'

'Er, whistle?'

'If he could whistle then he could speak, couldn't he? No, he clapped!'

'Goodness,' Eleanor said.

'Yes, like summoning a performing seal. So degrading.'

'Are you wanting the truckle?' the cheese woman asked.

It was all getting a bit surreal, Eleanor thought, a

feeling reinforced by their arrival at the house, where her father spat out a succession of clucks and gasps, as though he'd mastered some African tribal tongue since she last saw him – disconcerting in a cardiganed man of sixty-five.

'What would everyone like to drink?' her mum asked. 'We've got a new bottle of lovage?'

'What's that?' Will asked, eyes opening fully for the first time.

'It's a local herbal spirit, might do you some good, it's supposed to be medicinal. I've been giving it to Dad.'

Giant measures were swiftly distributed.

'Well, this is a very cosy village,' Will said, politely. Thanks to the instant properties of the lovage he seemed to have regained some colour, Eleanor was relieved to see. She wasn't sure he'd made the greatest impression so far. 'Do you ever get any murder mysteries around here?'

'You know, like Miss Marple,' Eleanor said, helpfully. 'Will's writing a murder play.'

'Are you, how exciting, like "The Mousetrap"? Is that still on?'

'Still the longest-running play in London,' Will said.

'Anyway, nothing like that happens here,' Carol said. 'In reality no one would live in these places if there were murders all the time. I'm not saying there isn't the provocation, though.'

On cue, her father made a painful croaking noise.

'He's asking where you live, Will?'

'Putney,' Will replied.

'But he's moving in with me soon,' Eleanor said. 'I told you on the phone.'

'Oh, is there room?' Carol asked.

'I've got two bedrooms. I might get a lodger as well, eventually, to help with the mortgage.' She didn't mention that Will wouldn't be contributing; he had debts he needed to pay off.

'How can there possibly be room for three of you in that confined space?'

'Oh, you'd be surprised, Carol,' Will grinned, finally finding his charm. 'Obviously it would be fantastic to have a house like this, but in Clapham this would cost, well, two million, maybe.'

'Two million!' Eleanor's father managed to rasp out.

'Well, I simply don't believe that,' Carol said, with an air of hers being the final word on the matter.

At her side Will fell silent; he was subject to sudden plunges. 'Is there any more lovage?' Eleanor asked.

The next day the weather changed completely, revealing the idyllic village of thatched cottages and Sunday strollers Eleanor always pictured when she thought of home. She went upstairs to get Will out of bed; he'd been sleeping for eleven hours and even her father had begun signing concern for their guest's welfare.

'Will, are you still in bed? Mum wants to know if you want breakfast. It's almost midday.'

His face emerged from under the duvet, sulky and boyish.

'What's up, babe? Still not well?'

'Bored,' he said, nuzzling her neck.

'Bored?'

'Can we get an earlier train?' He looked very appealing with his mussed-up hair. She began stroking it back from his face.

'Oh, I'd rather not, Mum might be offended. Come on, if you put in a walk I'll see if I can get us away by five.'

'It's a deal,' Will said, pulling her down on to the pillow. 'This is the worst thing about staying at girl-friends' parents, you can't shag them. It feels wrong, somehow.'

Eleanor laughed. 'You've obviously forgotten last night. How much of that lovage did you actually drink?'

Thanks to the Limoncello frenzy – and its curiously appropriate hangover, consisting as it did of a sticky throb in her head and dry, sweet choke in her throat – Eleanor was late getting to the office on Thursday morning. This was how she'd come to think of the roof terrace, and her morning glimpse of Will certainly seemed workaday now, barely worth the energy it took to fiddle with the zoom on her camera and frame a shot of him standing around in exactly the same clothes with exactly the same people. What she wanted was a chance to observe him more closely, like a visit to the lions' enclosure at the zoo when everyone else had left for the day.

She had a sudden image of herself concealed in a wardrobe inside that whitewashed house in Iditella . . .

Meanwhile, she hadn't forgotten the lunch date with Frannie, set for tomorrow. It made her nervous, as though she had a job interview lined up. She tried to tell herself that she would be the interviewer this time, get right to the bottom of this Frannie business. She considered making some preparatory notes.

Noises began to float up from one of the rooms below, the unmistakable groans and creaks and giggles of sex. She tried not to listen, didn't need any reminders of her own passionless status, but without clamping her hands to her ears it was impossible not to. Tim and Sophie, she supposed, enjoying an anniversary clinch, no curious little Rory at the door. She imagined Sophie tearing off Tim's shorts with her teeth, hell-bent on the creation of new life. It seemed to be going on for ages.

She pulled out her guidebook and tried to concentrate on the book's recommendations for restaurants. Then she looked up Vulcano and read about the mud baths, thinking of Lewis with all that yellow stuff smeared over his arms and chest. Hadn't they had a conversation in this very spot last night? She wondered if she'd told him about meeting Frannie – how irritating not to be able to remember his advice. She had an idea she hadn't been entirely sensible, would need to apologise later, maybe lay off the alcohol at dinner and get his calm pragmatic slant on this new development.

Finally, the squeaking of shutters signalled the end of her discomfort, and she had to smile when the smell of cigarette smoke wafted upwards. Unable to resist, she peeked over the terrace wall and froze immediately. The cigarette was being shared not by Tim and Sophie, but by Carlo and Nathalie. They were leaning out of the window, both naked to the waist. Eleanor tried to edge back but her body had cast a shadow over the couple and they both looked up as it shifted again. Carlo looked unnerved and guilty; he withdrew from the window at once. Nathalie's laughing face turned first blank and then contemptuous, and she held her gaze without blinking until Eleanor looked away.

She stepped back, not sure what to do. She was amazed by their boldness. Right in the hotel, a pair of underage lovers sitting naked at the window for all the world to see. Quite apart from the matter of Nathalie's parents, Giovanna could have appeared at any time to discover her grandson . . . neglecting his duties. Or was Rico covering for him again – their work rota was obviously of the flexible Sicilian type.

Eleanor wondered at her own outrage. She had no idea if they'd actually been having sex, though it certainly sounded like the real thing, and she had even less idea if fourteen was still considered too young; it seemed like a different lifetime for her. It was probably best to ignore the whole thing, she decided, and was just about to pack away her book and sneak off when there were footsteps on the spiral stairs and Nathalie emerged. The tennis T-shirt was back on and she'd twisted her hair into a braid, which made her look younger than usual, closer to her real age. She folded her arms in front of her and looked unpleasantly at Eleanor.

'You will not tell the parents of this,' she said. It sounded more like an order than a request, but Eleanor decided to give her the benefit of the doubt – the girl had probably inherited Katharina's brusque command of English. Annoyed with herself for colouring slightly, she replied: 'No, I won't. Don't worry. None of my business.' She stood up to leave, but Nathalie didn't budge from the top of the steps and Eleanor couldn't get by. She stopped awkwardly, twiddling with her bag.

'If you do tell,' said Nathalie, coldly, 'I will tell the man you watch.' Her voice had a flinty American inflection.

'What are you talking about?' Eleanor asked, startled. Did the girl take her for some kind of kinky voyeur?

'I saw you with this telescope. The English man, he has a blond head.'

She meant Will. How could she possibly know about Will?

'Look, I think you've got it all wrong,' said Eleanor, trying to wrest back some control over the conversation. 'If you're talking about my monocular, that's for looking at flora and fauna.'

This seemed to stump Nathalie for a moment and Eleanor hurried on, anxious to seal her advantage. 'It's an instrument designed especially for birders, you know, it's called a spotter.'

'No,' Nathalie replied, coolly. 'His name is Will. I have spoken with him.'

Curiosity now got the better of Eleanor. 'You've spoken to him? What did he say?'

'We are talking only about this Panarea. He learns diving. He is very nice man, I like him. He is very good-looking.' She pronounced it the American way, with the emphasis on 'good'.

For an insane moment Eleanor wondered if Nathalie might turn out to be of some use. She could see it perfectly: the strumpet would lure Will away from Frannie, and after a series of undetermined but soul-destroying events he would tire of both of them and return to Eleanor for secure, uncomplicated love. Frannie would be fine, she'd just take her pick of the remaining males at her feet, and Nathalie would return to her tennis camp, or wherever it was creepy German teenagers went to hang out. But, no, Nathalie would be no match for Frannie, and as far as she could remember Will had no taste for schoolgirls. Eleanor felt a bit ashamed.

Nathalie was continuing to eye her stonily. 'I have seen this man speak also with Lewis.'

'With Lewis?' The girl was clearly a more adept spy than Eleanor. 'You mean the same one who's staying here, at this hotel?'

'Of course this is the same. They are talking yesterday night in the harbour – after dinner.'

Obviously the harbour was exactly the danger zone she'd imagined; everyone seemed to be bumping into each other there. But Will and Lewis? That was a bit close for comfort. But Lewis had seemed genuinely compassionate when they'd talked about Will in Vulcano, even if his interest did turn out to be short-lived. He'd surely have twigged who Will was as soon as they exchanged names, if they'd even got that far; there couldn't possibly be any other Wills from London on this tiny island. She just hoped he'd been careful not to mention her name. And with any luck he might even have dug up some useful information to report back to her. It occurred to her this might have been what he'd been doing last night. Her mind was still sticky and yellow on that score; she vowed never to touch Limoncello again.

'I think we can both keep a secret, Nathalie,' she said to the teenager, feeling like a nanny outwitted by her charge. 'But you should be careful to do . . . well, what you were doing. Giovanna could have found you.'

'She is at Lipari, she is nothing,' Nathalie snorted, with such scorn that Eleanor felt quite frightened. The girl then skipped off down the steps and there was the

171

sound of a whispered exchange with Carlo followed by a door closing.

Eleanor was left to the sound of the bees buzzing around the potted plants. She closed her eyes and massaged the lids with her fingertips. They creaked and itched to the touch. She sighed. Nathalie and Carlo, Will and Lewis, Frannie and her: it was all starting to get a bit out of hand. But what was the alternative: to leave now and return to London with nothing resolved?

She couldn't bear the thought.

Picking at a prosciutto sandwich she'd procured at the bar, she was finally able to get hold of Lizzie.

'So have you seen them yet? Will and the girl?'

'Better than that, I've spoken to her. I bumped into her yesterday. She's super charming, sort of difficult to dislike.' She told Lizzie all about her encounter with Frannie, amazing herself with her own verbatim recall.

'I wonder if she's Francesca de Luca,' said Lizzie. 'I'm sure that was the name of the girl I saw in *Blithe Spirit* last year at the Haymarket. Not the main part but, God, she *is* gorgeous. I'm so sorry.'

'She's going to be on TV soon. I can't bear it, she'll be famous and there'll be features about their lovely home. Or their love nest in Italy. They'll pose with a puppy. God, Lizzie, they'll go to the Oscars together. He'll write a screenplay and she'll star in it!'

'Well, at least you'll be able to sell your side of the story for silly money. That'll buy you a few months off work. I assume she has no idea who you are?'

'No, no, she just thinks I'm a tourist called Jane.'

'What, Jane Doe?'

'Don't laugh, I'm not very good at thinking on my feet.' Just talking to Lizzie seemed to warm her from the inside out; she was starting to get that business with Nathalie in proportion.

'What about Will?' Lizzie asked. 'Have you spoken to him?'

'No, I've seen him, but he hasn't seen me. He's doing a diving course.'

'Will, diving? What is this place, Wonderland?'

Eleanor had to giggle. She wished Lizzie were in Panarea too.

'By the way,' Lizzie said, 'are you sure Miranda doesn't know where you are?'

'I just told her I was down with my parents for the week.'

'It's just that she rang me to ask for their number, needed it for your boss or something, and I got the feeling she didn't believe you were really at your mum's.'

'Bugger, that's not good.'

'Maybe it was just a bit of lame Miranda innuendo, she's not very subtle, is she?'

'You didn't tell her I'm here? Or give her Mum's number?'

'No, of course not. She's done enough damage already.'

'They're trying to get me to go into work,' Eleanor said, 'but obviously I can't. I don't see what the problem is, if I'm in Exeter or Italy it's none of their business. I've got agreed holiday.'

There was a pause. 'I suppose sometimes it's just easier to tell people the truth,' Lizzie said. 'Then you don't have to keep track of the stories.'

This was something Eleanor certainly didn't need to be told. 'So what's been happening there,' she asked. 'Any news or gossip?'

'Oh, you know, work's a nightmare. I'm having dinner with Simon tonight. Same old same old, basically.'

Suddenly Eleanor wanted same old back.

Chapter 12

To her disappointment, Lewis didn't turn up for dinner again that evening. He seemed to have dropped out of evening meals altogether. By now, she was bursting to ask him about the encounter with Will that Nathalie had reported and to tell him about her own with Frannie.

She even felt half attractive for once. Cheered by her contact with Lizzie, she'd gone back to the roof and spent the whole afternoon sunbathing and snoozing. She'd got quite a good colour, evened out a bit, although there was an unfortunate white handprint on her left thigh where her hand must have rested when she dozed, more like a large paw print, really, but no one would see that if she avoided shorts for a day or two.

Then she'd poked around more of the little boutiques in San Pietro, all crammed with beautiful items: scarves that were just silky little wisps and hand-embroidered cardigans in fresh blues, greens and pinks – island colours. She'd seen a sequinned bag exactly like Frannie's and almost gasped out loud at the price: about half her month's salary. In the end, she'd bought a pale-green dress, knee length and very low at the neck, the fabric tissue-fine and beautifully soft. After shopping she showered and spent half an hour massaging lotion into her hot skin until it gleamed to her satisfaction. The dress made her feel light and cool as she walked down to the dining room, hair still damp and dark from the shower, the evening breeze pouring soothingly on to her skin.

Sophie, sitting alone at the dinner table, greeted her like a favourite little sister.

'You look fantastic, Eleanor, that dress looks so pretty with your eyes. And you did catch the sun today, didn't you? It makes such a difference!' This linked straight into an anecdote about Rory ('I don't want to catch the sun, Mummy, it will burn my fingers and I'll hurt'). Tim was on the phone to the little monster right now, Sophie explained. She always spoke to him first, but tried to keep it short because it made her so tearful, whereas Tim was strong enough to rattle off a bedtime story, stay completely dry-eyed throughout, and still be in the bar in time for cocktails. She'd already downed a few glasses of wine, Eleanor noticed; the carafe was half empty.

Stefan and Katharina arrived next and they too

began drawing heavily on their tumblers of wine. For once, they both seemed subdued, remaining silent while Sophie and Eleanor chatted about their day, but every time Eleanor looked up she saw Stefan's close-set eyes fixed on her neckline. The beach was one thing, but here at the dinner table? She tried to ignore him and concentrate on Sophie.

'Has anyone else been plagued by bees all day?' Sophie asked. 'I hadn't even noticed them until today. They just seemed to follow me everywhere, the beach, the café, it was so unnerving, have you seen how huge they are?'

This she asked to the table at large and Eleanor nodded her agreement. Stefan didn't respond at all, just transferred his gaze briefly to Sophie, then back to Eleanor's breasts, while Katharina gamely replied, 'Size of fist,' clenching her own dramatically to demonstrate. Eleanor found this vaguely menacing. She had no idea what to make of Stefan and Katharina, and their child was hardly a ringing advertisement. They'd definitely had a row, she thought; there was a new element to the tension tonight. This was one part of life as a couple that she didn't miss at all, the post-conflict atmosphere that never failed to fill everyone else with unease. It killed the party spirit without a word being uttered. She was glad she'd engaged in that pact of secrecy with Nathalie; she didn't fancy being the one to break the news to Katharina that her

177

underage daughter was having sex with the barman. What was more, now Sophie was happily bandying the 'Will' word around, she didn't need Nathalie mentioning that she'd met a Will in Panarea, a very *good*-looking Will. If the full story came out there'd be no stopping Sophie getting involved in the amateur sleuthing.

But for now Sophie was in full Rory flow. 'You know what he said to me the other day,' she sang on, eyes teary with fondness. 'We were in the garden and he suddenly asked: "What does beeline mean, Mummy?" "It means it makes a straight line for you, darling," I said, but he looked suspicious and said: "But bees don't fly in a straight line. They fly in curves."' She laughed. 'Little monster won't take a straight answer, it's like being cross-examined every day over the most basic things, everything you just take for granted normally.'

Katharina chuckled loudly. Eleanor wondered if she were even listening.

'It does make you think about language, though. Stops the brain from creaking to a complete stop.' There was a long pause and Sophie looked to Eleanor for help, as though struggling with a business dinner she was hosting for foreign dignitaries. There was definitely a peculiar atmosphere brewing this evening.

'He sounds a real sweetie,' Eleanor said, on cue. 'And very advanced for his age.' Sophie beamed and modestly accredited Rory's teacher, which made Eleanor think of Lewis's girlfriend. 'No sign of Lewis?' she asked the others.

Stefan spoke for the first time: 'He is not with us again. Dinner with friends.'

'What friends?' asked Sophie. 'He's on holiday alone. Well, he is becoming Mr Popular, isn't he?'

Before Eleanor could ponder this, Tim and Nathalie arrived, along with the first of the Italian guests. Tim was wearing a satsuma-coloured Hawaiian-print shirt, which vied with Katharina's leopard-skin affair as the most eye-popping item Eleanor had seen on the island that week. Immediately, the atmosphere picked up.

'He's absolutely fine,' he said to Sophie, kissing the top of her head before sitting down. 'Cute as a button. Being fed Ben & Jerry's by Granny as we speak. Chunky fucking Monkey. He'll probably choke on the stuff.'

Nathalie sat down, insouciant as ever. She didn't even glance in Eleanor's direction, just cracked open her Coke and started drinking from the can, ignoring the iced glass Rico had delivered for it. Too young to drink alcohol, thought Eleanor. She couldn't believe the arrogance of the girl; was she really so glacial, so self-possessed, or was this just typical teenage sullenness? Eleanor's mother had told her how exasperating she herself had been at that age, yet at the time she'd viewed herself as perfectly sociable.

'No Lewis again?' Tim asked, draining the rest of

the carafe of wine into his tumbler and sloshing it down his throat with no discernible swallow reflex.

'He is with the archaeology friends,' said Stefan, and Eleanor couldn't help feeling disappointed at this new detail. If Lewis was finally concentrating on his original plans for his trip, would that mean they'd be seeing nothing more of him, just when she needed his advice the most?

As usual, Tim bulldozed his way through any awkwardness in the conversation, and they all started demolishing the pasta, little twists sticky with gorgonzola and sundried tomatoes, while chatting about their days and making the usual appreciative noises about Giovanna's kitchen. For once, Eleanor was the most animated of them all, the last to finish eating she was talking so much. She was finally starting to feel like she was really on holiday.

As soon as the meal was finished, Stefan and Katharina left the table, thankfully taking Nathalie with them, and Tim immediately started campaigning for a move to the harbour bars.

'Why don't we just stay in the bar here?' suggested Eleanor. 'It's so lovely, with all the candles.' She felt in the mood to extend the evening but knew she couldn't risk the waterfront, not at night. To her relief, the other two agreed, and since several of the Italian guests had had the same thought the bar was busier than usual. Even non-residents were wandering in from the lane, attracted by the laughter. What a lovely, welcoming hotel it was, thought Eleanor, sinking into the same seat she'd taken the evening Lewis had confronted her. That seemed like weeks ago now.

'Nice bloke, Stefan,' Tim said, as they started on another round of red wine. 'Usually these Germans are a bunch of humourless hopheads, but he's actually got some interesting views. Complete layabout, of course, all this jazz malarky.'

'Don't you mean all *that* jazz malarky?' asked Sophie, and they both heaved with laughter.

Eleanor had noticed that Tim liked nothing better than to make unflattering generalisations about the other nationalities holidaying in Panarea. His view of the stocky Italian males who escorted the pin-thin women around the island was that they were 'hairy as apes'. 'I'll tell you what,' he'd said to Eleanor the previous evening when he'd seen her mouthing hello to the Italian with the square head, 'he should be in a cage. You watch long enough and you'll see him pick a tick from his armpit.' She'd had to smile, even as she gasped in protest, it was such an absurd image. Sophie, meanwhile, had been in stitches at the remark, rocking around like a weeble. Eleanor supposed her supremely tolerant sense of humour was a big factor in the success of their partnership.

The three of them speculated for a while on the state of play in the German marriage. Sophie, like Eleanor, had noticed a distinct chill in the atmosphere. Stefan and Katharina had spent every day in separate activities, she pointed out, except for yesterday, and Lewis had hinted that the visit to the Bronze Age village hadn't exactly been a runaway success. Perhaps they'd even been tempted to hurl bits of old stone at each other's heads, she thought, or trip one another over the cliff edge accidentally on purpose. They certainly weren't speaking by the time they got to the beach. But of course she didn't want to pry, and Katharina was always much more eager to talk about Nathalie and her tennis achievements than her husband.

'She's a complete nutbar,' Tim declared, interrupting. Eleanor assumed he meant Katharina and not his own wife. 'She's in a totally different mood every time you speak to her. Keep your pet bunnies out of her way, that's what I say.'

'Well, I think she might be medicated,' said Sophie. 'And in her defence, babe, she does hold that marriage together financially, you know. He doesn't earn a bean and they send Nathalie to some kind of sports and arts academy. That must cost quite a bit.'

'Hippie crap,' said Tim.

'I must say Lewis is being very mysterious about *his* relationship,' said Sophie, as if it was every man's duty to publicly declare the true state of his love life. She had pinched one of Eleanor's cigarettes and was puffing away with relish as she chatted. 'Do you know he admitted to me that he hasn't phoned his girlfriend once this whole week? They can't be very close, can they?'

'Bollocks,' said Tim. 'Why would they need to be nattering every hour of the day? Sounds perfectly reasonable to me.'

'Well, you always call me every day when you're away with clients, darling,' protested Sophie. 'But then I suppose you have to check in to make sure there hasn't been some domestic calamity.'

'Oh, you'd track me down soon enough; I can run but I can't hide!' said Tim, guffawing. Eleanor laughed, recognising a set piece for her benefit.

'You remind me of my boss, Rufus,' she told Tim. 'He's not ready to join the politically correct world yet, either.'

'You mean he's a shameless xenophobe as well?' Sophie said.

'Nothing wrong with shagging the boss,' Tim said, incongruously.

'What? Did I miss something?' laughed Eleanor.

'Attractive is he?' Tim was slurring now. 'Well, if it's good enough for Sophe . . .'

'I had no choice, you were such a persistent old dog,' Sophie drawled, causing Tim to woof and accept a pat on the head. Eleanor could only imagine what bedtime stories were like for Rory. They were an entertaining double act, she thought, delighting in her newfound holiday spirit. She'd been lucky to team up with them.

Sophie was still keen to pursue the subject of Lewis. 'Anyway, if you ask me, he's got a bit of a roving eye. Did you see him flirting with Nathalie at the beach yesterday? It was outrageous.'

'Yes,' Eleanor said, 'I did notice that.'

'With the überbrat?' Tim asked. 'I'm not sure he's into jailbait. He's a bit principled for that, don't you think?'

Eleanor, tongue loosened by the wine, considered telling them about Nathalie and Carlo, but managed to resist. Nathalie had gone to bed, but Carlo was still working behind the bar, shooting the occasional wary glance in Eleanor's direction. She had to keep her word: Tim would never be able to resist a cheeky quip in the youngsters' direction. She felt uncomfortable being in possession of such dangerous information.

'Well, I did wonder if there might be a bit of a spark between you two?' Sophie said, meaningfully, to Eleanor. 'Maybe he's just what you need to get over this ex of yours? He did whisk you off to Vulcano the other day, didn't he? That was quite masterful, I thought.'

'You sound like Barbara Cartland!' Eleanor said, although after a litre of wine she had to admit the idea of being whisked off and mastered was far from abhorrent. 'Anyway, if Nathalie's too young for him, then I'm too old.'

'Too old?' said Tim. 'You can't be more than thirty-five.'

'Er, thirty, thank you very much,' Eleanor said.

'Tim!' cried Sophie. 'You're going to get a slap at this rate.'

But Tim was a difficult man to shame. 'Just wait till you're looking forty-five in the eye, then you'll know what old feels like.'

'Anyway, age isn't an issue,' said Sophie, briskly. 'Up to ten years either way is absolutely fine.'

'Well, even if I did like him,' Eleanor protested, 'which I don't, I'd never muscle in on someone else's boyfriend. I know how that feels, don't I? He's not attractive, anyway.' She wasn't sure she really believed the last bit.

'Not *un*attractive,' Sophie said. 'Tim, will you stop looking at Eleanor's tits!' She gave her husband the threatened slap. 'Sorry, Eleanor, holidays bring out the beast in a man, have you noticed?'

Tim gave a very lifelike wolfish growl and Eleanor half expected him to drop on to all fours at their feet. 'Actually, I was just wondering if there's anyone back home who might suit . . .'

The two of them now began systematically running through every available male in their circle, even consulting their phone contacts and considering each in turn before rejecting it and calling out the next. Most of the candidates seemed to be divorced, alcoholic or dysfunctional in some sordid, irreversible way. Dan, said Sophie, finally, was the best bet: wealthy, generous, loved a gossip; in fact, he'd be ideal if it weren't for the fact that he was barely five feet tall.

'Not technically a dwarf, though,' put in Tim. 'You could get him to wear lifts?'

'No!' cried Eleanor. 'Stop! I'm not looking for a new boyfriend.' She noticed other people in the bar were now looking over at their noisy table. Carlo was watching them with growing concern.

'OK, you just need some steamy sex,' Sophie said, getting carried away. She was holding her cigarette like a dart and Eleanor noticed it had burnt down into the filter.

'Exactly my point! You won't notice Dan's miniature proportions when you're horizontal,' Tim insisted.

'I think I would,' laughed Eleanor.

'There more than anywhere else,' put in Sophie, raucously.

'Good God, you women are difficult to please,' said Tim with another thick slur. He grasped each of them by the wrist and grinned, lips wet and wine-stained.

'Oh, I'm going to have to go to bed,' said Sophie. 'Those cigarettes have gone to my head. I think I've burnt my finger.'

Eleanor found herself hoping faintly that she wouldn't be left alone with Tim. She'd definitely lost her touch when it came to managing male attention. 'I'm heading up, too,' she said, standing. She was surprised how dizzy she felt. It wasn't quite the moderate evening she'd planned, though she'd at least avoided the Limoncello.

'Better get you to bed, darling,' Tim slurred, almost falling into Sophie. 'Now, Eleanor, think how useful a little friend like Dan would be at a time like this, when the old married fools have stumbled off to bed. You could do a lot worse.'

'Thank you, Tim, but—'

'Look, I'll write down his number. Give him a buzz when you're back in London. Gotta pen?' Tim dropped his phone, reached unsteadily for it. 'Where does he live again? Hobbit House . . . no, I mean Holland Park?'

'Shut up, darling, you're far too drunk to handle a writing implement.' As they turned towards the stairs, Sophie whipped round and hissed to Eleanor, 'I'd go for Lewis if I were you, he's soooo yummy.'

'Sleep well,' Eleanor replied.

She let herself into her room, undressed, and hugged herself beneath the bedclothes. Perhaps Sophie was right and Lewis was worth consideration. There was obviously nothing between Nathalie and him, after all, he didn't seem particularly serious about the girlfriend, and he was attractive. Everyone seemed to think so; he was one of those people with natural magnetism, not in a flamboyant way like Frannie, but in an unknowing, unexpected way. What did Will have that he didn't?

No, it was just one of her fleeting fancies, she decided as she lay in the dark waiting for sleep. Such optimistic bursts had a habit of sneaking up and tricking her, usually after a few drinks and a particularly forceful suggestion from a girlfriend. But in the morning Will would still be there, she knew he would, the face she saw before all others.

Chapter 13

At Friday's breakfast – just Sophie, Eleanor and Katharina today – Eleanor marvelled at Sophie's lack of hangover. Years of sleep deprivation was the key, Sophie explained. 'It doesn't matter if I drink one unit of alcohol or a hundred, if I have the luxury of eight hours' sleep these days, I feel like I've had a weekend in a spa.'

Eleanor thought having a baby might be a rather drastic way of putting hangovers into perspective. In any case, she felt remarkably bright herself; her body had obviously adjusted to its challenging new consumption levels. She'd also managed her first dreamless night since arriving in Panarea, her preference these days over the Will-filled interludes that usually jammed the space between her last thought of him at night and her first thought of him in the morning.

Talk turned to the subject of little Rory's scheduled transfer from Tim's parents to Sophie's for the second half of their holiday.

'Does he get on with all the grandparents?' Eleanor asked, sipping her espresso. She'd decided to switch from cappuccino.

'Yes, he seems equally happy with both sets,' Sophie said. 'But he probably likes going to mine a bit more – only because they've got two dogs, mind you. One of which is a Dalmatian puppy, which is all it takes. Four-year-olds just aren't that discerning, are they?'

Watching a pair of Italian men at the next table follow the exit of a female guest half their age, her lean bottom swaying under a skimpy white sarong, Eleanor wondered if forty-year-olds were any better.

'We're so lucky they all get on so well,' Sophie went on. 'Believe me, Eleanor, the last thing you need is rivalry between the in-laws. God, I'm getting bored with the breakfasts here, aren't you? It's the only meal the Italians don't seem to have got the hang of!'

Katharina, less done up than usual with face free of make-up and her hair in a ponytail that revealed an underlayer of crinkly grey, looked glum as she chomped through a third *cornetto*.

'What's Stefan's mother like?' Eleanor asked, trying to include her.

Katharina made an explosive 'pah' noise: 'She is horrible, this Joanne of the ark.'

'Who's that?' Eleanor asked. 'Noah's wife?'

'She means Joan of Arc,' Sophie said. 'What, she's a bit of a martyr, is she?'

'She is always being right,' Katharina sighed. 'In Germany, I think we spoil the boys. She is spoiling my husband.'

'Just like in Italy,' Sophie said. 'Or Britain, for that matter. I hope I'm not going to be Rory's ruin, the kind of mother who freezes out all his girlfriends and thinks no one's good enough for their little prince.' She paused. 'I have a horrible feeling I will be, though.'

'I've always got on quite well with my boyfriends' parents,' Eleanor said, considering. 'But then girls make more of an effort, don't they?'

'Understatement of the year,' Sophie replied. 'Have you kept in touch with Will's folks?'

'His mother rang me after we split up. I think she was a bit embarrassed – we'd already had a few conversations about the wedding and I'd invited them to meet my parents. It was my mum and dad who were the most disappointed.'

'Poor you,' Sophie said, cocking her head in sympathy. 'He really picked his moment, didn't he? Well, no doubt he's giving the new girl exactly the same runaround.'

'Mmm, maybe.'

The conversation reminded Eleanor that she should call her parents. There she was, using them as an alibi for work and to keep Miranda off the scent, blithely inventing illnesses for her father, and yet they didn't even know she was out of the country. What if disaster struck, either here or at home? It wasn't as if she was just an easy direct flight away. She decided she would phone later, send a nice postcard describing her impulse holiday, take them back a bottle of Limoncello.

But for now she needed to consider Frannie. How was she going to handle their lunch, the awkwardness of playing Jane? Could she really hope to fool an actress? ('Never bullshit a bullshitter' was one of Rufus's golden rules, possibly the only one of his she had ever understood.) Her aim was to deftly slide questions about Will into the conversation at every opportunity, while taking extreme care not to let slip any detail that Frannie hadn't already offered herself. The idea of exposing her real identity was too mortifying to contemplate. Frannie would surely be appalled – maybe even frightened – to learn that it was her own presence that had drawn Eleanor to Panarea in the first place.

Sophie had ordered more coffee and the new cups were set down with satisfying little clinks. 'I'll tell you what, ladies,' she said with determination. 'One thing you need to avoid in life is a mother-in-law more glamorous than you are. It's almost as bad as dealing with a glamorous ex.'

Eleanor began fidgeting with her napkin. That was the other question: what on earth was she going to wear?

* * *

'Isn't it funny,' said Frannie, 'the way we seek out these little holiday islands. I mean, we leave Britain for a smaller island like Sicily, and no sooner are we there than we're on a boat for a more remote one.'

They were following the progress of one of the striped fishing boats transporting a group of tourists to the islets in the distance. One jutted out of the water like a pointed finger issuing its disrespect. 'They must be heading for Basiluzzo,' said Frannie, 'always looking out to sea for that smaller dot on the horizon.'

She had a theatrical way of putting things, ponderous but somehow romantic. Eleanor found it very engaging. She was keenly aware that she herself had not discovered Panarea by searching for ever-more remote islands, but by simply following her ex-boyfriend across the continent in an irrational bid to cling on to the past. She didn't say this to Frannie, of course. She was nicely in control so far.

They were having lunch on the terrace of a trattoria not far from Eleanor's hotel: spaghetti with sardines, pine nuts and raisins, a Sicilian speciality recommended by Frannie. Eleanor had arrived first, which gave her the best seat in the house for watching heads turn when Frannie made her entrance, sleek and sexy in white Capri pants and a tight blue halter top. Though Eleanor felt she'd rarely looked better herself, having spent the whole morning trying on different clothes, taming her hair and conjuring up maximum sparkle and gloss around her eyes and lips, one look at Frannie's effortless, camera-ready beauty made her feel instantly second-rate. It wasn't difficult to imagine how euphoric Will must feel to have landed a woman who drew sighs of admiration even from other gorgeous creatures.

'There's obviously some human instinct to get off the mainland,' continued Frannie, gazing out at the rocks.

'What are we looking for, I wonder?' said Eleanor, gamely, though she was more interested in the pasta and wine; they were absolutely delicious.

'Oh, a beach, usually. People will go to any lengths to lay their bones on virgin sand.' Frannie laughed. 'I quite like having other people around on the beach, don't you? Someone to save you if you get pulled down by the current.'

Eleanor doubted Frannie would have any shortage of volunteers to rescue her in the event of a snorkelling mishap. As she looked out to sea, Eleanor took the opportunity to scrutinise her rival once more. She looked even more beautiful than she remembered from Wednesday. Her hair was pulled off her face and neck, exposing her fine brow and nose and silky olive complexion. The searchlight eyes were wide, unblinking, and each time they turned their beam on Eleanor it was impossible not to feel specially selected for attention, the recipient of an unexpected gift.

A hydrofoil was now disgorging its latest round of visitors. There were quite a few today, Eleanor noticed, all shaking off the passage like new puppies adjusting to the light. With each glass of wine she saw herself distanced a little further from these rookies and day-trippers and aligned a little more closely with the locals, the ones who really belonged to all this easy glamour. People like Frannie, who had family villas to retreat to.

Frannie was warming to her theme: 'Just look! It's incredible, all these crowds in the middle of the ocean Can you imagine that handful of islanders years ago, no electricity, still fishing for their food, I bet they never expected their home to become Milan-on-Sea.' She turned to Eleanor with a dazzling smile and added, 'I'm glad it has, though, otherwise we wouldn't have this scrummy wine shipped in from the mainland!'

'Did you come to Panarea, back then, when there was no tourism?' asked Eleanor.

'No, I only came to the Aeolians for the first time as a teenager. After my parents split up my mother decided to deny our Sicilian heritage, pretend my father had never happened. He just disappeared off the scene, crawled back into his hole as far as she was concerned. They had a very acrimonious breakup. Of course, she couldn't deny our Italian names, Salvatore and Francesca. And my middle name is Salina, after the island. You probably saw it on your way here. It's lovely there.'

She was sure the wine had something to do with it, but Eleanor felt she was being pulled slowly under a spell. Either that or developing a plain old-fashioned schoolgirl crush.

'How old were you when your parents split up?' she asked, thinking fleetingly of Lewis.

'Oh, very young, about seven or eight. We didn't see our father for years. He was in Italy and my mother kept us out of reach in our little boarding-school prisons. And prison life just turned us into complete terrors. I can't remember the number of times we were almost expelled and Mum had to come and charm them out of it.'

Eleanor thought of her own schooldays at the local comprehensive. It had never occurred to her to rebel or subvert school rules; generally, she'd liked her teachers and worked steadily hard. Of course, she'd sneaked in the occasional cigarette and once caused a minor scandal in art class by painting a flower in the style of female genitalia, but she'd never viewed school as a prison sentence, never come close to being seriously disciplined. Now her experience seemed bloodless compared to Frannie's.

'Then, between school and college my parents put their heads together – they were speaking again by then,' went on Frannie. 'They decided I needed a dose of reality to stamp out my wickedness.' She gurgled with laughter at the memory. 'So they sent me to Salina to work in a hotel. For the whole summer! Dad knew the owner, and that was the first time I came out here.'

'What happened?'

'Well, of course it was hardly a labour camp. The hotel was absolutely gorgeous and it didn't feel like work at all. And I seem to remember some very wicked liaisons with one or two guests . . .'

As Frannie described the hotel, with its rooms carved into the cliff face and private cove for nude sunbathing, Eleanor reflected that it was entirely appropriate that someone so beguiling should be the product of an exotic, drama-filled childhood. A small-town two-up, two-down just wouldn't have thrown up such a creature. She wondered if Frannie had ever stepped inside a two-up two-down, even visited the English provinces. She imagined her growing up in some modernist villa with a curved swimming pool on the edge of Hampstead Heath or a Georgian townhouse with a blue plaque in Bloomsbury. She thought of her own upbringing: ordinary, no more no less. Safe, predictable, drab. In her parents' part of the world, style was expressed in the way you trimmed your garden hedges and stuffed your Sunday roast. Perhaps people now looked at her and saw that same safeness, predictability, drabness.

With every minute of this lunch it was becoming abundantly obvious why Will had fallen in love with Frannie so quickly and convincingly. Had he ever even entertained the question of a comparison, weighed up their relative attractions and considered staying with Eleanor?

'So is this your boyfriend's first visit to the islands?' she asked, horrified that her heart had started drumming heavily in her ribcage, independently sensing a fight or flight ahead.

'Yes, he wasn't going to come at first, but when he met my father in London he was persuaded. Honestly, Dad should get commission from the tourist board.'

How seamlessly Will had slotted into Frannie's life, Eleanor thought. It had been several months before he'd met all *her* friends, a further indecently long stretch before that less-than-triumphant visit to her parents, and yet here he was, just a few months after first laying eyes on this girl, turning Italian, reshaping his life. Getting into watersports, for goodness' sake.

'How did you guys meet?' The violent thudding was showing no signs of abating, but Frannie didn't seem to notice anything was wrong.

'I was in a play, just a short run at the Hampstead Theatre. Will came to the first-night party; he knew Matthew – the director – from college.'

Eleanor remembered the occasion. Will and Matthew had studied English together at university, both had been active in the drama society, both had aspirations to write and direct for a living. And now one of them had opened his first play in London and it wasn't Will. He'd grumbled about going along; simple jealousy, Eleanor had assumed.

She'd wondered if he'd still be in a grumpy mood when she came back home from her weekend in Devon – he'd cried off that at the last minute, to her parents' disappointment; they'd wanted to celebrate the engagement. She had even picked up some nice wine on her way back from Paddington to cheer him up. Instead, she'd found him elated, claiming to have been re-inspired by his friend's success. Had he known straight away that Frannie was the one he wanted? Even before speaking to her? Later, he'd told Eleanor that it wasn't only about Frannie appearing in his life, but that he'd fallen out of love with her; their relationship no longer felt right.

Once again, she asked herself if it had been her intention to come to Panarea specifically to pit herself against the new girlfriend, to offer Will a second chance to choose. How had Lewis put it in Vulcano? *You seem to believe your relationship can be resurrected* . . . He couldn't have made it plainer that *he* didn't think it could, but he'd been right in his observation: she *had* hoped fortune might still be reversed.

But sitting here now, the question was irrelevant: Frannie was invincible, anyone could see that. Eleanor couldn't imagine what sort of person could possibly challenge the girl's charisma, even if they had the good fortune to match her beauty. The best she could hope for was that Will might hit his head on a rock while diving and forget that the last few months had ever happened. She sighed. How she wished it were she who possessed this utter self-assurance, this anecdote-filled past, that it were Frannie who sat in attendance, the plain Jane.

'So, Jane, how about you? Are your parents still together?' Frannie pushed away her pasta dish half eaten. She seemed keen to stay on the subject of families, clearly a favourite with her.

'Yes, nothing exciting there. They still live a few miles from the village where I grew up in Devon. They did have a big row once, but I'd already left home for college. I remember the phone calls trying to get me on-side. It was ridiculous.'

'Tell me about it,' said Frannie. 'We were young when Mum and Dad split, but old enough to manipulate the situation. Mum's way of making it all up to us was holidays. She was fantastic at holidays. As soon as we were packed off to school she said it was our decision to choose the main summer holiday; she would make any wish come true.'

'How wonderful,' exclaimed Eleanor. 'What did you choose?'

'Well, of course, Salvatore and I couldn't agree. I wanted Disney World every time, he would want things like the British Grand Prix – can you believe he was willing to waste the whole holiday on a race that lasted two hours, and in our own country?' She looked so indignant, Eleanor couldn't help laughing again.

'So we had to take it in turns, one year each. My first three turns were Disney World. Then one year Salv got ambitious and asked to go to the Moon. So Mum took us to California, where there was a theme park called Lunarland or something. So it was like my turn after all. I still think of that as one of the greatest victories of my life to date.'

Eleanor couldn't imagine such a magical style of family life. She'd once badgered her mother about Disney World; all the kids thought it was paradise on earth, and those lucky enough to go in the summer break rode the wave of celebrity well into the autumn term – or at least until the Mickey Mouse ears had been stolen from their locker and snapped apart by some jealous classmate. Eventually her mother had lost her patience and said, 'We're going to the Lake District, Ellie, like it or lump it!'

Frannie refilled both their wine glasses to the brim and went on: 'When we were little we thought Mum was so powerful, whisking us off all over the place. Now I see it just took a few phone calls to a travel agent.'

'And cash, of course,' said Eleanor.

'Yes, well, my father supplied plenty of that.' Frannie

didn't elaborate on the subject; as with her beauty, wealth seemed to be just a natural part of who she was. Will was not from a particularly moneyed family, Eleanor reflected, though his parents were eccentric and funny. She had adored them.

'So are you going out with anyone back in London?' Frannie asked, tone light, as though she half suspected some bitter tale. It reminded Eleanor of Lewis's thoughtfulness when he wanted her to think he hadn't really noticed her embarrassment.

'No,' said Eleanor. 'I recently split up with someone. We were engaged, actually, but I'm getting over it.'

As was becoming a familiar experience to Eleanor, saying the words aloud seemed to validate the notion, and she suddenly felt that she was getting over it. After all, it was only a broken heart, not a real fracture or horrible disease, like the kind of life-threatening situations some people had to deal with. She had a sudden, overwhelming recognition of her own self-absorption. She vowed to call Lizzie, ask her how she was getting on, how things were going with Simon – goodness, she had to think to remember his name and he'd been going out with her best friend for over six months now. It was time to stop monopolising everyone's emotions.

'I'm sorry,' said Frannie, peering at her with compassion. 'You must still feel down. I remember how I felt when my first boyfriend at college dumped me. Right at the end of the first year, when we were about to go to France for the summer. I was in shreds.'

She appreciated Frannie's lightness of touch. She'd calculated correctly that Eleanor had been the rejected party and had left it at that. And it wasn't surprising that she had to delve back a few years for her own most recent rejection. Eleanor realised she didn't know Frannie's age; mid-twenties, she guessed. For a second, she saw her differently, as the striving young actress who hadn't made it yet, running out of time, still awaiting her first TV airing, nowhere near the big screen, where she surely aimed to belong. What had Sophie said: 'Not tall enough for modelling and too stupid for a real job'? Well, that plainly didn't apply, but even so, being beautiful and charming was just what you woke up with in the morning when you were Frannie; being accredited as an actress was rather less easy.

Again, as though reading her thoughts, Frannie said, 'Now I've got so much experience of rejection through my work, I'm not sure the end of a relationship would feel as traumatic as it did back then. It's all relative, isn't it? Like when you're little and just going over the lines in your colouring book seems like the end of the world.'

'I guess.' Eleanor didn't think that having her whole future with Will obliterated in the space of five minutes was in any way like making a mistake in her colouring book. Could it be that Frannie wasn't taking this new relationship as seriously as Will? Perhaps she would one day subject him to the same agony Eleanor had endured. This wasn't as satisfying a thought as she'd hoped.

'Shall we have some more wine?' asked Frannie. Red wine seemed to be consumed like water here, it was so warm and bright-tasting, barely seemed like alcohol. Eleanor was certainly downing more of it than she would at home. Frannie, she noticed, drank rapidly and with practised relish. She didn't smoke, though; one nod in the direction of an actress's self-preservation, perhaps.

'Maybe half a carafe,' suggested Eleanor. 'My evenings are always huge drinking sessions. I don't think I need too much of a head start.'

Frannie giggled and dictated the order to the waitress. 'I thought we might like some *malvasia*, too,' she said. 'Hideously sweet, I know, but I love it. We used to be allowed a bit when we were kids.'

'I'm up for that.' Eleanor lit herself another cigarette.

'So tell me about the other guests at the hotel,' said Frannie in a low, conspiratorial tone that reminded Eleanor of Sophie. 'Who will you have dinner with tonight?'

Eleanor described Katharina, Stefan and Nathalie, including the episode with Nathalie and Carlo, eager to amuse her new friend with the spiciest tales she could offer. They both hooted with laughter at the teenagers' stolen passion, and Eleanor thoroughly enjoyed this new light-hearted perspective. She quite forgot the checkmated hopelessness Nathalie had made her feel at the time. Then she told Frannie about Tim and Sophie, leaving out Tim's less flattering observations about the Italians and focusing on Rory.

'He's not here but he's like one of the group,' she said. 'Every evening we all hear what he's been up to during the day, his little commentary from his granny's in Woking.'

'Well, they should have brought him with them,' said Frannie. 'Italians adore children, especially boys, they just flutter around them like bees around a honeypot. Turns them into monsters, though, according to my mother.'

Sophie and Katharina said the same. Eleanor realised she had deliberately omitted Lewis from her list, partly because Frannie might connect him with the man Will had bumped into – she felt sure Will would have mentioned his encounters, he was as keen a gossip as any woman she'd met – but also because, for reasons she couldn't quite place, she wanted to keep Lewis to herself. She still hadn't had a chance to catch up with him properly and hoped he would be at dinner that evening. She was dying to know what he'd talked about with Will, what he thought of him.

'Here's the latest delivery,' said Frannie, gesturing to

the port. 'Must be overnighters, it's getting too late for a day trip.'

Eleanor recognised the Stromboli-bound hydrofoil, often stuffed with determined-faced hikers bound for the next island's crater. She could barely remember a time when the comings and goings of boats weren't of key interest to her day. In Panarea, it was pretty much the only thing that ever happened. She'd noticed some of the boats were named after Italian artists: Donatello, Giorgione. She thought she might have arrived on Masaccio.

'It feels like there's such a divide between the people staying here a while and the ones passing through on their way to Stromboli or Lipari,' she said.

Frannie agreed. 'That's if they can pass through. You know, in bad weather you can get stranded here for days, because the *aliscafi* can't run.' Eleanor had noticed Frannie always used Italian vocabulary and, again, it reminded her of Sophie. 'There've been cases of islanders going off to Lipari in the morning to do a bit of shopping, then ending up in Napoli because they couldn't get the *aliscafo* back and took a chance on the big ferry.'

Eleanor shuddered at the memory of her own battered arrival. 'Why, don't the ferries stop here either?'

'Not if it's really bad weather. Can you imagine? Going off in the morning to get a pint of milk and then finding yourself in the port at Naples? But it doesn't happen very often. There's a wedding here tomorrow, so it would be a disaster if the *aliscafi* weren't running.'

'What a lovely place to get married,' sighed Eleanor, unable to resist a fantasy of herself with Will on their wedding day in Panarea, posing for photographs by the smooth green water. She wondered if Frannie was picturing her own version, and couldn't help blurting out: 'Do you think you'll get married here one day?' So much for deftly sliding in the questions, she thought; that sounded far too nosy. But Frannie just smiled.

'Salina, possibly. But that's years away, I hope! You both have to be a hundred per cent sure, don't you?'

Eleanor was at a loss as to how to reply to this.

'Anyway, it'll be lovely tomorrow, I can't wait. We're all going. The church is just by our house – it's so pretty, with a little spotted steeple, you've probably seen it.'

Eleanor felt a prickle of disappointment as she sipped her malvasia. It was as though the popular girl at school had started acknowledging her with a 'hello' here and there, only subtly to let her know that she still wasn't going to be invited to the party everyone was talking about. It was almost more painful than being ignored.

Frannie suddenly jumped up excitedly. 'There's Will, he's back from the dive already! They must have finished early because it's the last day . . .'

Instinctively, Eleanor reached for her bag to find her monocular but stopped herself just in time. She craned to see him, but could only catch glimpses of the back of his head, half a shoulder, a hand slapping the back of one of his course mates. Meanwhile, Frannie was organising the bill, giggling that she felt drunk and Will would joke that he couldn't leave her to her own devices for five minutes without her getting sozzled.

'Coming down to the harbour, as well?' she asked Eleanor, as they pushed back their chairs and pulled bags over shoulders. There was something in her tone this time that suggested she was just being polite.

'No, I think I'll head back for a siesta.' She couldn't possibly accompany Frannie down to the jetty to meet Will. She imagined his look of confusion, maybe even terror, as his girlfriends old and new approached together.

'OK, maybe a coffee tomorrow morning if you're about?' Frannie delivered soft kisses to Eleanor's cheeks and, without waiting for a reply, wafted off down the restaurant stairs.

Eleanor didn't head for her room, of course, but went straight to her customary perch on the roof terrace. She was just in time to see Frannie swing her hips tipsily up the jetty and grab Will around the waist. A full minute of kissing and shoulder-caressing followed

208

as a couple of the other divers stood around awkwardly, trying not to watch the lovebirds too openly.

And just as she had now every day since June, Eleanor wished with every nerve ending in her body that she were Frannie.

Chapter 14

'Will, you're back early!' Eleanor and Miranda, faces caked with deep clay moisturising masks, looked up from their mugs of tea and TV comedy marathon. The room was reverberating with studio laughter and they hadn't heard the key in the door. The tiny Clapham flat the three shared was as chaotic as it had ever been, with mugs, magazines, clothes and toiletries all over the place. Will always complained that the mess levels rose a foot or two when he was out of town, but in fact he was just as hopeless himself. Somehow the arrangement seemed to work.

It was obvious he was not his usual self, and it took a while for Eleanor to realise what was different: he looked serious.

'What's up?' She gestured for him to join her on the sofa.

'Miranda, can you give us a minute?' he said.

There was something about the way Miranda meekly

disappeared that struck Eleanor as odd, but she dismissed this and focused on Will's face. He looked totally stricken. Had he lost his job? She heard the front door click shut.

'What's up? Why don't you come and sit down.' Some remote instinct told her to delay whatever was coming. 'We were just deciding whether to go to Claire's party tonight or not. Want some tea?' Although he didn't reply, she got up and fetched a mug from the kitchen, then poured him some tea from the pot. It was black and treacly and she knew he wouldn't touch it.

'So shall we go?'

'Where?'

'To Claire's party?'

Will shuffled in his seat. 'I don't think so, Eleanor.'

She lost her cool. 'What's going on? Why are you calling me by my name – there's no one else in the room! You're being really weird.' She moved across to snuggle against his chest and felt an infinitesimal clench of his chest muscles, the faintest of pulls away from her. She sat up straight again and waited.

'I need to tell you something,' he said, finally. 'I haven't been in Leeds this week.'

Will's work frequently took him out of London. Miranda called him the travelling salesman, 'TS' for short, which amused him. He'd often have to stay overnight and would ring Eleanor to bemoan the fresh boredoms of provincial living. 'How's Cornwall?' 'Oh, very Cornish,' he'd reply. It had quickly become their little joke. How was Manchester? 'Very Mancunian.' Northampton? 'Very Northamptonian.' Will did a great camp Noel Coward voice for these pronouncements.

'Not in Leeds? How d'you mean?'

'I've been here,' he said.

'In London? Why stay in a hotel then?'

'I didn't. It wasn't work.'

However she delayed it, the penny *would* drop, and now she wondered if she hadn't sensed its roll towards the edge in recent weeks. Will had been away far more than usual, was noticeably less keen to talk about the engagement, and, crucially as far as she was concerned, had never followed up his proposal with the choosing of a ring. Since they'd come back from New York he hadn't had a single Saturday free. Even when she'd arranged a celebratory dinner with Lizzie and Simon he had dropped out at the last minute for a long-standing arrangement he'd just remembered with a friend from work. He'd been the barest bit more irritable with her and Miranda, his humour just a little less fond. Day by day, he'd been retreating by a whisker.

'I've been seeing someone else.' Now his voice cracked with guilt.

Eleanor found that she felt completely calm. 'Who is she?' she asked.

'You don't need to know.'

'I repeat: *who is she?*'

But he stood his ground. 'No one you know.' He

212

paused. 'The thing is, I don't want to stop seeing her.'

Eleanor grappled numbly with the implications of this. Was he suggesting that he continue seeing both of them? That was crazy, surely.

'You want to break up with me?' She marvelled at the lightness of her voice.

'Yes.'

'When did you meet this person?'

'A few weeks ago, a month or two. April, whatever.'

Soon after the New York trip, then.

'But we were already engaged.' She sought his eye without success. 'You asked me to marry you,' she added.

'I know what engaged means.' Will smiled for the first time, but he still looked as though he was battling an eyeball-wringing migraine.

'But weren't you in love with me?'

'Yes, I was. I still love you.'

This wasn't making sense. 'I don't understand. How can you get engaged to someone, love them, and then . . . then be available for a new relationship straight after?'

'I wasn't *available*. Something extraordinary happened.'

'What, exactly?'

'Meeting her. Feeling like I do.'

There was a long silence, during which time Eleanor's head began to roar. Will still wasn't making eye contact, just looking in the general direction of her face with his eyes cold, disconnected, unreachable. It occurred to her briefly that she must look like Coco the Clown with the face pack still on.

'Where did you meet her?'

'Does it matter?'

'Yes. Where?'

'Oh, Eleanor, I can't talk to you properly with that stuff on your face.'

A diversionary tactic; he obviously wasn't going to reveal anything about the girl. But she would find out. She would not rest until she did.

He sighed. 'I think I'd better leave. Can I just get some stuff from the bedroom?'

'It's your bedroom. I can hardly stop you.'

She heard him moving round the room, the sound of a buckle hitting the wood of the bed frame, pictured the big leather bag on the armchair in their New York hotel room; it had been a surprise trip and he'd secretly packed her clothes with his in one bag.

She stood up and marched into the bedroom. 'I don't understand what's happening.' Now there were tears and her voice was desperate. He stopped what he was doing, looked as though he were about to comfort her, then seemed to decide against it and carried on cramming shirts into the bag.

She felt a lurch of gratitude that the flat was hers and not theirs or, worse, his. How would he have handled this then? She imagined the horror of being dismissed from her home within minutes of being ditched from his life.

'I don't understand,' she repeated.

This time Will seized her hand. 'Nor do I, I really don't. But something has happened. It just feels right. I have to go, I have no choice.'

The bag was zipped, strap buckled and he was gone. She rewound her mind twenty minutes: she was lounging on the sofa, laughing through a mouthful of chocolate brownie as Miranda disparaged the fluffy new hairstyle of the actress on TV. Everything had changed.

Later – she wasn't sure how long she'd been sitting there, on their bed, now her bed – Miranda returned and crept into the darkening room. Her face was scrubbed clean now, and there was something in it, a shadow – what was it? Pity? Guilt? – that made Eleanor see that she already knew.

Lewis was back for dinner, but to Eleanor's frustration she wasn't able to talk to him for long. They'd all shuffled round a place for the meals he'd missed and now he had to slot in next to Stefan. The two of them spoke almost exclusively throughout the meal, giving Tim free reign to entertain the women.

It was Friday and several of the Italian guests were leaving the next day; Giovanna was hosting a farewell buffet, a weekly tradition at the hotel. Dozens of non-residents arrived for dinner, too, and the place heaved with glowing flesh and white smiles. Candles covered every surface and the light fluttered seductively around the diners' faces. It felt like a film set.

Eleanor waited for Lewis to head up to the buffet to fill his plate and followed closely behind. 'Hi there, I feel like I haven't spoken to you for ages. We missed you last night. How are you?'

He was busy spearing pieces of smoked swordfish and adding them to a pile of rolled aubergine slices on his plate. 'Very well, very well. I've been out and about, making some notes. And you? You're looking a lot happier than the other night.'

'Yes, sorry about that. Was I a bit painful?'

'Not at all. You were very entertaining.' He turned to smile down at her, his face wearing that easy, dependable expression she now realised she'd needed to see. She felt a rush of affection for him, followed by a fierce urge to hug him.

'A bizarre thing has happened, Lewis, I seem to have got quite friendly with Will's new girlfriend, Frannie. We had lunch today. She's actually very nice. Doesn't know who I am, obviously.' She waited impatiently for his expression of surprise, desperate to dissect the details, but he just nodded, as if nothing she said could surprise him.

'I met them both myself the other day,' he said. 'I have to say I thought they were great. Your Will seems like he might be a decent guy, after all.'

'Oh!' *Both* of them? Nathalie had only seen him with Will, and Frannie certainly hadn't mentioned meeting him. But as Eleanor had neglected to include him in her tales of hotel living, Frannie had obviously had no reason to make the connection; to her he would have been just another English tourist she had bumped into in a café and left bedazzled in her wake. Not for the first time Eleanor felt pride and pleasure at having struck up this friendship with Frannie, who presumably could take her pick of companions and summon the likes of Lewis at her whim.

'Did they say anything about me?' she couldn't help asking. She wished she could find a way of presenting herself to Lewis as just a little less consumed by her own dramas, or at least give him the impression that the dramas weren't all of her own making.

'No, of course not, why would they if they don't know you're here?' asked Lewis, pleasantly. 'Frannie was very helpful, though, put me in touch with someone in Iditella who's got a fantastic private collection, by the sounds.' Eleanor looked blank and he grinned. 'You know, pots and urns and stuff; I know you're not interested in archaeology.'

'No, I love urns,' Eleanor cried. 'Especially really old ones, with all the dust and chips and stuff. That's great news. So, Frannie seems to know everyone on the island . . .'

'Yes, I suppose she must have spent a lot of time here before. She's half Italian, isn't she?'

They were being edged apart by some new arrivals hungry for the buffet. Eleanor grabbed a dinner plate and began manhandling bits of fish and salad. Lewis was already turning away from her and she felt sheer panic that this might be the end of the discussion.

'Lewis, perhaps we could do something else together? I really enjoyed our day in Vulcano.' She thought she caught a twitch of something in his face – Irritation? Amusement? – and turned quickly away again, pretending to concentrate on her food selection. She forked the nearest thing, a whole wedge of dolcelatte, and dumped it on to her plate before she noticed the odd looks around her and slid it back to the buffet table again. Lewis watched, face impassive.

'Er, yes, why not,' he said, after an excruciating pause.

They walked back to their table, where Tim and Sophie were waiting with heaped plates, full glasses, and eyes avid for the latest diversion. Trying to ignore them, Eleanor rushed on before she lost her nerve. 'Well, how about a drink after dinner?'

'What, Limoncello?' Lewis chortled to himself at this. 'I'm sure Giovanna will supply it with coffee, as usual. You could lead the singing, Eleanor.'

She swallowed. 'No, I mean just the two of us, and we can catch up properly on everything?'

From the corner of her eye she saw Sophie gasp at this and nod pointedly at Tim, who responded with a pantomime of a coughing fit. 'Early night for us, eh, Sophe?' he spluttered, too loudly.

Eleanor shot them a pleading look, but was rewarded with a none-too-discreet wink from Sophie. To crown her mortification, Lewis was taking ages to respond to her invitation, obviously wishing to decline it. 'Sorry, I can't,' he said, finally. 'Today's been a bit exhausting. I really need an early night myself.'

'Oh, fine, OK, no big deal,' said Eleanor, crumpling into her seat. She nibbled at an olive in what she hoped was a nonchalant manner, but it was slippery with oil and escaped from her fingers, rolling off under the table. She toyed with the idea of going after it and spending the rest of the evening down there.

As Tim and Sophie began chatting conspicuously together, Lewis leant across the table towards her, keen to ease the blow: 'But Stefan and I were just talking about hiring a boat and going out to Lisca Bianca and the other islands tomorrow. Why don't you come with us?' Lisca Bianca was the farthest of Panarea's islets, Eleanor remembered, the one that glowed a rainbow of colours in the milky early evening light.

'I'd love to. Sounds fabulous.' Except for the bit about Stefan coming, she didn't add.

'Good,' said Lewis, his attention turning to his plate. 'Let's all meet at breakfast. Nine-thirtyish?'

After dinner most of the table made their customary trek down to the waterfront for last orders – not that the term applied here, where bars and restaurants stayed open as long as the tourists were willing to divest themselves of their euros – and Eleanor made her customary excuses. She was reluctant to let go of the atmosphere, however, which, after a substantial amount of wine, felt more festive and liberating than at any time so far. But of course she couldn't risk the harbour: it was no longer simply a question of bumping into Will, but of bumping into Will with Frannie. That would mean Frannie would discover that her new lunch mate was nothing less than Will's deranged ex-girlfriend unable to accept that she'd been given her marching orders. Some women would be very disturbed by that knowledge; they might alert the authorities. At the absolute best Frannie would be disappointed, confused, and that was bad enough for Eleanor.

She now hated this pitiable state of affairs. She felt she'd lost her grip totally on the various strands she'd been trying to work together: they were now just a hopeless tangle on the floor at her feet. She'd somehow managed to create deceptions and restrictions with just about everyone she'd run into, and there was not a single person to blame but herself. Even her life at home was getting too complicated to handle: God knew what versions of her absence Miranda was circulating at work; she owed Rufus an explanation for her failure to come back at his command and his recent silence was more dangerous than the previous pile-up of voicemails; and she still hadn't contacted her parents. Even Lizzie seemed unusually difficult to get hold of – they'd spoken just once all week.

But the days were passing quickly, she told herself, it was already Friday evening and she was due to return to London on Tuesday. With any luck she'd be able to sail off undiscovered, some semblance of dignity intact; it would have to be by the skin of her teeth, but it was possible.

She found herself wandering inland, in search of somewhere to set free the old uncomplicated Eleanor and bury her fraught replacement, not to mention this new twin, Jane. The path was unlit, so she followed the lights from the houses and terraces ahead. There was no one about and she allowed herself to relax and enjoy the night air – it smelled of sweet baked fruit. It felt delightful to be off guard; she'd never been anywhere that felt so warm and safe late at night.

Bearing left in the direction of the beach she soon came to a lively terrace bar packed with islanders, or so she judged them to be on the basis that they were more weather-beaten and less bejewelled than the holidaying Italians. A group of men were standing in a ring, raising their voices in good-humoured debate. One or two glanced her way: she still had the sleek hair and dramatic eyes she'd styled for Frannie's benefit and it felt good to turn an appreciative head or two herself. This was how she should feel after a week in Italy: attractive, glimmering, at ease.

She ordered a glass of red wine and sat in the corner, transfixed by the men's camaraderie, the cigarettes brandished like sparklers, the way the volume rose and fell as if conducted. She had no idea what they were discussing, certainly not the price of fish, she thought to herself; Frannie had told her that very little fishing took place in Panarea now because the fishermen could get ten times as much money taking tourists on boat trips. She wondered where these men's wives were; perhaps preparing for the big wedding tomorrow. Within minutes she'd finished her wine. How many glasses had she had today? She started to count them in her head, but drifted off once she reached double figures.

Presently the group parted to allow the entry of another man, this one more smartly dressed and with the moneyed aura Eleanor now recognised as that of the visiting Northerner. All the others issued little nods of recognition. He moved with absolute confidence in this local enclave, clearly hadn't stumbled in accidentally as she had. He was probably forty, maybe even fifty, she couldn't tell. What she could tell was that she found him extremely attractive. It was an unfamiliar sensation, shocking and elating.

He didn't even glance in her direction, so she was able to gaze openly and indulge in the physical details. He had smooth, slightly greying dark hair pushed away from the forehead, black, low-lidded eyes with shadowed sockets. He looked tired. His lips barely parted as he muttered an order to the barman. He was surprisingly slight, his arms noticeably less powerful than those of the other men. Definitely a city creature. She prayed he wouldn't take his drink to join the others, but would seek her out in her corner, drawn by the same impulse she felt towards him. He did neither, as it turned out, just remained standing at the bar, drinking quickly and wordlessly.

Eleanor wished wildly that she knew enough Italian to go and strike up a conversation; the wine had certainly made her bold enough to make the approach. She searched her memory for 'Good evening, how are you?' and wondered if it was acceptable to say 'ciao' to a stranger. Probably a bit too childish, she decided, more of a greeting sung by the schoolchildren she'd seen around the island, cute and photogenic in their starched housecoats. It was no good, and yet she couldn't possibly speak to him in English, she'd just be dismissed as a tourist buffoon.

She left her table and went into the tiny toilet cabin. There was no mirror, so she used her finger to slick on some lipstick, before dropping it into the toilet pan and, after much agonising, opting to leave it there.

Remembering that Tim's tongue had been almost black by the end of dinner – 'It's unusually porous,' he'd explained, displaying it proudly – she stuck out her own and tried to peer down the side of her nose at it. It was pinkish-grey.

After this, she ferreted in her bag for her phrase-book and searched for the words that might help her, repeating the Italian to herself over and over. At last, realising she had no idea how long she'd been in the toilet, she unlocked the door, desperately hoping the man would still be there. He was, still standing at the bar, still drinking alone. She chose to view this as a sign that their meeting had somehow been pre-determined.

'*Ha un accendino?*'

He did have a lighter, of course; she'd yet to meet an Italian man who didn't smoke. He looked at her with courteous interest before lighting himself a cigarette as well – his eyes were extremely black, they reminded her of the lava monsters in Vulcano. He was definitely the sort of person to search beyond face value, she decided; he looked far too intense to care about a grey tongue. Certainly, he didn't object when she settled on the bar stool next to him. She looked at his face in profile; there was an endearing weariness about the jaw.

'You are *Americano*?' he asked in curt, accented English. She felt mesmerised by his lips and had to will herself to raise her gaze and make eye contact.

'English. *Inglese*. I'm on holiday here. It's very beautiful.'

No reply.

'Are you from the north of Italy?' she asked.

'Yes, but I know these islands, I have houses here. Panarea is very different now. Once it was more simple, honest. I miss that very much.' He sounded as though he were pronouncing on life, not just the island, and Eleanor felt another drunken lurch of kindred spirit.

'What was it like before?' She felt she would say anything, however idiotic, to extend the conversation and hear his voice again.

He looked at her for several seconds as though judging whether she was capable of an intelligent exchange, and she tried with all her might to look in control of both mind and body. She realised she was holding her breath and allowed herself to relax again. Immediately every nerve in her body flared with lust. He rattled out an order to the barman, who instantly placed two mismatched flutes of red wine in front of them. This was another sign, Eleanor thought, happily, an excellent one.

'It was not, what is the word, fashionable as it is now,' he said. 'Everywhere was like this bar, wood tables, ancient chairs. Just one hotel or two. There were families in the hills, growing fruits. The villas now, they were sheds for the cows.'

'Wow, really?' Eleanor felt as though his lost paradise were the most romantic thing in the world. 'But the island still feels very simple and relaxed,' she added, watching his lips again.

'It is all *turista*, businessmen with the big money.' He shrugged dismissively.

'But don't you fall into that category?' she asked.

He laughed loudly at this and flashed his eyes at her. 'Yes, you might say this. But I have my houses when they were the sheds. I like this bar, not the ones in San Pietro with the *turista*. How did you come here, to this bar?'

Clearly being a tourist was doing Eleanor no favours in the desirability stakes. She hurriedly tried to make amends. 'Oh, I wanted to get away from that scene. I prefer small, local places like this, too, with genuine native people.' This sounded nauseating even to her own ear, Miss World gushing out memorised lines, but the idea of explaining her self-exile to this man was totally out of the question.

'Where are you staying?'

'In San Pietro,' she admitted. 'At the Albergo delle Rose. It's quite old.'

He merely snorted at this, no doubt preferring to remember it as the humble waterside shack Eleanor had seen in the black-and-white photos on the wall behind Giovanna's desk. Lewis had told her that when it first opened the hotel had no plumbing or electricity.

'Whereabouts is your house?' she asked. She realised she was aching for him to suggest he might show her for herself then and there. This feeling of attraction was overpowering, filling her with a mad glee that was beginning to frighten her.

'Near here, in the hill,' he gestured vaguely.

Eleanor ordered two more glasses of wine, too drunk to care about her hopeless accent, but sober enough to realise that it might take more than a couple of glasses of red to seduce this jaded creature. She'd had quite a head start. She pictured herself pursuing him to his door, pinning him against a pillar and kissing him furiously. It was so farcical she let out a yelp of laughter. He laughed, too, seeming to cheer a little.

'You are enjoying Panarea.' It wasn't a question but Eleanor seized on the remark to display her passion for the island. She chatted on and on, including opinions about the Bronze Age village, before realising she'd been saying 'bronze village', as though the houses were actually carved out of bronze. She hoped the blunder was lost in translation, along with the rest of her personal flaws.

'All these exclusive gated villas,' she drawled, aiming for a deeper, more nostalgic tone, rather like Frannie's. 'The little private compounds – it's all so mysterious. I'd love to see inside one of them. It's my dream!' This was far more overt than she'd intended, but she made no attempt to retract it. She waited.

He laughed again into his glass, then turned slowly to look at her. 'Well, your dream is coming true. You can see inside my "compound".'

Eleanor gasped. This was perfect. In her head, nothing else registered. She watched him push over some euros to the barman and turn to leave. The remaining locals chorused '*Buona notte*' to their backs.

They walked in silence up a steep pathway she didn't recognise. It had dry-stone walls and was too narrow for two people to walk side by side, so Eleanor followed, feeling like an obedient child. Before long he turned to the left and pushed at a broad, heavy gate. A short path led through trees and shrubs towards a long, low villa. The terrace was vast, with fat white pillars and tiles of green and red, and inside a series of stone arches led from one large stylish space to another. The floors were covered with antique kilims and what furniture there was was simple – cane chairs with pale cushions, a glass table or two and a pair of dark linen sofas. The walls were randomly dotted with paintings, just a few spare strokes here and there, watery evocations of island life, nothing like the slick, detailed paintings she'd seen for sale in the boutiques. And all around there were the tall, curvaceous silhouettes of terracotta pots, which made Eleanor think of Lewis and his stories of shipwreck booty. In the living room area stood an unpacked suitcase, with a jacket slung over it. He must have arrived that evening.

'What a beautiful house,' she exclaimed, but he'd disappeared and there was no answer. There was to be no formal tour, then.

She wandered through the open doors to the terrace, breathing in jasmine and lemon and the fainter restaurant smells of grilled fish and garlic. Then cigarette smoke: he was back, with an ashtray and two glasses of wine. 'From the vineyards in Salina,' he said, 'the next island from Panarea.'

'I hear Salina is even prettier than Panarea,' Eleanor said, thanking God for all the snippets she'd picked up from Frannie and Lewis. 'I'd like to go there.'

The wine tasted wonderful, warm and rich, layered with liquorice. She moved to join him as he stood by the terrace wall, longing for him to kiss her. Instead he took her hand. It felt like the sexiest thing she could imagine, dizzyingly good as he pressed at her palm and fingers. She didn't dare look at him, continued gazing blindly into the dark, but sensed that he'd now turned to look at her.

'I like your cowshed,' she said, weakly.

'I like you. What is your name?'

'Eleanor.' Now she looked at his face. He didn't offer his own name, just set down his wine glass, took hers from her hand, then moved forward to kiss her. Being so close to him, feeling dry male lips pressing hard against her face, made her feel wild and accelerated. He, however, was totally controlled, dictating every move. Very slowly he unbuttoned her top and she could barely contain a tremor of lust. He moved his hands over her shoulders and breasts, then unzipped her skirt, pushed it over her hips to the floor. She hoped her skin didn't feel too hot from the sun, remembered the hand-print on her thigh and tried to distract him by pulling open his shirt: he seemed too cool and protected in his clothes. The shirt slipped off. He was more muscular than she'd thought.

Then they were on one of the sofas and he was pulling her on to his lap to kiss her neck and breasts. 'Here is right? Or in the bedroom?' he asked her, between kisses.

'Bedroom,' said Eleanor hoarsely. Drunk as she was, she had no idea if any other houses overlooked this terrace. She couldn't even tell if it was quiet outside, could barely hear his voice any more, because the inside of her head was in uproar.

They didn't make it to the bedroom, but fell on to one of the sofas inside; at first she didn't realise he was inside her, then gave a long sigh and bit at his shoulders as he moved deeply, abruptly. She couldn't believe how extraordinary this felt. She knew she'd allowed her body to shut down over the last few months, hadn't wanted to imagine sex with anyone but Will, sustaining herself on the memory and a prayer for his return. But now the new smell and touch of this stranger made her feel sexier, giddier than ever before. It must have been an hour, longer maybe, during which he didn't once stop touching her.

She lost all sense of everything else after that, feeling herself being lifted, slotted against his body for sleep.

Chapter 15

When Eleanor woke up her head felt as if it had been set in concrete: there was no question of independent movement. Instead, she used her left hand to adjust the pillow under her cheek and, with some effort, was able to open a pair of squeaky, dehydrated eyes. There was a large purple-grey stain on the pillow: she must have been dribbling. But now her lips seemed to have dried together like two flattened figs and she couldn't prise them apart with her tongue. She would have to slather some lotion on them and wait for the moisture to release them. Exactly how many bottles of wine had she drunk her way through last night? Was it any more than on previous nights? She seemed to have several days' worth of hangover, some kind of weird accumulator.

It was a minute or two before she noticed a faint ache in her left knee. Now she remembered scraping it against a wall as she made her way back to the hotel in the half-light of early morning. Thank God she'd left the villa and not remained, a drooling freak show, in the bed next to him. The man. She hadn't discovered his name in the end: once they'd had sex a couple of times it seemed disingenuous to ask. In the morning she'd just uncurled her arm from under his back and slid silently out of the bed, leaving him sleeping deeply, neck arched right back with his mouth half open. On the way out she'd checked the label on his suitcase, but there was no name, just an illegible scribble of an address in Milan.

More images of their night together began to play in her head in an unsettling kaleidoscope and she felt a remote twist of lust. There was another sensation, too, not quite freedom, but a feeling of lightening. She wondered if she could make it to the bathroom for some water, and tried to move her head again: it seemed the smallest bit more willing. But moving it even a couple of inches set in motion a hideous ricocheting of soft tissue against skull that went on for minutes afterwards, like that executive toy Rufus had on his desk, with its row of metallic balls that swung to and fro eternally – a Newton's Cradle, that was it. Her head was a Newton's Cradle.

She reached for her phone to check the time: 10.45 a.m. She'd missed a call from Lizzie and the voicemail promised news. She closed her eyes again; even the stale, shuttered darkness was too much to bear. She hoped she'd been sufficiently stealthy that morning not to wake any of the other hotel guests on her return. It would have been obvious even to a groggy simpleton that she hadn't been studying the flora by starlight. Sophie would approve, she thought, but perhaps not Lewis.

Lewis! She remembered their boat trip to Lisca Bianca with Stefan. They would surely have left by now. And even if she managed to catch them at the jetty her body would never permit a trip across water; that horrible suck and swell of the sea, the mere thought of it made her queasy. She groaned; it was so rude of her not to turn up or send a message – after all, she'd invited herself along in the first place.

She eased out of bed, inch by wretched inch, twice having to place her head back on the pillow before persevering, then dressed in the easiest clothes with the fewest buttons and hobbled down to the hall. The boys were there, clearing up after breakfast. The sight of half-eaten croissants and flaps of pink ham was nauseating.

At the reception desk stood a line of suitcases and bags. Of course, it was Saturday, some of the guests would be leaving, perhaps new ones arriving.

She approached Giovanna. '*Buon giorno, signora.* Has Lewis left already?'

Giovanna beamed at her: ''E is to Leesca Beeanca, with Herr Stefan.'

234

'Any message for me?'

'I 'ave only message for Jane,' Giovanna said, turning back to her papers. This sounded faintly familiar and Eleanor stood for a moment, goading her brain into life.

'Yes, I am Jane, Eleanor Jane!' she cried.

Luckily, Giovanna accepted this without interrogation and said, 'Ees Francesca who call. She will not see you for the *caffè*. She ees engaged.'

'OK, right, thank you.' Eleanor took this to mean that Frannie was too busy for coffee, rather than newly proposed to by Will. This was good news, at least. Much as she'd enjoyed lunch with Frannie yesterday, she was in no fit state to face that flawless radiance all over again, not to mention the stomach-turning *malvasia*.

'I'm going back to my room, Giovanna,' she said, weakly. 'I don't feel well, so don't worry about sending the maid today.'

'You want *dottore*?' Giovanna was suddenly full of concern. 'I call Lipari?'

'No, no, thank you, I just need to sleep. I'll be down later.'

She shuffled back upstairs, invalid-slow, feeling as though her body's entire volume of blood had been replaced by mercury. But she couldn't sleep for long; a slow tingle was reanimating her rag doll limbs and her mind had started its daily racing, thoughts rushing to unstick themselves from one another and pulse around as frantically as ever. She dialled Lizzie's home number.

'Lizzie? I've had sex!'

'Good morning to you too, Eleanor. I'm very glad I was the one to answer the phone.'

'Ha ha!'

'Come on, then, who with? Not Will?'

'No, a complete stranger. Italian and older. I don't even know his name.'

She heard Lizzie wheeze with laughter. 'Excellent! Just what the doctor ordered. Are you going to see him again?'

'I very much doubt it, especially as I spend most of my day hiding from other people. It's more difficult to sneak around than I thought.'

'Still, once is all it takes.'

To forget the one before, she meant; to forget Will. But life wasn't that easy, everybody knew that.

'How old are we talking, exactly?' Lizzie asked.

'I think mid-, maybe late-forties.'

'And you didn't even get his name? You are so funny.'

'I wasn't exactly behaving in character. I was genuinely out of control.' The back of Eleanor's throat felt skinned; she vowed never to smoke again. 'But what was your news? You said you had something to tell me?'

'I'll tell you next time.' Lizzie sounded dismissive, in a hurry to return the subject to Eleanor. 'When are you coming back?'

'Tuesday is the plan, but I may try to come home a bit earlier.' This was news to her own ears, and somehow welcome, too. 'Listen, I'm worried about what you said about Miranda not believing I'm in Devon. Has she been on to you again? Should I phone her?'

'Oh, forget about that ninny, of course you shouldn't. The less you involve her in your life from now on the better.'

'You might be right.'

'I've got to go now, Simon'll be waiting for me at the gym.'

'Is everything going OK with him?'

'Yes, great, I'll tell you later. Take care!'

'Bye.'

Puzzled by Lizzie's abruptness, Eleanor wandered down to the bar. It was too early for lunch and Katharina was the only guest still there, sitting reading a German newspaper, brow creased and lips jutting forward in an exaggerated pout. She was wearing an orange sarong and a purple bikini top at least a size too small, the two garments separated by a trio of unevenly tanned fleshy tyres. Eleanor wondered if she'd also been invited on the boat trip. She told herself it was fortuitous that she'd missed this outing – at least she'd been spared another session of Stefan's beady inspection. And the men probably fancied a day of male bonding; she pictured them trying to spear fish and light a beach barbecue by rubbing damp sticks together. She couldn't imagine Lewis being particularly good at fishing, though he'd no doubt be able to classify and dissect the creatures once captured. She smiled fondly.

'Hi, Katharina, what are you up to today?'

Katharina looked up with a start. 'I put myself into hot water,' she said, 'in Calcara.'

'Hot water?' Eleanor was determined to avoid getting into any more of the stuff herself.

'Bubbles, very healthysome.'

'Oh, you mean the thermal springs!' Lewis had mentioned these. Apparently, somewhere on Panarea hot water bubbled up delightfully in a rock pool just a few feet from the water's edge. The idea was suddenly overwhelmingly soothing.

'You are coming *auch*?' asked Katharina, merrily.

'Yes, why not, I'll just change into my swimming stuff.'

She and Katharina walked steadily up the lane, not saying much. Eleanor still didn't feel entirely comfortable in the German woman's company: they hadn't really struck up a friendship, or even the good-humoured familiarity that Sophie managed so well. She wasn't sure why Katharina had invited her along, but she was glad for the distraction, as she didn't want to waste the whole day daydreaming about a one-night stand. She knew she wouldn't return to the bar where she'd met her man, even if she could remember exactly how she'd got there. Something so unexpected and self-contained was not going to be rekindled. Perhaps Lizzie

238

was right: it had been just what the doctor ordered, a one-off antidote. After all, she wasn't on the roof terrace with her trusty spotter, and that had to be considered an improvement.

Two tall, well-dressed men in their thirties strolled by, both pushing babies in old-fashioned prams, as though they'd been accessorised for a magazine shoot. She would have liked to have gazed more openly, but was concentrating on keeping her head down. Calcara was evidently beyond Iditella, and they were on the pathway leading directly to Will and Frannie's villa. This was the greatest risk she'd taken so far, walking in broad daylight on enemy terrain, knowing Will wouldn't be out with the diving boat and with no inkling of where he might be instead.

As they approached Casa Salina she moved directly across Katharina's path to hug the wall and therefore remain out of sight from the windows and terraces above their heads. She prayed Katharina wouldn't ask her a question or, worse, use her name, but luckily her companion just stared dreamily ahead, swinging her straw bag, puffing a little as the path climbed and giving occasional little sighs. Not for the first time Eleanor wondered if the German woman wasn't a bit touched; there was something very unpredictable about her manner, which veered without warning from intensity to vacancy. What a pair they made, she thought, the orange-clad madwoman from Cologne and the English girl skulking around like someone on a witness protection scheme. Of all the new people she'd met over this last week, was Katharina not her closest match? It was a frightening thought.

Once they were ten or fifteen feet beyond Casa Salina, she allowed herself to relax for the first time. Katharina, however, chose the same moment to make her move, springing with surprising sprightliness on to a nearby wall and, from there, straight into a tree, where she began scrabbling around, forearms whipping back and forth.

Oh no, thought Eleanor, she really has gone nuts. Why did she have to choose here of all places? The tree was in a small courtyard just two doors up from Frannie's terrace on the opposite side of the lane. She watched, flummoxed, as Katharina clawed and tore at the tree, even swinging herself around at one point, which caused the branch to buckle under her weight. Eleanor glanced towards Will's terrace; there was no one there, but the door that led into the house was ajar, which meant someone must be at home.

'Stay calm, don't panic,' she told herself, trying to crank her brain into constructive thought. What could she do to get Katharina out of the tree, and without delay? Should she climb in, too, and give the woman a slap to shock her? She wished Lewis were there: he would know how to quieten a lunatic.

'Katharina!' she hissed, not daring to raise her voice.

'What are you doing in there? Katharina!' There was no response, just a snuffling sound from the tree. She stood helplessly, looking up and down the lane for help.

A male voice now shouted out in English: 'Hey, are you all right? Hello, who is it?' The clear, confident tone was unmistakably Will's. Eleanor went rigid, felt as though she'd been rolled in snow. What had she been thinking: of course he and Frannie would be lazing around the villa, it was their first day together all week. She slunk back against the wall and began easing sideways up the hill out of sight, her breathing fast and shallow. Next she heard Frannie's voice, 'Come on, babe, we need to leave.'

'There's someone in the tree,' Will said, sounding more amused now.

'Which tree? Let me see . . .'

The last Eleanor heard as she scurried safely out of reach was Frannie calling out in Italian. Terrified by this close encounter, she huddled in a doorway and waited for several minutes with no idea what to do next. Perhaps she should go back; what if Katharina really was having some sort of fit? It was irresponsible not to go to her aid, but what kind of help would she offer in a confrontation with Will? She decided she'd have to count on him and Frannie to administer any necessary first aid – he'd done a course at work, if she remembered rightly – which meant that she would need to plan an alternative route back to San Pietro.

She stood up, patting down her clothes – the ducking

in doorways reminded her too much of that first time in Iditella, when Lewis had seen her. She tried to look about her sensibly and formulate a plan. The lane upwards seemed to be snaking inland, and she squinted up at the hills, densely covered in gorse and cacti: it seemed wild and hostile up there, more like Scotland than Italy. There was no way she could trek back through that; her legs would be scratched to shreds.

Just as she was debating whether it was possible to loop back to San Pietro via a lower coastal path, Katharina made her reappearance. She was alone, wandering up the lane as though nothing had happened, just looking a little pinker in the face. She waved fistfuls of round pink-and-green fruits in Eleanor's face. 'Fig! Fig! Fresh from the tree,' she announced. 'You are resting? That is splendid.'

Eleanor laughed with relief. 'I thought I heard someone calling, I thought it might be the police, you're probably not supposed to take fruit from the trees . . .' she babbled, aware that this excuse would put her in an equally cowardly light as the truth.

Luckily, Katharina roared at this idea, her laughter like cymbals clashing at Eleanor's ears. 'No, no, just this people in the villa; they think I make hurt. They are the *Engländer*, you know them?'

'Nope, never seen them before in my life. Shall we get on?'

Moments later, Katharina set about pilfering lemons,

too, again pressing them into Eleanor's face to demonstrate their ripeness. The sweet, aromatic smell was comforting after the scare. In contrast to Eleanor's state, the scrumping episode seemed to have revitalised Katharina, who now picked up the pace, almost skipping along.

'So where are these springs again?' Eleanor asked, puffing to keep up; she realised she had no idea where they were headed.

'Soon arriving,' answered Katharina. She veered to the right and began leading the way down a steep cliff path. The view was beautiful, the sea as flat and heavy as double cream, no murmur of a breeze. The archipelago of rocks glinted at them over the water. Eleanor looked out at Lisca Bianca, wishing it were she there with Lewis, and Stefan here with his wife. Would Lewis have been even faintly disappointed by her failure to turn up? Or just relieved at eluding another 'date' with her?

Below them was a stony cove, larger than Cala Junca but evidently far less popular, for there wasn't a soul to be seen. This is more like it, thought Eleanor, no unexpected visitors here. It was no mean feat getting across the stones in little leaps; Katharina was much better at it than she was and she marvelled again at the light-footedness of so lumpen a woman. Perhaps she'd been an athlete in her day, Eleanor thought, as slim and nimble as Nathalie. It was simply the difference between two or three decades.

'The thermal rocks,' said Katharina, pointing to a sunken area at the edge of the shore, filled with about a foot of bubbling water. She bent over to test the temperature and exclaimed: '*Fantastisch!*'

She promptly stripped bare and Eleanor, trying not to look, settled for keeping her bikini bottoms on. For once, she didn't feel self-conscious, even with the bruised knee and fading handprint – there was no one else about to care. She followed Katharina into the water and lowered herself into sitting position on a large, flat stone. The water was as warm as a bathtub, bubbling gently through the rocks. Leaning back on her elbows Eleanor almost gave a shriek as her arm collided with heavy flesh and bone. It was a naked man. She had no idea where he'd appeared from: he must have been lying there all along. His body was very tanned, the chest hair grey, and he was perfectly camouflaged against the pepper-coloured rocks. For an appalling second she thought it was the man from the previous night, her man, but, meeting his gaze, realised he was a stranger. She watched as his tongue darted out between his lips like a lizard's, then told herself she'd just imagined it and looked quickly away. Now her eyes fell on his penis; it was small, pale and shiny, like a freshly caught sardine. Again, she looked away. Her head hurt horribly.

'Katharina,' she whispered, indicating with her eyes their new companion. Katharina just shrugged, which made her slack white breasts swing from side to side.

Evidently this was the naturist spot on the island and not one to attract the perfectly formed crowd that inhabited all other public spaces.

'Well, what a beautiful spot for a Jacuzzi,' Eleanor sighed, finally settling in. It was lovely the way the dark bubbles tickled her body, with nothing but the quiet sea beyond.

'There is something more,' said Katharina, climbing out and disappearing across the rocks. Eleanor tried not to think about being left alone with the naked lizard man just a foot away from her head; she wondered what fruit tree Katharina had spotted this time. But Katharina returned half a minute later with handfuls of thick red clay. She passed a ball of the stuff to Eleanor. 'Mix with the *wasser* and spread across your skin,' she instructed, as though dictating the method for a recipe.

This was fun, Eleanor thought, watching Katharina bring her feet up in front of her face and vigorously massage the clay between each toe. It was much stickier than the yellow gloop in Vulcano, and it looked fierce and tribal smeared all over their arms and faces. Again Eleanor wished it were Lewis with her, instead. He'd be able to tell her about ancient rituals and urns salvaged from the sea nearby. It occurred to her she'd thought about him rather a lot today.

'You like the fig?' Katharina suggested, and began digging open the fruit with her thumbs. The two of them greedily sucked out the sweet contents, not speaking. Eleanor couldn't remember the last time she'd felt so weightless. She closed her eyes for a doze.

'Stefan and I make divorce in Köln, you know this?' said Katharina suddenly. Her tone was matter of fact, no different from when she'd offered the figs.

Eleanor forced her eyes open. She couldn't nap through a confession of this sort, much as she would have preferred to. 'Oh, I'm sorry to hear that. Have you been having problems?' She strained to think of something more helpful.

Katharina shrugged. 'We are deciding this for long time, but we are worried for Nathalie.'

'Does she have any idea you're separating?'

'We think no. She is just baby. She care number one for the tennis.'

Eleanor suppressed a snort. 'So when will you tell her?'

'When we are back in Germany, next week.'

Eleanor pondered this, averting her eyes from the older woman's gaze. She had no idea whether Nathalie would be traumatised by such an event.

'Are you close to Nathalie?'

'Oh yes, she is telling me all the news. We are like cistern.'

Eleanor paused. 'Sisters? Right, sure. Katharina, I wondered if she and Carlo might, you know, like each other?'

246

'They are friends. They go today to Lipari for the tennis courts.'

'Doesn't Carlo have to work?'

'Oh, he is *Italiano*. He has always the free time.'

Sly little things, thought Eleanor. She had to admire the teens' technique: they were far more skilful than she was at giving people the slip, outfoxing the adults daily with little real effort. She felt a rush of pity for Katharina, abandoned by her husband, hoodwinked by her daughter.

'Stefan, he want stay married,' Katharina now announced, surprising Eleanor again. 'But I have friend in Köln and we want Mary.'

Who on earth was Mary? Eleanor wasn't sure her dried-out brain could cope with this narrative. Or did she mean 'marry'? She felt more disarmed than ever by the German woman's conversational style, with its dramatic pronouncements tossed out to listening ears like hoops.

'So you definitely don't want to give Stefan another try?' She made it sound like he was a pony or a car.

'Oh no. He devil man.'

This was unexpected news, though not something Eleanor felt inclined to dispute. 'Are there any more figs?' she asked in desperation, hoping she might plug this confessional stream with a return to the safer subject of Panarea's many delicious fruits. As Katharina shook her head slowly, tragically, Eleanor suddenly wanted to yell out with laughter, felt a shudder working its way through her body from the inside out. She turned her face away, lips twitching at the corners as though tugged by strings by a puppeteer above her head.

Now the naked man was standing up and grinning at them. He had a very large, taut paunch, which he proceeded to slap with both hands like a bongo drum. He looked oddly at Eleanor's grinning face, evidently mistaking her laughter for a reaction to his physique, and murmured something in Italian.

'You should no laugh,' Katharina told her. 'Only the children are laughing.'

'I'm not!' But she *was* laughing, and she *was* like a child, and it felt quite wonderful.

'We go snorkel,' Katharina said, as the man crouched at the water's edge rinsing his goggles, white bottom sticking out towards them. She hobbled over to join him. 'You have mask?' she called back.

Eleanor shook her head, couldn't risk opening her mouth in case more giggles gurgled out.

'Here is Nathalie's *auch*,' said Katharina, tossing her a purple snorkel. 'We swim, yes?' Then she and the naked man both snapped on their goggles and plunged into the still sea, synchronising their acceleration like a pair of fleshy dolphins.

Finally alone, Eleanor shouted with laughter at the top of her voice. She felt completely out of her mind, incapable of judging what she might do next. Snorkelling seemed as useful as anything else, so she pulled herself together, splashed the mud off her face and eased her limbs into the cool sea. It was the ideal anaesthetic, seeming to wash away her hysteria and knead her headache down to the faintest push and pull. She stared through the goggles at the strange tinsel plants that grew between the rocks. Christmas all year round, she thought, admiring their tentacles and watching the transparent fish dart about, fast as radar. What an amazingly beautiful place Panarea was, even underwater.

All of a sudden she felt her right ankle being tugged down, and her brain was impaled with a red-hot bolt of fear as she realised she'd swum quite far along the coast. Frannie flashed into her mind first, her fear of deep water and warnings of hydrofoils unable to master the currents, followed by Lewis, with his tales of ship-wrecks. Was this how it was all to end, then, a silent drowning as two middle-aged strangers frolicked in the distance, her lifeless body pulled from the water by people wearing nothing but snorkels? The terror passed and then she felt nothing, not even surprise. Finally, remembering to look down, she saw that her foot was tangled in some seaweed, and she was able to dislodge the slimy ropes with her hands without much trouble. There were no currents, no horrors of the deep: the water was as still and gentle as it had been all day. She swam in gluey slow motion back to the shore.

Katharina and the man were sitting on adjoining

rocks, speaking together in low, sultry Italian. It struck Eleanor that they seemed to know each other rather well. She put on her T-shirt and went over to join them, lighting a cigarette and trying not to catch either's eye. Still she felt like a child, *their* child, forced to suffer the appalling shame of having parents who insisted on taking their family holiday in a naturist resort. For a moment she felt a yearning to be back in England, on the train down to Exeter, or sitting in her parents' living room, drinking hot tea from an oversized mug, probably the one painted with wood mice, waiting for her mother to bring in the cake.

Katharina was in buoyant mood as they walked back to San Pietro, telling Eleanor all about their naked companion, who, it emerged, she'd met at the thermal pool a couple of days earlier and was one of Sicily's best-known sculptors. She pointed out his villa in the distance: it was probably the largest on the island, its flat rooftop crammed with potted cacti.

They were safely past Frannie's villa and approaching the little clifftop church in Iditella when a warm swirl of chatter began to drown out Katharina's voice. Of course, Eleanor remembered, the wedding. Frannie had mentioned it. 'We're all going,' she'd said.

They arrived to find a crowd of guests on the sun-drenched terrace, apparently just released from the service. Hanging back, Eleanor took in the scene over

Katharina's shoulder: everywhere dark heads dipped to kiss honey-coloured cheeks, men and women dressed in black and white and red clustered and crowded in little groups, gold jewellery and white teeth flashed in the afternoon sun. The bride and groom stood together on the church steps, clogging the spillage. She wore traditional white lace and a long train, veil thrown back to reveal a startlingly youthful face – couldn't be any older than nineteen or twenty, thought Eleanor. The groom, also young, gripped his wife's hand, as though for protection; even when she was pulled away by the current of well-wishers, he always kept hold of her little finger.

'Come on, Katharina.' Eleanor pawed at the German's arm. 'Let's head back, we're intruding.' But they plainly weren't, as a gaggle of tourists had now gathered to coo encouragement at the photographer as he ordered kiss after kiss between the bride and groom. Next the groom was making a cartoon dash for it, with the bride catching him by his coat-tails, which caused whoops of hilarity all round. It was less funny the second and third times as the photographer perfected his shot. Before long, guests and passers-by were mingling and the tourists set about getting their own snaps of this unexpected local treat.

Eleanor tried to imagine taking the bride's place on the steps with Will at her side. Their parents would be there, of course, and all their friends, sharing in the pride and optimism of the union. She'd feel that giddying feeling just-married couples said was like nothing else in life; her face would radiate a special joy. But there was something wrong: Will wasn't gripping her hand the way this groom – unbidden – kept gripping his bride's. He didn't need to know that her little finger was there, and never would. She sensed herself let go of the fantasy like a teenager realising for the first time that her crush on a movie star was simply that, no more no less: what she felt was one part terror, one part relief.

Then she saw them, just as she'd been expecting to. Will and Frannie, wedding guests, holding hands and looking so blissfully joined they could easily have been mistaken for the newlyweds. Will was in light grey, eyes proud as they returned over and over to Frannie's face. She wore a simple deep-blue shift dress, with an embroidered silk scarf draped over her upper arms, no hat or jewellery. She looked fragile and Eastern compared to the other women.

Eleanor's reverie was abruptly broken by the sudden suspicion that her lover of last night might have arrived in Panarea for this very event. She remembered his suitcase, no bigger than overnight luggage, really. Well, at least he wasn't the groom, she thought, gratefully. She wondered what Katharina would say if she shared her thoughts – probably wouldn't bat an eyelid. As more of the wedding party assembled on the steps for a group photograph, she scanned their faces again, half hoping, half dreading: her eyes moved over a clutch of teenage bridesmaids, with their ripening Sicilian features, big eyes and lips, strong noses and chins, gleaming skin; over Will and Frannie again, arm-in-arm, chatting with two other couples. She couldn't see him.

'Come on,' she said again to Katharina. 'I'm going back.'

Retreating to the outskirts of the group, Eleanor took a final glance at the newlyweds. Faced with this radiant display of compatibility, it was impossible not to smile for their happiness, for their simply having reached this far. Securely paired, their futures were as certain and optimistic as could be, she thought, while her own, right then, was anyone's for the taking. But wasn't there a little optimism in that, too?

They walked back in companionable silence, but as they reached the pathway to the hotel, Katharina suddenly turned to her and cried out in an absurdly doom-laden tone: 'You should not Mary this Lewis.' She squeezed Eleanor's shoulder so hard it hurt.

'You mean marry?' Eleanor sighed heavily. The poor dear had obviously misread the situation at the hotel and allowed herself to get carried away by the wedding. 'Don't worry, Katharina, Lewis and I barely know each other and he has a girlfriend back in London.'

Katharina gave an urgent whinny. 'No, he is hiding something. You must not trust him.'

'He's not hiding anything,' Eleanor said, with as much patience as she could muster. How very wrong Katharina had got it; it was she, Eleanor, who could not be trusted. 'He's a perfectly friendly, normal person. There's nothing to worry about.'

She laughed off this melodrama. It felt rather good to have regained enough faith to laugh something off.

Chapter 16

She was early for dinner and had a Coke in the bar. It was time to take a night off alcohol. The TV news was on in the corner of the room, presented by an ancient, smokily tanned man in a dark suit and a glamorous blonde woman masked in make-up and wearing an oversized crucifix at her throat. Every so often the man would turn to address the woman with theatrical solemnity and she would respond with identical gravity. It was a day of perfectly compatible couples, Eleanor thought, and one divorcing pair. A strange day.

She had made a decision. After dinner she would go to Frannie's villa and try for a last look at Will. If he turned out not to be there, if he was still at the wedding reception or off somewhere else with his new love, then she would accept that her glimpse at the church had been her last. Either way, it would be a goodbye. Then tomorrow she would check out of the hotel early. She needed to head home and get on with her own life.

The decision made her feel serene and charitable. As everyone trickled down for dinner she smiled happily at them in turn and ordered another soft drink. She was determined to resist the wine and enjoy her final meal with the group with a clear head.

At the table Katharina's high spirits seemed to have returned as she described the wedding with such enthusiasm that even Nathalie showed signs of thawing.

'What a stunning place to get married! Not quite Wandsworth Register Office,' Sophie said. 'Wine, Eleanor? Not drinking? Good lord, you must have it bad!'

'I'd heard there was a wedding this weekend,' said Lewis. 'They're great, aren't they, men in black and all that, always reminds me of *The Godfather*.'

As Sophie and Katharina began exchanging memories of their own wedding days, Eleanor smiled soberly at Lewis and replied, 'Yes, they looked so happy, it was lovely.' And how lovely he looked, she thought, with his deepening tan and reliably sympathetic eyes. She felt drawn with every nerve in her body to the solidity of him, the down-to-earth, matter-of-fact thereness of him.

'I'm so sorry I didn't make it down in time for the boat trip this morning,' she said. 'I just slept straight through. I hope you had a good time?'

'No problem,' Lewis said cheerfully. 'It was great, thanks, we spent most of the day in Basiluzzo in the end, looking at the Roman stuff; the bits of mosaic floors are really cool.' He paused. 'And I'm sorry I couldn't have a drink with you last night. I didn't mean to be rude, I just felt exhausted. The sun is getting to me.'

'Oh, it was just a spur-of-the-moment idea,' Eleanor said, quickly. 'No big deal.' Part of her hoped he might suggest a drink after dinner that evening instead, but he didn't.

'Did you go for drinks with the others? I hear there was another historic session?'

'No, no.' She felt anxious to avoid discussing the events of the latter part of the previous evening, but somehow disliked lying to him. 'I just went for a wander and then straight to bed. I drank a lot at lunch with Frannie. Have you run into her or Will again?'

'No, I've been out in the boat all day, we just got back an hour ago. So you two are becoming quite chummy, are you?'

'I do like her, but it's a bit weird. I mean, it's nice to have got to know her a bit, but I'm sure she'd hate me if she knew who I really was.'

'Oh, you're not so much of a villain,' he chuckled.

'I saw her and Will at the wedding earlier. I suppose Frannie must know the couple getting married through her family or something.'

'How do you feel about it? Still bad seeing them together?' asked Lewis. His voice adopted the measured, professional quality she recognised from their previous heart-to-hearts. How kind he was; not many men would be willing to take on such a role on holiday.

'I feel a bit better about it, I suppose. Actually, a lot better. I'm getting used to the idea of them together. I just have to accept that my time is over.'

'You make it sound like you're terminally ill. Seriously, it's good that you're feeling more positive. I was worried about you, I must admit.'

'Really?' Without the armour of alcohol, Eleanor felt curiously shy.

'You are ill, Eleanor?' Stefan now broke in.

'No, no, we were just joking,' said Eleanor, meeting his gaze for the first time that evening and finding it typically acute. He'd been eyeing her again throughout the meal. Did he suspect Katharina had confided in her? Or Nathalie, for that matter? God, how had she managed to get entangled in this family's affairs?

Sophie broke away from Katharina and nudged Eleanor from the left. 'Any luck?'

'What d'you mean?'

'You know, with Lewis?'

'No,' hissed Eleanor. 'We're not interested in each other.'

'Yeah, right. You must think we were born yesterday.'

Eleanor rolled her eyes.

'And did I hear you talking about Will?' Sophie asked. 'Is there any news?'

'No, no, just that I feel I'm finally getting over the whole thing. Being here has definitely done me some good.'

'Superb news!' Sophie exclaimed. 'Though I'm not surprised, Panarea's like therapy, don't you think? How could anyone be gloomy here for long? No, with you here and him back in dreary old Blighty, you've definitely got the better deal. It's rained there every day, you know? You should pity him.'

Unable to think of an answer to this, Eleanor turned briefly away. It was much quieter in the dining hall, just four of the Italian guests staying on, most having left on the afternoon boat. It was now officially low season. Eleanor couldn't believe she'd been in Panarea a whole week, that she planned to leave in the morning and might never see these people again. She could barely remember her London life, the flat in Clapham, the low, white sky. It was almost that time of year when it was dark by the time you left the office.

'So when's everyone going home?' Tim asked, as though reading her mind. Only he seemed to be drinking as ferociously as ever that evening.

'Wednesday,' said Katharina. Eleanor didn't envy her that particular homecoming, what with her dying marriage and whatever Nathalie-related traumas lay ahead. For the first time in three months she had a sense of her own broken relationship belonging to the past, not the present, overtaken by the real, current dilemmas faced by other people.

'Tuesday for me,' she lied. 'How about you, Lewis?' She imagined them leaving the island together on that clapped-out hydrofoil, he reassuring her about the currents.

'Not sure yet,' he said. 'I've got an open ticket for Naples. I thought I might hang on till next weekend. I haven't done as much work as I planned and I fancy doing the Stromboli night climb.'

'My, you must be fit,' said Sophie, flirtatiously. 'Isn't that like a four-hour hike or something?'

'Something like that, and in the dark, as well.'

'I heard a woman got hit on the head by a big chunk of rock and had to be choppered to the mainland,' Tim put in, helpfully.

'I heard that, too,' said Lewis. 'I'm sure it'll be OK, though. I mean, it's got to be worth it. Just imagine standing at the lip of an active volcano – it must feel like you're looking down into the bowels of hell.'

There was a moment of collective awe.

'Rather you than me,' Tim said.

Eleanor excused herself early and spent some time in her room going over her plan. There was no other way of leaving the hotel than through the bar, but she felt confident that in an hour or so Tim and the others would have left for drinks in the harbour. As for Will, she had no idea how long wedding receptions went on for in the Aeolians – possibly until the early hours, maybe even all weekend. The perfect scenario would be that he had returned alone, perhaps weary of the Italian chatter he didn't understand, and had gone to sit outside on the terrace. Then she could finally have a moment or two alone with him, just looking at him. He'd never need know she'd been and gone. She felt she deserved that.

At eleven o'clock she slipped downstairs, torch, monocular and camera in the front pocket of her fleece, and paused before entering the bar. If challenged she planned to say she was getting cigarettes from the machine outside the *tabacchieri* – everyone knew that was the only place on the island you could buy them. But luckily the bar was unusually quiet, with just the two Italian couples drinking coffee in the corner and watching TV.

Exiting the hotel into the lane, she began hurrying towards the turning to Iditella, but almost at once a broad figure sprang out of nowhere and blocked her path. She smelled warm, sour breath inches from her face and felt no alarm, just impatience.

'Stefan, what *are* you doing?'

He moved forward and forced her back against the wall, placing a muscular arm on either side of her shoulders as though holding her in some kind of wrestling lock. To her horror he then pushed his face against hers. His chin felt bristly, the cheek warm and greasy.

'Leave me alone!' She wriggled and tried to duck under his right arm, but he reacted in a flash, pressing his whole body flatly against her, almost crushing her. She could feel her camera and torch digging painfully into her ribs.

'What are you doing? You're hurting me, you nutter!'

'You are very, very sexy girl.' His lips, slippery and repulsive, were now sliding about on top of hers, and to her disgust a stout tongue inserted itself into her mouth and began moving around in a circular motion.

'Urggghh! Get off, I can't breathe!'

He muttered something in German and began gnawing at her throat, his long hair tickling her face. With a gigantic effort she managed finally to dislodge his body and duck away, stumbling briefly before scuttling back to the hotel gate. With the safety of distance came brief, hot anger.

'Get lost! What did you think you were doing, Stefan? Are you mad?' She wished she had the strength to bundle him to the ground and kick him in the crotch.

He was skulking against the wall, eyes narrowed to tiny raisins.

'You are not liking me?'

'No, no, I am not liking you, you . . . great beast!

262

Don't dare touch me again or I'll call the *carabinieri*, OK? *Polizei*. I will call. I mean it!'

He didn't respond and she felt reluctant to march past him up the unlit lane in case he grabbed her again. She considered calling for Giovanna, but quite what assistance she'd be able to offer once she'd trailed out to join them Eleanor wasn't sure. She was intent on seeing through her plan. 'I'm going up there. Don't follow me or I swear I'll get the police.'

She stormed off without looking back, then waited around the corner to listen for his footsteps. Soon she heard his tread receding down the lane. She could make no sense of the encounter as she hurried up the lane to Iditella, torchlight bouncing ahead of her, but could only marvel at how swiftly she was able to shake it off. She prayed it was the last she would see or hear of Stefan until she was safely aboard the hydrofoil on her way home tomorrow. Gradually, as she walked on, she forgot about him, for the path was more demanding in the dark; it seemed longer, more twisting, and she needed to concentrate on every step.

Frannie's voice reached her first: louder, raspier than usual – it sounded very drunk to her sober ear.

'. . . So amusing to sit through the whole thing and not understand a word, though I s'pose it's easy enough to guess, it is a bloody wedding! You should have seen his face, it was hysterical.'

Loud laughter followed; it sounded like several people.

Then Frannie again: 'Or maybe you were thinking about how close you came to being joined in holy matrimony yourself?'

'Don't remind me,' came Will's voice.

'Aww, why not? I love this story, it's great fun!'

Eleanor stopped in her tracks. They must be talking about her. What fortunate – or unfortunate – timing.

'Go on, tell us! You down on one knee, the Empire State Building, her left high and dry – hey, I made a joke, did you get it . . .?'

'I've never seen you this hammered, Fran, it's hilarious. Hey, I thought I heard something in the lane. What was that?'

'Maybe it's that crazy German lady again, hurrah!' Frannie squealed. 'Just chuck some old figs down, that's all she wants! There's some in the fruit bowl, I think . . .'

There was another round of laughter at this and Eleanor took the opportunity to tiptoe past the villa and up the lane until she reached the house beyond Katharina's fig tree. There she was able to sit on the wall and peer through the branches at Frannie's terrace lit up in the darkness below.

There were three figures sitting around the little table, which was crowded with glasses, empty wine bottles and triangular saucers filled with cigarette butts.

On the inside of the open back door, which Eleanor now saw led to a whitewashed living room, hung a pair of flippers and a snorkel. Frannie was still in her blue dress from the wedding, skirt ridden up over her glossy brown thighs, one strap down to her elbow and the scarf draped over her seatback. Will was opposite her, now in denim shorts and a shirt, hair tousled, face grimacing with laughter.

The third figure was Lewis.

Eleanor went rigid with shock. How on earth had this friendship developed so quickly? Clearly she was not Frannie's only new friend. She gazed in bewilderment as he poured the last of a bottle of wine into the various glasses, saying something to the others as it dribbled empty. He looked perfectly at home, certainly not the polite visitor waiting for his glass to be refilled by the host.

Eleanor strained to hear the conversation but, other than Frannie's dominating ring of laughter, failed. She eased herself several feet along the wall towards the group, at which point all voices seemed to rise together at once. She heard Lewis calling out, 'Claudio? Claudio?', followed by a question in Italian.

Eleanor cursed her lack of the language. Who was Claudio? Wasn't that the name of Rita's boyfriend, she thought, racking her brain. No, that was Enso or Emilio or something with an 'E', she was sure.

Suddenly the silhouette of a fourth figure appeared

in the doorway on to the terrace, and a new voice responded to Lewis's question – Eleanor couldn't hear the words to know if it was English or Italian. She couldn't have been more surprised if Stefan had swaggered into view: it was her lover of the previous night. He went to stand behind Frannie, idly stroking her hair, while Will and Lewis looked on in approval, even admiration.

Now Will's voice carried crisply across the air. 'Well, won't the bars sell us some? What time does that little shop close again, Fran?'

'God, hours ago. There's the steak restaurant down the road, you could try there?' Frannie turned to look up at the man behind her. 'Hey, what about your place?'

Now the man was nodding and Will was standing up. 'I'll walk with you if you like, Claudio, I need to stretch my legs.'

'*Eccellente!*' cried Frannie. 'See you in a bit. Bring as many bottles as you can carry – I don't want to go to bed at all tonight!' She threw her arms above her head and shrieked with excitement. The scarf floated to the ground. Will and the man disappeared into the house and then, seconds later, reappeared in the lane and wandered off in the direction of San Pietro.

Eleanor returned her gaze to the terrace. Frannie was on her feet now, standing against the far wall, staring out into the darkness. Eleanor realised she must be looking at Stromboli. Lewis swirled the end of his wine around in the glass and poured it into his mouth in one gulp, then stood up and went to join Frannie. To Eleanor's amazement, he put his arm around Frannie's waist and she responded by threading her arm neatly through his and around his hips. Suddenly they were hugging, facing each other and smiling, practically nose to nose as he stooped forwards and she tipped her head back as though expecting to be kissed.

'So how long will it take them to get to Claudio's?' Lewis asked.

'About ten or fifteen minutes. They won't be back for at least twenty minutes, longer if they stop for one on the way. Hope they bring loads of lovely booze. I want Limoncello!'

Lewis chuckled. 'What is it with women and Limoncello?'

'How d'you mean, babe?'

All at once Eleanor's bottom leapt about a foot in the air at the sound of a dog's bark from behind her – it was coming from inside the nearby house, couldn't be more than five feet away. Then came a shout in Italian. Slithering off the wall, she felt her way back down the lane towards Frannie's villa as fast as she dared without using her torch. She knew the darkness hid her totally; so long as she was silent she was safe. Presently, the dog lost interest and she could hear Frannie and Lewis again loud and clear.

'It's that ridic'lous mutt next door to Rita's,' Frannie

said, slurring slightly. 'It's the size of a ferret but you'd think it was one of those giant ones the way it barks, what are they called, you know, the ones like small donkeys?'

'A Great Dane?' Lewis's voice was quieter, full of fond indulgence.

'You're so clever, Lewis, clever, clever, clever boy.' Then, 'You know what? Rebecca's a very lucky lady.' This was followed by hysterical cackles from Frannie and a snort from Lewis.

'Thanks, darling, I'll send her your regards.'

'I'll probably see her before you do,' said Frannie. 'I've got Sarah's wedding in November and Becky's one of the bridesmaids.'

'Then you'll have to send her *my* regards.' They both laughed again.

'Well, you're a very bad boyfriend, that's all I can say. Bad creature.'

'Not that you'd have anything to do with that, of course.'

Frannie now seemed to be close to hysteria, her voice bubbling up one second, muffled the next. She must have her head against his chest, Eleanor guessed.

'Oops, careful,' Lewis said. 'You almost fell.' How happy he sounded. Their banter reminded Eleanor of the trip to Vulcano, now a lifetime ago. The closeness she'd felt to him that day must have been some kind of illusion.

She tuned back in. 'What's Claudio's place like?' Lewis was asking.

'Oh, it's gorgeous, loads bigger than here, I'll show you before you go. Lots of pretty pots everywhere – you'd love it. Oh, I forgot! He's got a new Vespa this time, so I bet they'll come back on that. I'm dying to have a go!'

At this information, Eleanor was torn. She longed to continue eavesdropping, was morbidly rooted to the spot, but if she left her return too late she'd bump into Will and the man, Claudio, on their way back here. There was, after all, only that one path for them to take. She imagined them running into her on their bike, rushing to check she was still breathing, only to discover that each knew the victim better than the other realised . . .

She shivered. She really needed to leave now if total and irrecoverable humiliation was to be averted. Slowly, soundlessly, she started moving away.

Lying in bed, eyes closed, she grappled with what she'd seen and heard. Exactly how many of that strange little gathering was Frannie sleeping with? Clearly not just Will, but Lewis too, very possibly, and perhaps even Claudio as well – he'd been openly petting her. Was this normal holiday behaviour for Italians? Had Will agreed to some sort of open relationship?

And how did Frannie know Lewis's girlfriend? Was

it one of those 'small world' discoveries that people made on holiday and insisted on boring their friends with back home, when the coincidence never seemed quite so extraordinary after all? Presumably, with all the talk of weddings, they'd realised they'd been invited to the same event in England, had distant friends in common. But why had they spoken about Rebecca as though Lewis wouldn't be seeing her for months? It sounded as though she lived in another part of the country. It didn't make sense.

Frannie had obviously got very close to Lewis very quickly, in which case shouldn't Will be feeling suspicious or threatened? Eleanor knew that wasn't his style, he'd never behaved jealously with her, though she'd given no good reason for it, whereas Frannie had flaunted her intimacy with other men right in front of his eyes. 'They won't be back for at least twenty minutes' – that's what she'd said to Lewis, the implication surely being that this was long enough for the two of them to enjoy some time alone together. Her dress had practically been falling off her shoulders; his mouth had been just inches from making contact with her bare skin.

Eleanor felt the old heaviness refill her ribcage.

She hadn't liked that reference to Will's lucky escape from marriage, had liked even less the idea of them all talking into the night, each with secrets to share about her. Will might tell Lewis some unflattering anecdotes of life with his ex – there were some episodes, she knew, that wouldn't present her at all well – and Lewis might prompt a tale out of curiosity, might even let slip that he'd come across just such a spurned lover in his hotel here in Panarea. And that was even before this loose cannon Claudio got involved in the conversation.

She turned off the light and tried to ignore the buzz of a mosquito that had adopted some kind of holding pattern in the air above her face. But there was something more serious to fend off: a livid new jealousy that had been rearing up inside her since she made her way back to the hotel from Casa Salina. It was a jealousy of Frannie, of course, but no longer that provoked by Frannie's possession of Will, nor even by her connection with the mystery lover.

What she could not bear was what Frannie had with Lewis.

Chapter 17

Eleanor was dreaming she was being pulled out of a strong current, roughly scooped to safety. But when she looked down at the water it was only a narrow canal, the water was beautifully still and so clear she could see right down to the bottom.

She heard a wail; it sounded like someone in agony. She wasn't sure where it had come from, she couldn't see anyone but herself. Then a different, more familiar voice floated up from below the surface of the water. 'Yes, double four six seven, that's our landline number. Eleanor, wake up! Can you hear me? Yes, female, and she's thirty.'

She felt her wrist being prodded, then the voice again, rising. 'She's not conscious, but I'm pretty sure she's breathing. Hang on, she seems to be snoring!'

She eased open her eyes and was startled to make out the half-dressed figure of Miranda by her bed, hopping about frantically and talking into the phone:

'What shall I do? What? Yes, I'll just check. It says "Tem . . . temazepam, 12 tablets, 20mg" . . .'

'What's going on, has something happened?' Eleanor's voice was a rudely awakened croak – she needed to get some water.

'Eleanor, thank God! She's gaining consciousness, I think. What should I do now? Will she need her stomach pumped?'

'Miranda, who are you talking to?'

'Eleanor,' Miranda replied, speaking slowly and clearly. 'How many of these pills have you taken?'

'What pills?'

'These ones. It's really important you tell me.'

Eleanor looked at the little brown bottle Miranda was holding in front of her face.

'Just one,' she said. 'They're sleeping pills. They help me sleep,' she added, unnecessarily. She saw that Miranda had tears streaming down her cheeks.

'She says just one,' Miranda repeated into the phone. Eleanor began to have an idea of what might be happening here. She sat up and grabbed the phone from Miranda's ear.

'Hello, can I help? Yes, my name's Eleanor Blake and I'm absolutely fine. I've just woken up. I think there's been a misunderstanding on the part of my flatmate. OK, of course . . .'

Ringing off, she turned back to Miranda. 'Right, I think you'd better explain what you were doing calling 999.'

'But, Eleanor, the bottle's empty, I assumed you'd taken the whole lot!'

'There was only one left, you idiot. They have to run out at some point! You know I've had trouble getting any sleep since Will left.'

'I thought you'd . . .' Miranda trailed off, still weeping. 'I couldn't wake you up, you seemed, like, comatose.'

'Well you couldn't have tried very hard! I was just fast asleep, like any normal sleeping person. For God's sake, you've completely wasted their time, it's people like you who clog up the system with crank calls!'

'Well it's better to be safe than sorry,' Miranda snuffled, sitting on the edge of the bed.

Eleanor tried to get a grip on her temper. She was less surprised by this episode than she might have been; Miranda relished a 'situation', it was just like her to jump to conclusions, typically the more colourful the better.

'And I saw the empty wine bottle in the kitchen, as well,' Miranda said, defensive now.

'Oh, for Christ's sake, we've got empty wine bottles in the kitchen every day of the year – there'd be more cause for alarm if there weren't any! You're just being a drama queen. Why on earth would I want to take an overdose?'

'Because . . . well, you know.'

Because she was a hopeless reject whose life wasn't worth living, presumably.

'You've seemed so down this week,' Miranda said.

'I just thought, you know, when I saw the bottle by your bed . . . It's almost like I've been expecting you to do something to yourself, something like this . . .'

'Well, thank you for your faith in me! And why were you trying to wake me, anyway? I'd have woken up in an hour or two. It's Saturday. Whatever happened to a lie-in?' Eleanor pulled herself out of bed and checked the clock with a groan: 8.30.

'The phone wouldn't stop ringing. It was for you, it was Will. I came to get you.'

'Why was he phoning so early?' Great, Eleanor thought, now Will would know about this bogus suicide bid – that was all she needed. She felt like wringing the girl's neck.

'Something about his passport, but he's on his way over now. Eleanor, I'm so sorry . . .'

Eleanor interrupted her. 'Right, I'll call him and explain. You go and put the kettle on, and try to manage it without involving the emergency services, OK?'

'OK.' Miranda looked thoroughly distraught, her face was blotchy and her eyelashes caked together with last night's mascara. She looked as though she was the one who needed a paramedic. Eleanor sighed. She was a bit dense, but she meant well.

'And let's keep this to ourselves,' Eleanor said, more gently. 'I appreciate you're worried about me, but there's really no need. I may look like the living dead, but I am not suicidal.'

Miranda trotted off, wiping her eyes. Not for the first time, Eleanor felt she was living with a small child.

She reached for her mobile phone and dialled. 'Hi, Will? No, I'm absolutely fine. Look, I think Miranda might have given you the wrong idea . . .'

She woke early on Sunday and decided to get straight on with packing. She'd been in Panarea eight nights, stayed in her hotel for just seven, but she felt a stronger attachment to the little tiled room than anywhere else in the world. She folded the new green dress carefully, even though it would need to go to the dry-cleaners before it could be worn again: there was a pale-purple scar from spilled wine and another larger, rust-coloured one from pasta sauce or blood from her scraped knee.

After some consideration she decided to leave the monocular behind. She wouldn't be needing it any more, she'd had her fill of watching people too closely. Last night's tableau popped into her head again – the four faces, each separately familiar, separately powerful, somehow magnified beyond comprehension by their coming together. She was ready to leave.

But when she went down to reception to explain that she wanted to check out two days early, Giovanna exclaimed dramatically: 'No *aliscafi*, bad sea. Dangerous.'

Eleanor groaned. Frannie had warned her about this. She wondered if it happened to be the day that the big ferry came. It was three times as slow, but she'd at least be able to get on her way. But she didn't want to end up in Naples or detour to some other port she didn't know; her flight home was from Palermo and she'd have to buy a new ticket if she flew from anywhere else. She couldn't go on for much longer ignoring the financial damage of this little adventure.

'Thank you,' she said to Giovanna. 'Then I suppose I'll check out tomorrow, instead.'

'You ees unhappy? Not like Panarea, thees 'otel?'

It hadn't occurred to her that Giovanna might be offended by an early departure. 'No, I like the hotel and the island very much. I just need to get back to England a bit earlier than planned. Something's come up.'

'You waits and boat comes,' Giovanna reassured her, as if that were that.

Eleanor was deeply frustrated by this turn of events. For the first time she felt a powerful need to get away from Will rather than run to him, but here she was, forced to remain in his orbit after all. Suddenly, the idea of him being less than a mile away, embroiled in his strange love triangle with Frannie and Lewis, not to mention the mystery man Claudio, seemed appalling. And it was absolutely no business of hers. For the first time she saw herself as the half-crazy voyeur she supposed she must have been all along.

It was early and people were starting to appear for breakfast. She remembered Stefan's strike the night before and groaned again. It seemed there were now more people she wanted to avoid than those she didn't.

She hurried down to the harbour, to the offices of the hydrofoil operators, where scribbled notices confirmed that all morning services had been cancelled. There was an expectant buzz; this was probably as big as news got in Panarea. The cafés were already overflowing with people waiting for updates, their luggage propped in a neat row against the wall like a line of well-behaved infants. Everyone was looking up at the sky and out to sea, then turning to one another to speculate on the situation, raising their voices over the slam of the water, then looking out to sea hopefully, as though the weather might have brightened in the few seconds they'd looked away.

Eleanor looked, too. The slate-coloured sea was sloshing up wildly; the sky had the appearance of polished grey marble. Above and all around was an uneasy monochromatic version of the usual palette. Even the air felt thick and gloomy. It was strange to view Panarea without its usual shimmer. She felt an irresistible craving for coffee and a huge glass of water and decided to risk a public breakfast. Will and the others had clearly been set for a late-night spree when she'd seen them, they couldn't possibly be up yet. In any case, there were too many players in the game now and she no longer had the energy for strategy.

She ordered coffee and glanced around the café terrace. As usual, the beautiful crowd sat apart from the foreign tourists, prowling in parallel like big cats cohabiting naturally enough with the weaker creatures, lacking appetite for the attack. Eleanor barely noticed them any more.

She was gulping down her third coffee when she noticed Tim and Sophie weaving their way through the terrace towards her. She felt absurdly pleased to see them, as much for who they weren't as who they were.

'Giovanna said you were leaving early!' cried Sophie. 'We wanted to say goodbye.' She sat down, looking tired round the eyes but otherwise just as bright as ever. Tim squinted at Eleanor with sore, bloodshot eyes. He looked dreadful, skin slack at the jawline and deeply creased round the mouth.

'You're such an early riser,' remarked Sophie. 'Very good move to take a day off the booze yesterday. So why are you heading off early? You didn't say anything last night.'

'Oh, I've got a friend who needs me back home,' said Eleanor. 'She's having a bit of a crisis. But I can't leave Panarea today, anyway, so it looks like I'm staying.' She explained the situation with the weather as the waitress hovered for their order. Tim just muttered '*Birra*', allowing Sophie to take over with the specifics.

'Not sure one hair of the dog is enough for you, darling,' she laughed, tweaking his earlobe. 'You need the whole coat.'

'Hmm,' Tim growled. Eleanor smiled. She felt like

Sophie and Tim were her best friends in the world.

'Bugger it, shall we have a beer, too?' Sophie asked Eleanor. 'What about one of those beer and lemon *granita* thingies?'

'Lovely,' Eleanor agreed, with pathetic ease.

The drink was icy and delicious, sending a welcome shot of coolness through her whole body. Sophie leant back, stretched and began her customary chatter. That was soothing, too.

'They always walk in single file, don't they,' she remarked, turning her eye on a line of backpackers marching down the jetty. 'Something about that heavy pack must make them feel all military.' She started reminiscing about her own student travel. 'I just remember this huge thing squeaking along behind me, it was like having a Siamese twin.'

'What, your boyfriend?' Tim asked.

'No, you fool, my backpack!' Sophie winked at Eleanor. 'Can you believe he's still jealous of boyfriends from twenty years ago?'

They were all giggling, Tim also coughing painfully. He must have been on the cigars again, thought Eleanor.

'I've never been backpacking,' she said. 'I just couldn't bear the thought of dragging all those smelly socks around and never having enough clean underwear.'

'Very wise,' said Sophie. 'I remember we kept running out of clean knickers and there was one place, in Prague

I think, where they barely had plumbing, let alone a launderette, so we just fished out our dirty knickers and wore them inside out. I can't believe I have so little pride I'm willing to share this information!'

'Should have just gone commando,' suggested Tim, finding his voice again. Sophie just flapped a napkin around his ears as though swatting a fly.

'What time is it? God, we're supposed to be keeping an eye on Nathalie this afternoon.' She sighed. 'Katharina came and asked us at breakfast. She and Stefan want to spend some time together, amazingly.'

'Why does she need looking after?' Eleanor asked, knowing precisely why, even if no one else did.

'The older you are, the more trouble you can get into, I suppose. I couldn't really refuse, Katharina was so grateful, but I don't relish the idea of entertaining that little madam, I can tell you. She looks at me as if I've just crawled out from under a stone – she's friendlier to the geckoes.'

'A girl with tits that pert doesn't need charm as well,' said Tim. He'd perked up noticeably.

'Well, what do you expect?' Sophie laughed. 'She's only had them a couple of years. Gravity hasn't had a hand yet.'

Unlike Carlo, thought Eleanor. She realised they were on their second round of the iced shandy drinks and she suddenly felt a stab of reality – it was almost lunchtime, and who knew who might appear for a drink. What about Will, Frannie and Claudio? She imagined them strolling down arm-in-arm, Frannie the queen bee in the middle. Where did that leave Lewis? Bringing up the rear?

The harbour was packed; she'd never seen so many people down there; hotel karts were still delivering guests and luggage, presumably hoping the early afternoon hydrofoil to Stromboli would be operating. But no services had been announced yet. Her longing to escape returned with a physical punch.

'I was thinking I might walk up to Punta del Corvo and take some photos,' she said to Tim and Sophie.

'Punta del what?' Tim asked.

'The peak at the top of the island. It's only supposed to be a two-hour walk. D'you fancy it?' If she couldn't get off dry land then climbing as high as possible seemed the only bearable option.

'Well, it does look a bit clearer now,' said Sophie looking up at the sky again. It was a luminous, unearthly white. 'I would come, Eleanor, but all I want to do is read. Read a book from cover to cover with no interruptions. I don't think I've done that once since Rory. But you go, Tim, it'll get rid of your headache.'

'Not a bad idea,' said Tim. 'I could do with a bit of exercise of the non-horizontal variety.' As he and Sophie giggled and gurgled at one another, Eleanor wondered what it was about the island that seemed to bring sex fizzing to the surface. She flushed slightly at the thought of her own recent encounter.

'What about Nathalie?' she asked. 'We could see if she wants to come on the walk?'

'Oh, Eleanor, that would be wonderful,' said Sophie, beaming gratefully. 'I could really do without her sulky face every time I look up.'

'Where is she, anyway?'

'Presumably still at the hotel,' said Tim. 'Let's finish these, head up there and get sorted.'

But before they could get to their feet, Eleanor's body froze at the sound of a familiar voice, exactly as she'd dreaded: 'Jane! Jane! Over here!'

It was Frannie. She couldn't turn, felt certain of what was coming next, could already hear Will's voice in her head, the amazement in his cry – 'Eleanor! What are you doing here?' – like a terrible line from one of his own melodramas. Her breath quickened; it tasted thin and sour in her mouth. Here it was, then, the calamitous denouement she'd brought upon herself.

'Eleanor, is that girl talking to you?' asked Sophie, puzzled. Eleanor tried to slide a look to the left without turning her head. There it was, the unmistakable sexy bounce of Frannie, gorgeous in a tiny red dress, with huge dark glasses over her face, her hair falling down her back like a sheet of black lacquer.

Eleanor felt her heart catch as she saw who Frannie was with: not Will, but Claudio, her lover of Friday night. Thankfully he wasn't looking her way, but had turned to greet a tableful of people at the next café. Nearby tourists waiting around for the hydrofoils looked up at the noisy cries, no doubt speculating as to the identity of this man who was causing such a stir. He looked like he might be a more glamorous Cabinet minister or film producer. He struck Eleanor as being far more sanguine than she remembered, nowhere near as grave and intense. She watched as he was persuaded to take a seat, was practically pushed down into it, his back square to where she sat with Tim and Sophie.

'Who is she?' asked Sophie, curiously, still looking Frannie up and down. 'Why's she calling you Jane? Does she think you're someone else?'

'Oh, we met the other day,' said Eleanor as casually as she could manage. 'She got the wrong end of the stick about my name.'

'Absolute stunner,' said Tim in open admiration, and for the first time Eleanor thought she saw a flicker of disapproval on Sophie's face.

'I've seen her around, isn't she some sort of famous celeb?'

'She's an actress,' said Eleanor. 'Not at all famous, though, as far as I know.'

'Who's the silver fox?' asked Sophie. 'Looks a bit old for her, doesn't he? Sexy devil, though.'

'Yes,' Eleanor agreed, faintly.

Now Frannie was gliding over, all smiles and hellos, pulling off her glasses and tucking them in a tiny straw bag embroidered with flowers. There was not a trace of hangover in her face: she looked like a 1950s movie star, with her velvety orange lipstick and eyelashes batting down at them, like a young Sophia Loren flirting with her fans.

Praying the man would stay safely in his seat, Eleanor tried to concentrate on the introductions to hand. 'This is Frannie,' she said, barely hearing her own voice as she worked frantically on an escape plan in her head. 'Frannie, this is Tim and Sophie; they're also staying at the Albergo delle Rose.'

'Lovely to meet you,' said Frannie, holding out her hand and immediately taking control of the situation. Tim was flushed and gaping, Sophie smiling but glacial. 'You know, I'm sure I've seen you two down here before. Are you having a lovely holiday? It's very clever of you to have found Panarea. The English don't usually get this far.'

She was like royalty, thought Eleanor, Panarea's homecoming queen. Tim looked content as a royal lapdog being petted by his mistress.

'Sorry I couldn't meet for a coffee yesterday, Jane,' she said, swivelling her wide-eyed beam back to Eleanor. 'There's been a big wedding up in Iditella, I think I mentioned it, and, anyway, my father turned up unexpectedly in the morning.'

'Yes, we heard about the wedding,' put in Sophie. 'It was beautiful, by all accounts.'

Eleanor had gone limp. 'Your father?'

'Yes, he's just over there. You must meet him. It's just a flying visit for the wedding, we didn't think he was going to be able to make it. But he's off again this evening.'

'Your father,' Eleanor repeated, weakly.

Frannie smiled at her indulgently. 'Let me introduce you, I'll grab him.' She turned to frown over at the man – her father – who was still deep in conversation and now sipping at a shot of coffee, and threw up her arms with a theatrical shrug. 'Oh, he's ignoring me, of course, I'll never prise him away. It's always like this when he comes back.' It occurred to Eleanor that he may have spotted her, too, and was deliberately allowing himself to be waylaid to avoid an embarrassing meeting with her, the random English girl he'd picked up.

'No, no problem,' Eleanor cried, struggling to cover up her agitation. 'We were just about to head off, anyway. Weren't we, Tim?'

'Yes.' To her immense gratitude Tim sprang to his feet, still eyeing Frannie, and adopted a more athletic posture than usual, shoulders back and chin high. 'We're going for a walk. Miserable day, there's nothing else to do.'

'I know,' said Frannie, turning to him. 'We'd been planning a boat trip out to Salina later this afternoon, but not with those currents. You know the hydrofoil from Lipari tried to get here but had to turn back? We're all trapped. It's like an Agatha Christie – maybe there'll be a murder!'

Thank God for the weather, thought Eleanor, and the endless discussions about it that helped one avoid more delicate conversations. She backed away from the table, hand reaching for Tim's arm. 'C'mon, Tim.' Her voice sounded more urgent than she'd intended and she saw his look of bafflement.

'You guys head off,' said Sophie, coolly. 'I'll sort out the bill.' She turned back to Frannie. 'Would you and your father like to join me for a drink?'

'That's so sweet of you, thank you, but we're heading for lunch in a minute. More of Dad's chums to meet with.' Frannie named the smart restaurant near the *tabacchieri* and Eleanor made a mental note to avoid it on their route up to Punta del Corvo.

'Bye, Sophie, bye, Frannie, see you later,' said Eleanor. As she hurried away, she could faintly hear Sophie's voice. 'Do you know, I think we saw you at the Wyndham in *A Woman of No Importance* . . .'

'Kept that one to yourself,' said Tim, admiringly, as they walked up the lane. Eleanor didn't dare look over her shoulder.

'She is very beautiful,' agreed Eleanor.

'And the body – not often you get a face like that with a killer body. Those tits are for real, as well.'

'She's clever, too,' Eleanor said, in mock disappointment, but she felt temporarily elated. She'd escaped. If she could just lie low – or high – for the rest of the day, then she'd be off the island in the morning without coming face to face with either Will or Frannie's father. She rubbed her eyes and blinked. Frannie's father. She couldn't quite pinpoint her reaction. Relief that he wasn't just another of Frannie's admirers? Shame that Frannie, Will and Lewis might find out about the liaison? (She couldn't imagine any reason for them to be impressed by it, particularly not Frannie.) Maybe a smidgeon of pride at her conquest, too, for he was no less attractive in the light of day.

Discovering his identity did reinforce one thing very powerfully, however: her instinct to flee.

'Let's get Nathalie and head off straight away,' she said with determination.

Tim followed like a lamb.

Chapter 18

They found Nathalie reading a copy of Italian *Vogue* in the bar. She looked up with sullen resignation, her long hair fanned out over her shoulders, like Rapunzel.

'But where is Sophie?' she asked, sharply, as though suspecting some sort of plot. The wicked witch had met her match here.

'She's not coming, it's just us,' Tim said.

Having expected the girl to refuse to join them, Eleanor was surprised to see her accept her fate and begin strapping on her all-terrain sandals, huge and chunky below her delicate ankles and calves. 'Do you want to cover your legs, Nathalie?' she asked, feeling like a fussy maiden aunt. 'There's a lot of gorse on the path up – you might get scratched. I'm going to change into jeans.'

Nathalie just shrugged and pouted, reminding Eleanor of Katharina in the thermal pool. They were more alike than she'd noticed. She felt a stab of pity for the girl and the news that awaited her in Cologne. 'I'm sure you'll be fine like that,' she said, more warmly.

'Have we got enough water?' asked Tim, suddenly brisk and authoritative. 'And some high-energy snack foods?'

'It's not the Inca Trail, Tim,' laughed Eleanor. 'We'll only be a couple of hours – I think we'll cope without the Kendal Mint Cake.'

'If you say so.'

They headed off, Nathalie striding ahead, her slim legs dancing effortlessly up the steep path. Eleanor regretted the beers in the café as she felt the liquid sloshing round in her stomach. She vowed to cut down on the alcohol and cigarettes when she got back to London, to make a healthy start. She felt pleased with herself for viewing her return in a positive light; only days ago she'd dreaded the thought of going home, didn't feel she even had one any more in that sad, Will-free flat.

'Have you ever thought about giving up drinking?' she asked Tim, then realised that out of context the query sounded far more judgemental than she'd intended. His hoot of laughter told her she couldn't have come up with a more outlandish suggestion if she'd urged him to join a mass suicide cult on the dark side of the moon.

'Mother's milk, my dear, mother's milk,' he said jovially. 'It would be unnatural to stop sucking. Jesus, this hill's starting to feel like bloody Everest, isn't it?'

'I wish she wouldn't go so fast,' agreed Eleanor. They hadn't even reached the edge of the village and they were already puffing, but Nathalie was way ahead, streaking forward through the silvery gorse, hair flying. She looked frail against the thick fists of rock and stocky Indian figs. Once again, Eleanor was reminded of a fashion shoot.

'She's so attractive, isn't she?' she said to Tim. 'Not carrying an ounce of extra weight.'

'Oh, she'll be a fat old frau like her mother soon enough.'

Eleanor thought this was unfair. 'But Katharina's obviously attractive to some men,' she protested. 'After all, she's leaving Stefan for another man.'

'Oh is she indeed?' Tim hooted again and Eleanor was grateful Nathalie was safely out of earshot.

'Nathalie doesn't know,' she said hurriedly. 'Please don't mention it to her.'

'Can't say he'd be bothered,' said Tim. 'They obviously loathe each other. Probably on the lookout himself.'

Eleanor paused. 'Well, between you and me, Stefan did make a pass at me last night.'

'*Did* he? What happened?' Tim looked so amazed, Eleanor felt slightly offended.

'Oh, he was drunk, pressed me against the wall and tried to snog me, kept muttering at me. You know, German lovetalk.' She giggled.

'Surely that's a contradiction in terms,' smirked Tim. 'So what happened?'

'I just pushed him away and ran off.'

Tim let out a rattle of laughter and Eleanor saw Nathalie's head turn and look down at them.

'Shush, Tim, the poor girl doesn't know anything. Keep it to yourself.'

'Understood. God, let's take a break,' Tim said. 'No hurry, is there?'

They'd only been going half an hour, but both glugged heavily from the water bottle and surveyed the island below. The boats that had ventured out on to the shadowed sea were like motorised toys on a park lake, the houses tiny white blocks on an architect's scale model – their squat white chimneys looked like miniature snowmen. Eleanor searched for the villa where she'd spent the night with Claudio, but couldn't be sure which it was, they all looked too similar. She could just make out the church in Iditella, though, a lovely confection in the distance, its ceramic spots like chocolate buttons.

They set off again. The trail soon began to get more overgrown with gorse and other, unidentifiable, spiky plants that pricked savagely at their legs and arms. The dusty grey volcanic earth mixed underfoot with dried-up purple and brown leaves, a reminder that summer was close to its end. The route to the top was marked sporadically with dabs of paint, they discovered, so they were confident they were on the right path. However, it seemed to Eleanor that every time they reached a new splash of colour, the summit was just as far away as ever.

'God, what have you got us into? It looked so near from the village,' Tim complained, his face now very red and sweaty. 'We're nowhere near the top.'

Eleanor was enjoying it, though. She liked the intense concentration required to move one foot securely in front of the other, to find a solid rock or dried cake of earth, avoiding the bushes and cactus ears. It left no room in her head for Will and Lewis and the others.

On they went. There was no sign of Nathalie now, even when they reached a long, steep stretch where they needed to use their hands as well as their legs to push themselves up. After several minutes of this, they reached some kind of ruined hut, an old shepherd's shelter, perhaps, little more than a collection of old stones, which made Eleanor think of the Bronze Age ruins. Here, she and Tim took another break and wondered if they'd strayed off the path, but a faded daub of red ahead told them they were still on course.

The track got steeper and spikier still, and it was only after Eleanor's arms and neck had started to itch badly that they finally reached the top. They were both panting very heavily.

'Long bloody last,' said Tim. 'Remind me never to

go for a quick stroll with you again, mate. God, Sophie's well out of this.'

'Oh, come on, it's worth it, it's fantastic exercise,' Eleanor said, barely convincing herself. 'It counteracts the boozing, anyway.'

'Counteracts the will to live,' Tim said.

Nathalie was still nowhere to be seen. Instead, they were greeted with an alarming sight, for the sky in front of them was the colour of toxic smoke and a particularly impenetrable blotch had reduced the sun to a pale pinpoint. Below, hundreds of feet down, the sea looked black; it was far too dark to see any of the other islands. It was as though they'd left one part of the world and climbed through a screen into a completely different place.

'Fuck,' said Tim, 'just look at this sky. It's going to tip it down.'

'Where's Nathalie?' Eleanor asked, loath to take too many steps further: beyond the blunt hilltop there was a sheer drop, with no rail and no vegetation. The builders of Panarea's neat little stone walls had obviously not reached this blustery point. 'Tim, we haven't seen her for ages, you don't think she's lost, do you? Or, no . . . she can't have fallen over the edge, can she?'

'Of course not, she'll be skulking around somewhere, don't you worry.' Eleanor glanced at him. His face was still hot plum from the exertion. She sensed he was as unnerved as she was by this formidable spot.

'You know it's almost five o'clock,' he said. 'We've taken hours. I thought you said it was only two hours, there and back? The sun's practically setting, not that you can tell through that cloud.'

'Maybe we should head straight back before it gets dark,' said Eleanor.

'Not quite the photo opportunity you hoped for, eh?' said Tim. 'Well, we can't go back without Eva Braun. Where the hell is she?'

To their immense relief, Nathalie suddenly appeared, battling her way up through dense gorse. Her legs were etched all over in reddish brown and a couple of larger scratches were seeping fresh blood. She looked equally relieved to see them and came straight over to stand close by.

'It is dark and cold,' she said, sniffing.

Eleanor wondered if she'd been crying. 'Were you lost?' she asked in concern. 'You were so far ahead, we didn't know what had happened to you.' She suddenly felt close to tears herself.

'I waited for you,' said Nathalie, simply. 'I am very cold.'

Tim took control. 'Come on, girls, let's take a quick picture and head straight back. It'll take longer to get down and it won't be light for much longer by the look. We need to stick close together this time, OK, Nathalie, no haring ahead?'

Nathalie nodded. Eleanor watched her pull a pink

plastic camera from her back pocket and aim it with grazed hands at the horizon; the pink struck her as a strangely girlish, vulnerable colour for such a steely creature. As she fished in her bag for her own camera, a glum little drop of water landed on her shoulder. Within seconds the rain was coursing noisily down.

'Let's get off the top,' shouted Tim. 'It's bloody dangerous.'

They moved falteringly back down the steep path they'd just climbed, but already the stones were as treacherous as wet glass.

'We need to make it to that shelter thing we saw,' Tim cried, his voice battered to a hoarse cry by the rain and wind. Eleanor felt as though they were at sea, locked in the eye of a storm, using every last ounce of energy just to stay on deck. Visibility was worsening by the second: the clouds had come down even lower. After a few painful steps and turns, they reached the ruin and Tim leapt in first. Eleanor watched helplessly as his right leg slid and buckled under him, and reached out for his arm, almost slipping herself as she followed. He was cursing with pain. She gripped on to the half-collapsed stone wall and helped Nathalie down, pulling the girl towards her in a greasy hug. The contortions on Tim's sopping face told them the injury was serious.

'I must have twisted my ankle. Fuck, it's agony!'

Nathalie started to whimper and Eleanor gripped her more closely, trying to peer through the teeming rain at Tim's leg. She had no idea if she was crying herself – her face was slippery and stiff with cold.

'Tim,' she shouted through the wet roar, 'we should have known the weather wouldn't be any good – the hydrofoils were cancelled.'

'We're not bloody fishermen,' shouted Tim angrily. 'How should we know what the weather will do – it looked all right when we left.' The rain had pelted his thick hair flat to his head, making his eyes seem bright and animal; he was almost unrecognisable. 'Anyway, it's just a bit of rain, we'll just wait till it stops and carry on down. I'm more worried about this damn foot.'

'Look,' said Eleanor. She was shrieking at the top of her voice, but Tim had to crane closely towards her to hear. 'The sky's black – what if it goes on all night? We may have to stay up here for a while. I think we need to start thinking about survival techniques.'

'What?' he bellowed.

'I said survival techniques!'

'Right, OK,' said Tim, a bit calmer. Eleanor thought she felt Nathalie relax a little. The poor thing was shivering really badly. They waited for Tim to take charge.

'Know any?' Eleanor urged, after a few seconds.

'Any what?'

Eleanor just closed her eyes.

'Oh, yeah, let me think,' Tim shouted. 'I do know that if we encounter a mountain lion we should spread out our clothes to make us seem wider than we are – more threatening, you know? And Nathalie should sit on my shoulders so I look much taller. That'll scare the bugger!'

'Tim!' cried Eleanor impatiently. 'Mountain lions are not the issue here, you buffoon, I'm talking about getting dry and warm enough to survive a night up here!'

'Don't call me a buffoon!' The rain caught in his nostrils and he snorted and spluttered for several seconds. 'You're the dopey bird who suggested this ridiculous jaunt. I should have stayed in the bar. You could cost us our lives!'

'Well I hardly think that's going to happen.'

Nathalie was sobbing unrestrainedly now. 'Take me back home.'

'And you can shut up,' yelled Tim, face maniacal. 'If you didn't have such mentalist parents shagging around all over the place we wouldn't have to bloody babysit you in the first place.'

Nathalie pulled away from Eleanor's grip and made as if to punch Tim in the head.

'Please stop!' Eleanor cried, grabbing the girl's arms. 'He didn't mean it. We must all stay calm.' They were all on the verge of hysteria, she thought, trying to get a grip on her own fear and glaring murderously at Tim. She looked up at the sky again but all she could see were huge arrows of water shooting down out of the darkness.

'Well, we've got water supplies,' said Tim, patting his pack.

She didn't waste the energy pointing out that dehydration was even less likely than an assault by mountain lions.

'Let's wait till the rain eases off a bit,' she said. 'Then I'll go down and get help. There's no way you can walk with your foot like that and we can't risk taking a minor down on this terrain.'

'A minor pain in the arse,' Tim muttered. But it was a decent plan and they didn't speak for a few minutes as they watched the rain continue to pelt down. They were all shivering badly now.

'It can't get too cold at night,' said Tim, at last. The light was now so dim they could barely see ten metres beyond their camp. 'It's only September, and even if it does get chilly we could stay here all night if we have to, just make sure we stay awake.'

'It's all this water,' cried Eleanor, desperation rising once more. 'Where's it all coming from?' Thank God they'd got down below the peak; if they'd stayed at the top they'd surely have been dragged over the edge in a second. And how long before the water simply washed them away, even here? She had visions of it wearing away their bare skin, eroding the protective elastic – it seemed to fill her ears, nostrils, eyes, sealing off all the senses.

An obvious solution suddenly occurred to her. 'We should phone for help – if we can get a signal. I didn't bring mine with me, have either of you got yours?'

Nathalie had left hers in her room; Tim had his, but it was low on power and soaked in seconds. He tried to cup it in his hands and peer at the screen. 'There's a signal! Bit low on juice, though, enough for a couple of calls,' he snuffled. 'What's emergency services here? Is it 911, like in the States?'

None of them knew and Eleanor doubted emergency services even existed in Panarea. She thought of the plane and helicopter in Vulcano dropping water on the forest fire; they had flown in from the mainland, Lewis had said. Not quite what they had in mind here. And surely a helicopter wouldn't be able to operate in this weather, anyhow? Even if it did, the helipad was hundreds of feet below, she'd seen it on her walk to the beach. Or perhaps it would fly up here and hover in the air above them; she imagined some kind of SAS-style rope ladder catapulted down to them through the open door; they'd have to climb up in turn, swinging over the cliff edge like trapeze artists, a hair's breadth from death . . .

'We'd be better calling the hotel and getting them to sort out help,' she shouted. 'Don't suppose you've got the number programmed in, Tim?'

'No, there wasn't any reason.'

'What about Sophie, then, can you call her?'

'Good thinking.'

But Sophie's phone wasn't in range, it seemed; they couldn't even connect to leave her a message.

'I will call my mother?' suggested Nathalie, teeth chattering. 'I know this number in my heart.'

'Excellent,' said Tim. 'Well done, Nathalie. Katharina'll get some help organised. Here we go, tell her we're up at Punta del Corvo and we're stuck.'

Nathalie prodded at the phone keys while Tim and Eleanor attempted to create some shelter over her so she could see and hear more clearly. The number was ringing and Eleanor breathed heavily in relief when she heard Nathalie speaking rapidly in German. But the girl snapped the phone shut after a few seconds and looked more forlorn than ever. 'It is her voicemail.'

'Bollocks!' Tim exclaimed angrily. 'That's no use – if she's in the bar she might not pick up her messages for ages.'

And where else would anyone be in this weather, thought Eleanor. 'What about your father, Nathalie?'

'He does not have the phone.'

This incensed Tim. 'What? What kind of hippie arse-hole doesn't have a phone?'

Eleanor gestured for him to take it easy. 'Don't you think Sophie would call for help, anyway, sooner or later? She knows where we are. And if she sees Katharina, she'll tell her she's worried about Nathalie and Katharina will be sure to check her messages.'

'Not sure she'll remember exactly where we were going, but yes, yes, good point. They'll send for help eventually.'

Eventually. Eleanor was so cold and wet she could hardly speak. More minutes passed and their collective shivering got more feverish.

'We could try some random combinations for 999 and hope we hit on the right one by chance? It must be three digits?'

They all gazed at the phone. The fluorescent square flickered off and on. 'We'd have to get it right first time,' Tim said, miserably. 'Look, I'll call home – England – and get them to find the hotel number and get in touch with Sophie from there.'

The phone gave another pathetic bleat and Tim looked as though he were about to dash it to smithereens against the rocks.

'No,' Eleanor said. 'Give it to me. I know the number of someone on the island.'

'What?'

'I said I know a number.' Even as she spoke her heart started pulsing faster, louder even than the rain on her skull.

Tim just handed her the phone and he and Nathalie tried to huddle over her as she took her turn, hands shaking with cold. She could feel no warmth from their bodies, just thick, wet clothes and icy, waterlogged skin.

She dialled the UK country code and then the number she knew so well. A part of her prayed the phone would go dead or the voicemail would click in automatically, but the ringing tone sounded in her ear at once. It was so modulated, reassuring against the sound of the lashing rain, she felt herself relax. Then there was a gritty clunking sound and a male voice: 'Hello?'

'Will!' Eleanor shouted. 'Will, it's Eleanor! I need your help.'

Chapter 19

It took a monumental effort of will to recall the events of the night before. The first thing Eleanor did on waking was prod the skin on her face and arms in front of the mirror, half expecting to see external scarring from her battery by rainwater.

Will had been with the rescue party. She had also recognised one of the *carabinieri* she'd seen cruising round the island in his police kart. The team must have been just feet away before she, Tim and Nathalie picked up their voices and saw the flash of lights through the sheeting rain. Nathalie was weeping hysterically, Eleanor failing to comfort her, and Tim, who had by then totally withdrawn from them, spoke for the first time in an hour to say, in flat tones, 'Hallelujah'. There were thick waterproof coats to put on and hot liquid to drink – she was too weak to register what it was – and a kind of stretcher with a waterproof flap for Tim that made her think of skiing, the injured conveyed at top speed down the slopes in sporty fluorescent body bags.

They didn't speak much during the descent, which took almost three hours. Eleanor required nothing in the world but sleep. She was aware of Will – he had been assigned to Nathalie and occasionally she caught a scrap of his voice behind her through the tumult – but they hadn't made eye contact; it was too wet to keep their eyes open for longer than half a second without blinking or squinting.

The party moved as painfully as befitted three broken, waterlogged zombies. When they finally reached the paved pathways of outer San Pietro she felt no joy or relief, just back-breaking exhaustion. But she tried to brace herself for interrogation: Will's voice was clearer now, and, turning to look, she saw he was carrying Nathalie in his arms, saying, 'Just a few more minutes, sweetheart.'

Vaguely, somewhere deep in her brain, she wondered what he knew, if he'd already been told the full story by Lewis.

When they reached the hotel there seemed to be hundreds of people, though she later realised it was no more than twenty-five. There were cheers and cries, as though they were returning to base camp from the iced cliffs of K2. Only the next day did it occur to her that the reception was as much for the rescuers as for the rescued: she and Tim were simply foolhardy idiots, who'd endangered not only their own lives but that of a child, too.

The bar area had been converted into some kind of emergency room, with medical supplies, maps, torches and piles of blankets and clothes covering every available surface. Giovanna presided, alongside an elderly doctor unable to speak a word of English, who examined each of them in turn in one of the downstairs guestrooms. Sophie was there, eyes swollen with crying. She gave Eleanor a long, warm hug and helped interpret the doctor's instructions.

'They were worried they might have to take you all to the hospital in Messina. They've got a helicopter on standby. They think you're OK, though. Probably suffering from shock. And you're all freezing! Apparently it hasn't been this cold at night in September for about thirty years! You poor, poor things.' Her tender tone was so comforting Eleanor thought she might start sobbing again. To the exclusion of all other feelings, she longed for warm water on her skin. But there were no bathtubs in the hotel – a shower would have to do.

When she was finally allowed to go to her own room she felt that she was experiencing events myopically and with only partial hearing. Her head and body seemed to be stuffed with foam. Lewis appeared and, without saying anything, wrapped her in a big bear hug. He opened the door for her – her hands were still too shaky – and then helped her deal with the sodden clothes. 'Giovanna'll run these through the hotel laundry,' he said. His voice seemed to be carried to her from another continent.

She'd been told to take a hot shower and return for food. Someone had piled blankets on her bed – they looked so inviting, she almost got straight under them without showering. But Lewis turned on the taps, testing the temperature, insisting she get under the water. Neither of them referred to her nakedness. The hot water felt blissful, bringing the skin and muscle back to life inch by inch. As her face was pelted with warmth she couldn't imagine ever needing anything else.

She had no memory of drying herself or manoeuvring her body beneath the bedclothes, but somehow warm layers were piled on top of her, and she thought she felt a kiss on her forehead. She fell asleep instantly.

She was already wide awake when there was a knock at the door and Lewis came in with a tray of hot chocolate and croissants. He seemed to be her allocated nurse, her surrogate partner. Neither of them said anything until he opened the shutters and allowed daylight to lick into the room. She watched him sheepishly as he sloshed chocolate from the jug into a cup and handed it to her. His face looked paler again.

'Well, it's a perfect day,' he said, sitting on the bed by her feet. 'You'd never guess we had a storm yesterday . . .'

'How long have I been sleeping?' she asked, croakily.

'About fourteen hours, it's almost midday. Sweet dreams?'

'I don't remember having any at all. I think the nightmare was the waking bit. God, my legs really ache.' She pushed herself into sitting position and saw that she was wearing a blue T-shirt that wasn't hers.

'Mine,' said Lewis, seeing her confusion. 'You were all packed up.' Her zipped bag was still sitting on the desk where she'd left it the previous morning.

Greedily, she sucked down the hot chocolate. 'Were we in any real danger?'

'You certainly were.' Lewis tore off the corner of a croissant and handed it to her. 'Try to eat. You were up there for hours. You wouldn't have been cold enough for hypothermia, but the main worry was that the storm would cause rock falls. It's quite dodgy up there. I can't believe you only had one phone between you, though the consensus is you were lucky to get a signal at all.'

She looked at his face and felt she'd known him for years, the familiar set of his lips, the earnest brown eyes. Realising she was staring, she began cramming the croissant into her mouth. It was warm and buttery and she reached for more.

'I suppose Will wants to talk to me. Has he said anything?'

Lewis sighed. 'He's going to come and see you in an hour or so, take you for lunch. Don't worry, he's not annoyed or anything, just worried.'

'What about Frannie?'

'The same. She was great last night, ran off in the rain to get the doctor – he's someone from the mainland who has a holiday home here and isn't usually in Panarea in September. The rest of them didn't even know he was here – usually they call the medic in Lipari, but there was no chance of him coming across in that weather. Apparently this guy is a friend of her father's and Frannie had seen him earlier in the week. He lives all the way out in Drauto by the beach; he's retired now and doesn't even have a phone.'

'I suppose she knows who I am now,' sighed Eleanor. She wasn't sure she had the energy to deal with all of this today, but the niggles and queries were starting to form a queue.

Lewis just nodded.

'Lewis, I saw you the other night, you know, at Frannie's house. I know the two of you have got very close this week . . .'

He stood up abruptly and interrupted her. 'Look, Eleanor, things aren't exactly as you think.'

'How d'you mean?'

'I'll let Will explain.'

'Will?' She didn't think Will would be likely to know anything about that indecently flirtatious exchange on Frannie's terrace.

'Yes, Will. I don't mean to mess you around, but you really do need to talk to him first. I'll catch up with you later and I promise I'll tell you anything you want to know. Take care.'

And he left the room, closing the door very gently behind him, as though she were still sleeping.

She went down to the bar with half an hour to spare. Dutch courage was in order and Rico obliged with a large brandy.

'I think I could do with one of those, as well,' said Sophie, behind her. They hugged. Sophie felt soft and cosy and smelled of shampoo.

'How are you feeling, you poor sweetie?'

'Oh, much better,' Eleanor said, 'but very embarrassed. I can't believe we created such a massive emergency. How's Tim?'

'Dreadful. He seems to think he lost his rag with you two – did he?'

'A bit. He sort of shouted at Nathalie. But we were all out of control. We really panicked.'

'He's always a nightmare in a crisis. *Rory* would be more helpful and he's in kindergarten. Katharina and Stefan were worried sick about Nathalie, as you can imagine. Stefan really went off on one when he found out I'd let her go hiking with Tim . . .'

'And me,' Eleanor added, hoping she might extract herself from the situation without any further skirmish with Stefan. 'We didn't prove very good at keeping an eye on her, did we?'

'Well, I'm taking them all out to dinner tonight to try to make up for it,' Sophie said. 'Without Tim.'

'How's his foot?'

'All strapped up. He's out for the count at the moment, dosed up with painkillers. The pills they gave him were so big, I'm sure they're meant for cattle or something.'

'I should never have insisted on the walk,' Eleanor said, with fresh dismay. 'I just had to escape, I don't know how to explain it.'

Sophie smiled at her. 'I take it this Will character is *the* Will, then, is he?'

'Yes. Frannie's his new girlfriend. I'm meeting him for lunch in a minute.' She took a mouthful of brandy. 'I came to Panarea to sort of spy on them, in case you haven't guessed. I'm obviously barking.'

Sophie's face displayed nothing but affectionate sympathy. 'Don't be hard on yourself. I'd say he quite enjoyed the drama of last night. Anyway, you're not the first person to do something a bit, well, misguided. I once hired a private detective to tail Tim.'

'Really?' Eleanor giggled. 'What happened?'

'Don't you dare tell him, he still doesn't know. I was pregnant and a bit paranoid. I was convinced he was having an affair; he wasn't coming home till eleven or twelve every night. But it turned out he really was working late, doing that classic father-to-be thing. They work even harder if they know it's going to be a boy; bizarre, isn't it? Anyway, it must have been the most boring job the private eye ever had. When he gave me his report, I could tell he felt like he was taking my money under false pretences.' She chortled. 'But I'll tell you what, Eleanor, I'm not very impressed with this Frannie girl.'

'Why not? Everyone seems to adore her.'

'Oh, she's a dreadful luvvie. I hate that technique of making you feel like you're the most fascinating person in the world – it's so obvious. I could see her doing it with the waitress, for God's sake.'

Eleanor thought this a little unjust. 'I don't think it's a technique, you know, I think she just *is* very charming.'

'Well, she definitely will be once she knows who you are, my dear – she's exactly the type to keep her enemies close, I'd say. But I bet there's an edge there, you know, something a bit meaner that she doesn't like people to see.'

Eleanor wondered about Frannie's drunken teasing of Will. 'It's great fun!' – that was what she'd said about his broken engagement, the humiliation of his fiancée.

'Hopefully I won't see her again,' she said. 'It's all just so embarrassing.'

'You'll be fine.' Sophie squeezed her arm. 'Two more brandies, Rico, *per favore*. Anyway, you can see where Frannie gets her silver tongue from – that old rogue of a father. She couldn't stop going on about him yesterday after you left. Told me what a Lothario he

312

is, how he's got a revolving door of younger women. He's just married wife number four, apparently.'

'Really?' Eleanor could feel the colour rising in her cheeks.

'She's only twenty-two! Isn't that sick? She's a model,' Frannie said. 'Couldn't come with him this weekend because she's doing a shoot for Gucci.'

Eleanor couldn't stop herself from gasping.

'He's some kind of auto industry mogul, tyres or something,' she said. 'Anyway, your friend's heart definitely belongs to Daddy. She seems to find his womanising funny – talked about him like he's Mick Jagger and just can't help himself. She said she thinks he's even been playing away while he's been here, just picked up some tourist in a bar the other night. Everyone was gossiping about it at the wedding, she said, wondering who it was. Can you imagine being so brazen in a tiny place like this?'

'Goodness,' croaked Eleanor and drained her second brandy in one enormous swallow. Her eyes watered. 'It's all been happening.'

'Certainly has,' Sophie laughed. 'What a holiday.'

It was peculiar sitting opposite Will again. It felt both ancient and brand new at the same time. Sharing a meal face to face had once been a daily event, in the kitchen by the window in their flat overlooking the bus stop, in a hundred restaurants and bars. This was the face she'd expected to watch crease and fatten with middle age. Now it just made cameo appearances in her life.

At first, she took him to be the picture of vitality, all nut-brown tan and thick sun-bleached hair, wiry movements and wide grins. Then she noticed his eyes: the sockets were smudged with deep yellow shadows, as though he'd been punched a couple of weeks ago and the bruises were slow to fade. She realised that his aura of dynamism was partly the effect of fidgeting. He was nervous.

'How are you feeling?' he asked, as soon as they sat down, making instant, intense eye contact.

She looked straight at him, surprisingly willing to meet the accusation in his face. 'Fine thanks, much better. Will, thank you so much for helping last night. I didn't expect you to come up to the clifftop yourself – it was dangerous.'

'That's OK, and of course I came. They needed a volunteer. Lucky you remembered my mobile number.'

She supposed he'd probably forgotten hers, discarded it, just as he had his house keys, which he'd sent back to her through the post with a brief cheery note, as though he'd been flat-sitting for a week or two while she was on holiday.

'What an incredible downpour,' he continued. 'It just seemed to come out of nowhere. It was running down the lanes in rivers.'

'I'd just assumed it was always glorious weather here. That was stupid, I realise.' Stupid or not, Eleanor was interested to note how little shame she was feeling. Instead, she felt like an escaped prisoner who'd been recaptured after a few terrifying days on the run. The game was up and she felt only relief to be returned to custody.

Will took a deep breath. 'Eleanor, I need to talk to you.'

'Of course.' That was why they were sitting there, in the restaurant, just a basketful of bread between them. It was the same restaurant where she'd had lunch with Frannie, and all around them tables were filling up with gossiping couples, foursomes, sixes. Eleanor stared in admiration at all the young, contented faces. How could it be, amid all this sunlit bliss, that she'd been summoned to the headmaster's office to hear the terms of her expulsion?

'Well, you look very well, considering last night's drama,' said Will, smiling, his eyes crinkling in that boyish way she used to love. She knew how his conversation worked. It was typical of him to announce that he needed to talk, as though presenting the idea to himself, and then switch instantly back to small talk. Yes, she knew exactly what to expect from him. I understand you've gone through a bit of a crisis, he would say (he wouldn't risk the word 'breakdown'). No one wants to upset you, but we want to get on with our lives. You'll feel better if you try to do the same. Leave us alone, please. And he had every right to say it, no one would disagree with that.

But Will seemed to be having difficulty finding the right words. He was still fidgeting, running his fingers through his hair, one hand after the other, then patting the strands back down again. She waited, calm and still.

'I've known you've been in Panarea all week. I mean, even before last night. Frannie's known, too.'

Eleanor looked up with a start. This was not in the script. 'You knew? How?' She felt her face flush. 'Where did you see me? Was it at the beach? No, in Iditella after the wedding?'

'No, I mean I knew even before you arrived here.'

'What? How?' She was totally bewildered.

'Miranda phoned me the morning you left. She'd been feeling guilty that she'd told you where I was in the first place.'

'Miranda!' cried Eleanor. 'How did she know I came here? I told her I was going down to Devon.'

'She didn't believe you. The timing was too much of a coincidence. And then she saw your tickets. You must have left them lying around the flat.'

Eleanor knew she hadn't, she'd kept them in a drawer in her bedroom, but Miranda was a sneaky thing, she could easily have found herself 'stumbling' across them.

'She was worried,' Will went on, in the coaxing voice she knew of old; he'd always used it when trying to appease her over some minor source of conflict. 'She thought you were planning to do something crazy . . .' He trailed off and she knew he'd had to catch himself adding 'again'.

'Right,' said Eleanor sulkily. 'Like murder you and Frannie, perhaps, with a single sleeping pill crushed into your food?'

'You know that's not what I meant.' Will was getting impatient now. He had a surprisingly short fuse in difficult conversations. His eyes weren't crinkling at the corners any more. 'She was genuinely worried about what happened before.'

'Nothing happened before, that's the point. Taking a sleeping pill prescribed by your own GP does not amount to a suicide attempt. You're all mad!' When he made no reply, she added, 'I have no intention of topping myself, OK? I'm perfectly stable.' It was unfortunate that her voice rose to shrillness at this point. And of course Will would have every right to point out that tracking one's ex-boyfriend down to a remote island off the coast of Sicily was hardly stable behaviour. This conversation had taken a wrong turn somewhere. 'Anyway,' she said, eager to injure him, 'perhaps you shouldn't have announced to Miranda you were coming here in the first place and none of this would have happened. She's clearly been playing double agent.'

'Frannie let it slip,' he said. 'Miranda rang to talk to me a few nights before we were flying out and Frannie picked up, didn't realise she was a friend of yours.'

'I'm starting to wonder if she is,' Eleanor said.

'Look, don't blame her,' Will pleaded. 'I really think she thought she was doing the right thing.'

Eleanor gave a little splutter, unable even to begin to articulate her feelings about Miranda. Lizzie had been right: she was not to be trusted. A proper friend kept your secrets no matter what; she didn't feed them to the man who'd crushed your heart in his fist.

Their food arrived and Will spent some time selecting and chewing forkfuls of gnocchi. When he spoke again, he looked wearier than ever. 'Anyway, once we knew you were coming here, we all thought it would be a good idea to just go along with whatever you had planned. And I'm still not sure what that was, to be honest with you.'

God, thought Eleanor, cheeks ablaze, they'd discussed her like a psychiatric case, agreed to humour her delusions. She imagined him explaining the situation to an astonished Frannie: 'Look, Fran, she's crazy as a coot,' – that was the phrase he always used, it made him chuckle – 'we need to just play along, darling.'

'So did you know I was following you?'

'We heard some shuffling outside the villa. And I saw you standing on the roof terrace at your hotel a few times.'

'Oh.' Eleanor had assumed she'd been totally out of sight on the roof. 'I didn't realise you could see anyone up there.'

'Well, I knew where to look. I kept seeing a flash,'

explained Will, 'I suppose from binoculars or a camera or something.' He was becoming more relaxed, confident he'd regained the measure of this conversation.

'So Frannie knew who I was all along?'

'She twigged pretty quickly after talking to you that first time in the café. I knew it was you as soon as she described you. I like your short hair, by the way.'

Her hand instinctively went up to pat at her hair; it had taken on an odd shingled style today, having dried on her pillow as she slept. But Will had now turned away to wave to a couple settling at a corner table in the shade and Eleanor saw that it was Emilio and Rita. Rita looked stunning in an off-the-shoulder pink top, her hair loosely curled, like lengths of chocolate-coloured embroidery silk.

'*Ciao*, Jane!' she called over to Eleanor.

'Hiya.' She grinned limply at the pair.

'That's another thing,' said Will, his voice low and noticeably more self-conscious now he'd spotted Frannie's friends. 'You told Frannie your name was Jane. You don't need to be trained by MI5 to work that one out. Obviously I remember your middle name.'

'You surprise me,' said Eleanor sarkily.

'That's unfair.'

There was another silence. They both looked down at their food.

'Frannie was very sweet,' said Eleanor, finally. 'She seemed genuinely friendly.'

Will's eyes were suddenly eager. 'She is sweet, she is genuine. She liked you a lot, you know, saw straight away you weren't in Panarea to do anything bad. But we knew that by then, anyway.'

How awkward for Frannie, chancing upon the enemy who was broken and self-pitying. How skilfully she'd handled that first meeting; she'd made Eleanor feel interesting and valued, worthy of befriending. Then again, as Sophie had suggested, the whole thing may have been nothing but an act: the challenge of winning over the one person who should by rights like her the least. But Eleanor knew instinctively that Frannie's compassion had been sincere. She also knew that in the same position she herself would have been far less gracious. She'd have felt threatened, maybe even spiteful, certainly too protective of Will to offer friendship.

Something in her brain suddenly clicked back a notch. 'What d'you mean you already knew by then?'

Will put down the piece of bread he'd been using to mop up his sauce, half-heartedly, as though it were an unconvincing prop he'd given up on. She waited impatiently while he finished chewing.

'Aren't you going to eat that fish?' he asked, at last.

'Will! Answer my question!'

'OK.' The hands were running through the hair again. 'Lewis.'

'Lewis? What about him? I know you've all met, of course; he told me.' She felt desperate to regain some control over this conversation and demonstrate that she already knew the score on one issue, at least. 'I saw the three of you together, actually, a couple of nights ago.'

Will nodded. 'Lewis is an old friend of Frannie's. They were at college together. He's been with us for this whole holiday. He checked into your hotel to . . . well, to keep an eye on you.'

Eleanor's pulse accelerated. Her eyeballs felt as though they were buzzing. This really was preposterous. 'What are you on about? I met him on the boat, before I even got here.'

'I know, he went over to Lipari in the morning. The idea was that he'd introduce himself to you, make it seem like you were both arriving at the same time.'

'But how could he know which boat I was getting?'

'Miranda saw the time on your itinerary.'

'Fuck Miranda,' exploded Eleanor. 'I don't believe this.' She could feel the colour pulsating in her face. Her eyes brimmed with tears.

'Keep your voice down, everyone's looking!' Will was smiling apologetically at Rita and Emilio, half shrugging, as if to disassociate himself from his lunch companion's hysteria.

'Will, I don't give a damn about your new friends . . .' It was unbearable that he cared more about the reaction of strangers than her own distress. 'I really don't want to talk about this any more. I just want to go home.' She scraped back her chair.

'Eleanor, don't go yet, please.'

'Then concentrate on us, not them!'

'All right.' He pulled in his seat to huddle towards her, but she couldn't bear the closeness and leant back. 'I'm really sorry,' he said. 'I know it sounds ridiculous and I admit we were being over-cautious. But we were worried something *unexpected* might happen and we obviously couldn't stop you from coming to Panarea. Lewis just kept us up to date. When he realised you were harm— *fine*, he got out of your way.'

He had been going to say 'harmless'. When he'd said 'unexpected', he meant 'dangerous'. He had led Frannie and Lewis to believe she was a psychopath. She was not prepared for the humiliation of this new revelation. She felt punched in the head, woozy with pain. So Lewis, too, had not befriended her for her own merits; he'd just been doing Frannie a favour. Taking the inmate on day release to Vulcano, while the real object of his devotion sat in the sun with Will, the two of them pulling the strings from their perfect hideaway in Panarea with the perfect view of Stromboli.

'Well, you're obviously a very close team,' she said, finally, with a heavy note of insinuation.

'*They* are. I only met him a few times in London, but we've seen him every day here. He usually comes for a drink after dinner.'

'How civilised. Yes, he and Frannie do seem especially close.'

'Just friends,' said Will, shrugging. 'They've never got together as far as I know. Probably why they've managed to stay such good mates.'

Eleanor sighed again. She knew he was probably right. Good mates. Was there no end to the enviable contents of Frannie's dream life?

'He's a great bloke, Lewis,' said Will. 'And he really likes you, actually, thinks you're very funny.'

'I'm so glad I've been a source of entertainment to you all,' said Eleanor, amazed that her voice had returned to normal. 'Look, I think we've cleared everything up now. I'm grateful for your help last night. You can get back to Frannie and Lewis with your report. I need to go and sort out my travel arrangements.'

'Don't be like that,' said Will, his eyes showing real alarm. 'Please stay. We haven't been trying to trick you. After all, Lewis keeping tabs on you was no different from you trailing around after me, was it?'

'But sending him to get the same boat as me? As if I couldn't be trusted to behave even on my way here.'

'Well, he did need to go to the archaeology museum,' Will said, feebly.

'Yes, the fabulous archaeology museum. One of the best in Sicily.' She searched in her bag for her cigarettes, lit herself one and offered the pack to Will.

'No thanks,' he said, mock-stoical. 'I've given up.'

'You've given up? Well, you have changed. And while we're on the subject, what's with the diving course?'

Will laughed. 'Not very me, I know. Actually, I took Lewis's place. He'd booked it in advance and had to pull out once Miranda . . . once the plan changed. It was great, though, an amazing experience. You should have a go.'

Eleanor looked out to the jetty, remembering how she and Frannie had watched him return from his dive like a pair of proud parents. But now, just days later, she was ready to withdraw from the tug of love. She'd never really been a contender.

'And you and Frannie, is it serious?'

His grey eyes softened. 'Yes. I'm really sorry, Eleanor. Please don't be upset. You may find it hard to believe, but the last thing I wanted was to upset you.'

'I'm not upset any more,' Eleanor said, honestly. 'I'm just tired.'

Chapter 20

There were three new messages on her mobile. For a loser and an outcast, she'd never been so in demand.

'Eleanor, it's Rufus. Where the fuck are you? It's Monday morning, you didn't get back to me last week and Miranda now seems to think you're in Italy? Can you please let me know when you're coming in. Preferably today. This really doesn't look good with the client.'

The next message was from Miranda, recorded just minutes after Rufus's. 'Call me, El, there's some stuff I need to explain. Rufus is going ape. Bye.'

Finally, Lizzie: 'Eleanor, I can't get hold of you. I wanted to tell you my news in case you heard it from someone else. I'm sorry it's not the best way, but, anyway, Simon asked me to marry him. Last week. I said yes. Call me back when you get a chance.' Her voice was carefully tempered but Eleanor could recognise sheer delight when she heard it.

She deleted the first two messages and then dialled. 'Lizzie? Congratulations! I'm so happy for you, I really am . . .'

'I'm really sorry, Eleanor,' said Lewis. He was waiting in the bar when she came downstairs with her luggage.

'Everyone's apologising to me today,' she smiled. 'I thought it would be the other way round.'

'Come and sit down for a bit. You've got time. The hydrofoil doesn't leave for another hour.' He looked freshly scrubbed, handsome, incredibly huggable.

'OK.'

'*Caffè?*' asked Carlo. No doubt he'd be another person delighted to see the back of her; he'd been awkward with her since the day she'd discovered him with Nathalie.

'Is Nathalie OK?' she asked Lewis. 'I don't think I'll have time to drop by.'

'Yes, she's had a shock and needs to rest for a day or two. I saw Stefan just now – he was asking after you, by the way. They'll be travelling back to Germany later in the week.'

'Have *you* seen Nathalie, Carlo?' Eleanor asked. 'Is she better?'

Carlo shrugged and curled his lip. 'I do not know. You must ask my grandmother.' He splashed coffee into Eleanor's cup and moved away. Arrogant twit, she thought.

'Anyway, I've just had lunch with Will,' she told Lewis. 'He filled me in on everything.'

'It must all seem very Machiavellian,' said Lewis. 'I feel awful, this whole double-agent thing. I can't quite believe I did it.'

'Oh, don't worry,' said Eleanor. 'I'm the one who came here with the cloak-and-dagger ideas. It was very game of you to interrupt your holiday to babysit the nutter.' She'd intended this to sound light and humorous, but it came out with surprising steel.

'I'm sorry,' he said again. He looked thoroughly ashamed. 'I really did enjoy our day in Vulcano. It's been fun spending time with you all at the hotel. I guess I'll check out of here today as well.'

'Are you staying with Frannie for the rest of the trip?'

'Yes, probably. They've got two bedrooms at the villa.'

'So you know Frannie from university?'

'We were at Bristol together. Shared a flat in my third year when she'd just started. Her mother knew my sister, bought some paintings off her, I think. Anyway, we lost touch for a bit after college but hooked up again when I got my job in London. She was the one who invited me to Panarea.'

It made sense now; both Lewis and Frannie had an appealing earnestness, she could imagine them getting on well.

'I saw you on the terrace, Lewis,' she said, 'at

Frannie's, on the night of the wedding. You and her, you looked a bit more than friends to me.'

Lewis raised a puzzled eyebrow.

'You know what I mean,' said Eleanor.

'I don't, actually.'

'From what I heard, neither of you was too concerned about your partners.'

'Ah.' He began chewing at his thumbnail. 'Well, you're barking up the wrong tree as far as that goes. We've never been more than friends, believe it or not.'

Now Eleanor raised an eyebrow.

'She's very happy with Will,' Lewis continued. 'She was off her face that night, as I remember. Nothing whatsoever happened.'

'Hmm.' Wobbly as her judgement may have been elsewhere in conversations with Lewis, she was certain he was telling the truth now.

'I hate to tell you that the two of them are very serious about each other,' he said.

'So I gather. What do you really think of him? Be honest.'

'I like him, yes. He treats her well. They really do seem right for each other. Sorry,' he added.

'It's all right. I guess you wouldn't want to be unfaithful to Rebecca, anyway.' This came out sounding rather glum.

'That's another thing,' said Lewis, looking shifty and noticeably pinker in the face.

'What?'

'Rebecca. She's not my girlfriend. We do know a Rebecca, another friend from college, and she is a teacher, up in Leeds. But she's happily married. They've got a baby now, I think.'

'Then why—'

'I just wanted to make myself seem safe, more platonic, you know?'

To stop her latching on to him with the same loony obsession that had brought her across Europe to stalk Will, thought Eleanor, horrified. Even so, she was aware of her brain registering this news as extremely welcome.

'Does she have a ponytail?'

'Who, Rebecca? No, no, she's got short hair, or at least she did last time I saw her.'

'You weren't very good at fleshing out the details, I have to say,' Eleanor giggled. 'I think Sophie might be on to you.'

'I'll take my chances.' He handed her a little bundle of tissues. He's come prepared for tears, thought Eleanor, then realised there was something wrapped up inside; this was a gift. It was a bracelet made of silver and spikes of red coral.

'Just keep it away from volcanic mud,' said Lewis. He helped her do up the clasp and she felt an unbearable lurch of affection for him.

'Thank you, it's lovely. You didn't need to . . .' give me a consolation prize, she was thinking. But it felt like a

329

prize to receive something from Lewis, consolation or not.

'Are you really leaving now?' he asked, changing the subject.

'Yes. You?'

'I'll stay till the weekend, then I need to get back to London and sort out my visa for Libya. I got the confirmation yesterday, I'm going down there for a dig.'

'Libya? God, is that safe?'

'Should be fine. I'll only be there for a few weeks.'

A few weeks; this felt like devastating news.

'What time's your flight?' Lewis asked.

'Actually, I'm not going straight home,' Eleanor said. 'I've just changed my flight to Thursday.'

'Oh? Spending a few days in Palermo?' He sounded confused. At last she'd managed to outmanoeuvre her keepers.

'I thought I'd go to Salina for a while.'

'Salina?'

'Yes, it sounds peaceful.'

'I think it is. Quieter than here. It'll be a great place to get your head together.'

'And we all know I need to do that.' Eleanor felt an overwhelming urge to invite him to come along, to make their own private hideaway of wherever they pitched up, but forced herself with all her might to resist.

'What about your job?' Lewis asked.

'That's one of the things I need to think about,'

Eleanor said. 'I've been putting it off, putting everything off. But now I need to make some changes.'

Just then, Giovanna shuffled up in a pair of slippers to deliver two tumblers of some dark, gooey-looking liqueur, clearly the evil twin of Limoncello. She patted Eleanor's head with a look of wonder and a clucking noise, as though comforting her chick after a miraculous retrieval from the jaws of a fox.

'Thanks, Giovanna. I'll be over in a minute to pay my bill.' She turned to Lewis. 'I must remember to leave my phone number in London for Tim and Sophie.' She hoped he would volunteer to pass it on to them, which would mean he would have the opportunity to note it for himself, too, but he didn't.

She decided to try again: 'It would be nice to all meet up for a drink in London – all the hotel gang, I mean – when we're all back?' Too many 'all's, she thought; she'd overdone it.

'Yes, I'd like that,' said Lewis. 'You must give me your number, as well, or I suppose I could get it from Will.'

'He might not remember. I'll give my details to Giovanna when I check out.'

'How did you leave things with Will?' Lewis asked, perhaps a little too casually.

'Oh, we're going to talk in a month or so, maybe try to be friends, we'll see. The main thing is he seems convinced that I've accepted he's with Frannie now and we'll never get back together.'

'And are you convinced?'

'Yes, I am.'

'Was she at lunch as well?'

'No. To be honest I'm embarrassed about seeing her again. God knows what she thinks about all of this.'

'Oh, she'll be cool about it,' said Lewis. 'She doesn't have a jealous bone in her body.'

'No, I can believe that,' Eleanor said. 'Right, one more cigarette and then I'd better head down to the jetty.' She lit up, passed the cigarettes to Lewis, and the two of them drained their liqueurs.

It occurred to her it might be an idea to cut down on some of her vices when she got back home.

It felt sadder than she'd expected to see Panarea again as she had on arrival: from the very end of the jetty. The shimmering weather had returned, restoring all the glamour and colour she'd been so dazzled by when she first stepped off the boat. The gnarl of Punta del Corvo looked innocent now, just another set of soaring rocks at the top-centre of a postcard landscape.

And there was the white line of the roof terrace at Albergo delle Rose, a couple of dark heads visible, two glinting sets of dark glasses. Odd to think of Sophie and the German family eating on their own tonight. She imagined Lewis would check on them at some point, make sure Nathalie was OK and ask about Tim's ankle; it was the sort of nice thing he'd do.

She turned at the sound of the hydrofoil buzzing in the distance and stared out into the haze. Stromboli looked as though it was afloat in the sea, light as baked meringue. Lewis would be heading there, that evening perhaps, climbing the great cone. She felt a little leap of tenderness for him.

'Jane! I mean Eleanor!'

She jumped at the sound of Frannie's voice.

'Hello. It seems strange to call you Eleanor.' She was standing a couple of feet away, urchin-slender in cut-off jeans and sun top. Eleanor had no idea how long she'd been there, prayed for the hydrofoil to reach the dock with God's speed.

'I suppose you must be relieved I'm on my way,' she said.

'I'm relieved you want to go,' said Frannie, eyes as intense as ever. Eleanor thought about Sophie's criticisms, about the mean edge. She decided she would reserve judgement.

She held Frannie's gaze. 'When Will told me you'd known who I was all along, I thought your friendliness might have been, well, a bit of a performance, you know, to check me out.' Egocentric to the end, she laughed to herself.

Frannie just smiled. 'No, not a performance. I'm on holiday.'

'I hope you enjoy the rest of your break,' said Eleanor, meaning it.

'Thank you.'

'Is your father still here?'

'No, he left on the morning boat. Had to get back to Milan. It's a shame you didn't meet him, he's quite a character.'

'Yes.'

There was a pause. The sound of the engines was getting closer, the water slapping up against the jetty and rolling over the rocks.

'I'm going to catch up with my parents as soon as I get home,' said Eleanor. 'Go down to Devon.'

'Lovely,' said Frannie. 'Maybe there'll be an Indian summer? Miracles happen. Lewis said you were going to Salina first?'

They must have seen each other straight after she'd said goodbye to him, Eleanor thought. What a slick little network the three of them had going. Would it be possible for her to keep in touch with Lewis, after all, even develop things a little, with Frannie and Will hovering in the background for updates? Yes, she decided, Panarea was one place, London was quite another.

'Salina, yes, you gave me the idea, actually, you made it sound so . . . magical.'

'It is,' said Frannie. 'You'll love it, it's so green and beautiful. We'll probably go there at the weekend.' She didn't need to add that she assumed Eleanor would have left by then. There'd be no crossing of paths this time.

Finally, the boat arrived and the smell of fuel fill~
the air. Ropes were tied, tourist legs shuffled forward

Eleanor lingered, knowing she owed Frannie an apology. A few hours earlier she would have wept it out, but now the words refused to come.

Frannie spoke instead. 'I'm sorry, Eleanor, I feel terrible about how you and Will broke up, when it obviously wasn't what you wanted.'

'You've got nothing to feel terrible about,' said Eleanor. 'It was his decision.'

'That's generous of you.'

Though there was noise and activity all around them, there was a small observed silence between them.

'I have to go,' Eleanor said.

'Of course. Good luck with looking for a new job.'

'Yes, thank you, and I hope your TV thing goes well. Goodbye.'

'Bye, Eleanor.'

And then, at last, there were no more words, because she had boarded, stowed her bag and taken her seat. As the hydrofoil reversed into position, she struggled with the urge to go out on to the rear deck, where passengers had gathered to snap final photos of the island. From there she'd be able to see Frannie still on the jetty, maybe even waving, or perhaps already turning back to join Will and Lewis, whom she pictured lingering together in the shadows as they watched the boat pull away, exclaiming to each her, 'How weird was that? Do you think she's *really* gone?'

With her monocular she'd be able to watch the scene right until the boat turned the headland for the open sea. But she didn't, just settled back in her seat, closed her eyes tight shut, and cast the three familiar faces from her mind – for now, if not forever.

She wondered what the hotel maid would say when she saw the eyeglass in the waste basket.

Louise Candlish on updating her first novel

There is a modest-sized group of readers out there who read *The Island Hideaway* in 2004 when it was titled *Prickly Heat*. It was a little summer paperback with a red cover that featured a stick figure of a woman in an aqua bikini and wide-brimmed sunhat, cocktail in hand. Such was the typographical design, you couldn't clearly read the author's name; unless you held the book right up to your face it looked like it was written by someone called 'Oie Adih'.

Anyway, it was my first novel and has remained over the years very special to me.

Over time the book went out of print, I wrote eight others, the digital format revolutionised publishing, and the time seemed right to revive my debut for a new audience.

I knew at once that I wanted to change the title, tastes – including mine – having moved on. *The Island Hideaway* is, in all sorts of ways, more appropriate. The question was, would any of the book itself need to be altered? Reading it again, I saw that while the story itself remained universal – a rather disturbed young woman struggles to get over being rejected by

337

man she loves – in the ten years that had passed since I delivered it to my first editor, some of the details had become distractingly out-dated. So I decided to revise the text, not to such an extent that you wouldn't recognise it as the same work, but with subtle changes that have, hopefully, improved and refreshed the story.

Some of the tweaks are to do with technology. First time around, for instance, there were no iPhones or BlackBerries. When I was in Panarea in 2001 writing the first scenes, everyone had tiny little black phones that they would snap shut when a call ended. My own phone was prehistoric, several times as heavy as the one I use now; not that it mattered since I rarely bothered to pick it up and turn it on. In those days, when you went away, you really went away: you weren't available to those back home. Even if you could get a signal you pretended you couldn't.

And then there was the smoking. This was my biggest dilemma, because in the intervening years smoking has been banned in public places in most European countries, including Italy. But the people in this book smoke a lot! Eleanor has become 'somewhat reliant' on cigarettes since Will has disposed of her. Characters bond over cigarettes, they pick each other up by asking for a light (oh, innocent times!).

I decided to exercise a little artistic licence and keep the indoor smoking. This is Italy, after all. Though I haven't returned to Panarea since the ban, I like to think that the rules on all kinds of things are more flexible in that most special of island hideaways . . .

On island settings

There've been island settings as long as there've been stories: they are a gift for writers, an eternal source of mystery and fantasy. And emotional separation, too. Encircled by the sea, self-contained, often quite remote and hidden, islands represent an alternative way of life to that of mainstream mainland civilisation. They are much, much more than plot devices.

Like millions of children, I devoured the island classics, *Treasure Island*, *Robinson Crusoe*, *Five on a Treasure Island*, *Lord of the Flies*, to name but a few. I absolutely loved Agatha Christie's *And Then There Were None* and, later, John Fowles' *The Magus*. On my travels as an adult I've visited dozens of islands: Robben Island, Alcatraz, Fraser Island, Langkawi, Capri . . . the list grows as long as there are little grey bumps on the horizon. As tourists, we set our sights on them from the mainland and book our day trips with an explorer's sense of risk and adventure. Sometimes we stay over (not on Alcatraz, one hopes) and enjoy that feeling of having been parted from the pack; we watch with a certain superiority as the day-trippers depart the port at sunset and leave us alone to the elements.

On an island you are both safe from the sea and trapped by it, so tension is very easily conjured up, emotions heightened, both in life and in stories. Things just seem to happen. In my own life, my two medical emergencies to date have taken place on islands (Skopelos in Greece and Grinda Island in Stockholm) and both involved dramatic escapes to mainland hospitals. Personally, I can't help but associate islands with drama.

Nothing bad happened to me in Panarea, however, the most glamorous and seductive of the Aeolians, a group of volcanic islands scattered off the northern coast of Sicily. I also visited – and hope to return to one day – Lipari, Salina, Stromboli and, of course, Vulcano, scene of Eleanor's and Lewis's shared mud bath. But Panarea is the truly alluring one, at once lush and arid, gentle and brittle. It's also the best one for people-watching: the Italians who prowl its tiny dimensions are mostly beautiful and rarefied, big shots from Milan. Sometimes you think you've stumbled on a fashion shoot or film set. When Eleanor blunders into this elite community, seasick during the crossing, she is single-minded in her purpose: she, alone, is here for reasons other than hedonism. But when she finally comes to

her senses and decides to leave, she finds she is capti
the ferries have been cancelled owing to dangerou
currents. Maybe there'll be a murder, Frannie tells her.
But it's not that sort of book . . .

Panarea was my first island setting, but not the last. Since
then I've set stories on Santorini (*Since I Don't Have
You*) and the Ile de Ré (*The Disappearance of Emily
Marr* and *The Second Husband*). In *Other People's
Secrets*, scenes take place on the little island in the middle
of Lake Orta in the Italian Lakes. My poor stranded
characters have suffered loss, love, calamity and glory in
their island hideaways and yet none has been so tormented
by circumstances that he or she has struck out for the
mainland in a wetsuit. But there's always a first time.

My top island reads:

The Tempest by William Shakespeare

Five on a Treasure Island by Enid Blyton

And Then There Were None by Agatha Christie

The Magus by John Fowles

Into the Blue by Robert Goddard

The Disappearance of Emily Marr

Arriving on the windswept Ile de Ré off the coast of
France, Tabby Dewhurst is heartbroken and pen-
niless, unable even to afford a room for the night.
Then she overhears a villager repeating aloud the
access code to her front door and, hardly believing
her own actions, Tabby waits for the villager to
leave and lets herself into the house . . .

And so she enters the strange, hidden world of
Emmie, whose sudden offer of friendship is at odds
with her obsession with her own privacy. Soon
Tabby begins to form suspicions about Emmie,
suspicions that will lead her back to England – and
to a scandal with shattering consequences.

978-0-7515-4356-8

The Day You Saved My Life

A child falls into the river.
A stranger jumps in to rescue him.
And four lives are changed for ever . . .

On a perfect summer's day in Paris, tourists on the
river watch in shock as a small boy falls into the
Seine and disappears below the surface. As his
mother stands frozen, a stranger takes a breath
and leaps . . .

From the internationally bestselling author of *Since I
Don't Have You* comes a spellbinding story of
passion, heartbreak and destiny – an unforgettable
novel about mothers and daughters, husbands and
wives, and the extraordinary ways that life and love
intersect.

978-0-7515-4355-1

Other People's Secrets

Ginny and Adam Trustlove arrive on holiday in Italy torn apart by personal tragedy. Two weeks in a boat-house on the edge of peaceful Lake Orta is exactly what they need to restore their faith in life – and each other.

Twenty-four hours later, the silence is broken. The Sale family have arrived at the main villa: wealthy, high-flying Marty, his beautiful wife Bea, and their privileged, confident offspring. It doesn't take long for Ginny and Adam to be drawn in, especially when the teenage Pippi introduces a new friend into the circle. For there is something about Zach that has everyone instantly beguiled, something that loosens old secrets – and creates shocking new ones.

And, yet, not one of them suspects that his arrival in their lives might be anything other than accidental . . .

978-0-7515-4354-4